TALES FROM
THE ILIAD

THE CLASSICAL LIBRARY

BY H.L. HAVELL

TALES FROM THE ILIAD

FÉNIX

PRESS

FÉNIX
PRESS

Stories from The Iliad, H.L. Havell, Homer
first published by George G. Harrap Co.,1908.

Republished by Fénix Press,
Jordan Station, ON. L0R 1S0, Canada

Book Design: Steven R. Martins

Library & Archives Canada
ISBN 978-1-7380192-2-9

Table of Contents

Preface

The Classical Library is a collection compiled by Fénix Press of literary classics that should be read, studied, and enjoyed by every home, student, and teacher, whether in the context of the homeschool, elementary, highschool, college, university, or in the most informal and casual of settings.

Fénix Press is proud to republish these literary classics, bringing to the forefront the excellence and masterfulness of these literary contributions. In an age of "nostalgia", with most looking back at the years prior to the 2000s, what better occasion to revisit these classics and to reflect on what made these stories great.

There are arguably four characteristics that make a literary composition a "classic", regardless of the genre. These are: (1) Quality; (2) Longevity; (3) Appeal; and (4) Influence.

As it concerns Quality, classical literature can be appreciated for its structural composition and its commendable artistic features. It would have been highly venerated, or respected by its readers, when it was first published, and this was for the most part because of its masterful artistic quality. And though classics may not be the best-selling books of today, mainly because of their dated language and pacing, they are nonetheless the foundation upon which our Western literary tradition is built. If you are looking for quality that does not disappoint, turn to the classics.

In regard to Longevity, classical literature is known for being representative of its times. The reason many books are considered "classics" today is because they have stood the test of time. That is to say that it was not only read in its time, but it was read well *after* its time, and it *continues* to be read today. In other words, in order for a book to become a "classic", it must live well beyond the life of its author, and that means finding a home in subsequent generations. If it has achieved this longevity, then the work must receive recognition, and that recognition is the designation of being a "classic."

In regard to Appeal, classical literature touches the heart of almost every reader. Most often it is because classics weave different themes within their own narratives, and these themes — whether they be, for example, love, hate, death, life, or faith — draw in readers from a wide range of backgrounds and experiences. As readers have attested, in spite of the fact that they originate from different time periods, the characters and their situations of these "classics" are highly relatable. If they were not, then they could not have stood the test of time.

And finally, in regard to Influence. Classics often reveal the influence that other writers have had on their general composition. As any avid reader of the classics can attest to, classics are nearly always informed by the history of ideas and literature, and in turn, they inform the great works that follow after them. They are, in other words, the product of influence, and an influence themselves.

Altogether, classical literature is an expression of life, truth, and beauty. Or put differently, an expression of the human soul, reflecting both the human condition, and the remnants of the divine image man bears.

Enjoy this republication by Fénix Press for the common good of man, *bonum commune hominis.*

INTRODUCTION

I. THE STORY

IN ORDER TO understand the structure of the *Iliad*, we must keep fast hold of the guiding clue which is supplied by the author in the first line of his poem. The subject, he tells us, is the *Wrath of Achilles*. The motive of the greatest of epics is *wrath*—blind, unreasoning fury, which knows no law, and acknowledges no right. Keeping this in view, we are able to explain what seems at first sight to be a strange anomaly in the conduct of the story—the absence of the hero from the scene of action during three-fourths of the narrative. For Achilles is not less the hero of the *Iliad* than Odysseus is the hero of the *Odyssey*, and in both cases the character of the man determines the structure of the poem. Odysseus is a man of middle age, in the maturity of his splendid powers, with his judgment refined by experience, and his passions cooled by time. From the moment when he sets sail from Troy he remains faithful to the fixed desire of his heart. All the malice of Poseidon, all the spells of Circe, all the loveliness of Calypso, cannot shake him from his resolve to return to his home in

Ithaca, and live out his life in calm domestic happiness and peace. Yet he is entirely free from the narrowness which commonly belongs to a fixed idea. He knows the uncertainty which attaches to all human hopes, and is as ready to enjoy the passing hour as the youngest sailor of his crew. He has the hungry intellect, which would fain take all knowledge into its compass, and the spirit of soaring enterprise, which delights in discovery and daring adventure. But above all he has the patient, constant human heart, faithful through all turns of fortune to one sober ideal. It is this steadfastness of purpose and sweet reasonableness in the hero which gives to the narrative of the *Odyssey* its smooth and pellucid flow, and makes it the most delightful of all story-books.

Achilles, on the other hand, is the incarnation of the spirit of youth, with its passionate pride, its acute sensibility, and its absorption in self. He is like one of the great forces of nature—unreasoning, elemental, mighty to create or destroy. His inaction is as tremendous as his action. He is offended, and the Greeks, deprived of his aid, are brought to the brink of ruin—his friend is slain by Hector, and the current of his fury, thus directed into a new channel, sweeps the whole Trojan army before it in havoc and rout.

This, then, is the plan of the *Iliad*—to describe the effects of Achilles' anger, first on the Greeks, then on the Trojans. A brief review of the story will show how the plan is worked out. In the ninth year of the war, the Greeks have taken a small town in the neighbourhood of Troy, and Agamemnon has received a maiden named Chryseis as his share of the spoil. Chryses, the maiden's father, comes to the Grecian camp to ransom his child, but he is rudely repulsed by Agamemnon, and invokes the vengeance of Apollo, whose priest he is, on the Greeks. Apollo sends a pestilence on the camp, and Agamemnon is compelled in consequence to restore Chryseis, but he recompenses himself by seizing another maiden, named Briseis, awarded to Achilles as a prize at the capture of the same city. Achilles vows vengeance on the whole Greek army for this outrage, and Thetis, his mother, obtains a promise from Zeus, the supreme god of Olympus, that her son's vow shall be fulfilled to the letter. Accordingly Zeus sends a false dream to Agamemnon, bidding him lead the whole army against Troy, with the assurance of a decisive victory. Agamemnon obeys the summons in all good faith, and the two armies meet on the plain before the city. But just as the general encounter is about to begin, Paris offers to meet Menelaus in single combat, and a truce is made in order that the duel may take place. They fight, and Menelaus is victorious, but Paris is saved from death or capture by the intervention of Aphrodite.

Menelaus now claims the fulfilment of the conditions of the truce—the restoration of Helen with all her wealth. But before the point can be debated, Pandarus, a Trojan, at the instigation of Athene, aims an arrow at Menelaus, and wounds him in the side. This treacherous act leads to an immediate renewal of hostilities, and in the battle which follows the Trojans are reduced to such straits by the powers of Diomede that Hector goes on a mission to the city, to institute a solemn supplication in the temple of Athene, in the vain hope of diverting her anger from the Trojans. Having accomplished his errand, he returns to the field, bringing with him Paris, who, since his defeat by Menelaus, has been dallying in Helen's bower; and then follows a duel between Hector and Ajax, in which the Greek champion has the advantage. At the suggestion of Nestor, the Greeks fortify their camp with a moat and rampart; and this brings us to the end of the seventh book.

Hitherto the Greeks have had a decided advantage in battle with the Trojans, and nothing has been done to carry out the promise which Zeus made to Thetis. But now the father of gods and men begins to take decisive measures to fulfil his pledge; the gods are forbidden to interfere between the rival armies, and in the next day's battle the Greeks are driven back in panic to their camp, while the Trojans, contrary to their custom, keep the field all night, intending to attack the Greek stronghold in full force next day. So despondent are the Greeks that an embassy is sent with an offer of magnificent gifts to Achilles, if he will lay aside his anger and come to the help of his distressed countrymen. Achilles refuses all compromise, and the rest of the night is occupied by the bold raid undertaken by Diomede and Odysseus on the Thracian camp.

At the opening of the eleventh book our attention is concentrated on the valorous exploits of Agamemnon, who is at length compelled to retire by a severe wound in the arm; Diomede is pierced through the foot by an arrow from the bow of Paris, and Odysseus, Machaon, and Eurypylus are also disabled. Patroclus is sent by Achilles to inquire of Nestor concerning the fortunes of the Greeks, and Nestor then makes the suggestion which marks the turning-point in the first act of the great epic drama: if, he says, Achilles will not go to the field himself, at least let him send Patroclus to lead the Myrmidons[1] against the Trojans. Nothing comes of the proposal for the present, but it is to bear fatal fruit both for Patroclus and Achilles in the near future. The Greeks are again driven behind their defences, and a furious struggle ensues, at the end of which the gates of the camp are demolished, and the Trojans, led by Hector, are on the point of setting fire to the ships.

At this moment the attention of Zeus is withdrawn from the battle, and Poseidon seizes the opportunity to interfere in favour of the Greeks. By his influence the scale is turned again, Hector receives fearful injuries from a huge stone hurled by Ajax, and the Trojans are driven headlong across the plain. Zeus is lulled to sleep by the contrivance of Hera, and when he awakens it is to find his whole scheme of vengeance on the point of being frustrated. In great anger he sends a peremptory message to Poseidon to withdraw from the battle, and

---

1. The followers of Achilles.

lays his commands on Apollo, who brings back Hector, healed and whole, to the field, and leads the Trojans once more to the assault of the camp. In spite of the desperate valour of Ajax, the Greeks are driven back to their ships, and the Trojans bring torches, with the intention of burning the whole fleet.

Then at last Achilles, yielding to the earnest entreaty of Patroclus, sends him to the aid of the Greeks, equipped in his own armour, and leading the whole force of the Myrmidons. Patroclus easily drives the Trojans back from the camp, and slays Sarpedon, one of the bravest warriors among the allies of Troy; but he himself falls by Hector's hand, and the armour of Achilles passes into the possession of his slayer. A tremendous struggle ensues over the body of Patroclus, which is only ended by the appearance of Achilles himself, who comes, attended by strange prodigies, to the wall, and, by the mere terror of his presence, scares the Trojans from the field, and saves his friend's body from outrage.

The rest of the story may be briefly told. By the intercession of Thetis, Hephæstus, the divine smith, makes a splendid suit of armour for Achilles, and, after a solemn scene of reconciliation with Agamemnon, Achilles leads the Greeks to battle. The whole torrent of his fury is now turned upon the Trojans, and, after a wholesale massacre of lesser victims, he meets Hector in single combat, slays him, and drags his body behind his chariot to the camp. The funeral obsequies of Patroclus are celebrated with great pomp, and then Achilles, who is possessed by a demon of rage and grief, continues for a space of twelve days to wreak his vengeance on the lifeless body of Hector, which he drags repeatedly behind his car round the tomb of Patroclus. The gods interpose to make an end of this senseless fury, and Hector's body, which has been miraculously preserved from harm, is restored to Priam, who comes in the night, under the conduct of Hermes, and redeems the corpse with a heavy ransom. With the burial of Hector the poem reaches its conclusion.

Such, in the briefest and baldest outline, is the story of the *Iliad*. Space does not allow us to discuss the various objections which have been raised against some of the details of the narrative, still less to enumerate the reconstructions and mutilations to which the great epic has been subjected in the dissecting-room of criticism. Where opinion is still so much divided, we may be allowed to state our conviction that the *Iliad*, though wanting the structural perfection of the *Odyssey*, is one poem, and the work of one master mind.

II. THE DIVINE CHARACTERS

The gods in the *Iliad* play a very active and human part, and indeed they may be said in a sense to be more human than the men themselves. They are passionate, sensual, vindictive; they have no sense of fair play, but are always ready to help their favourites by all means, fair or foul. When Patroclus is to die, he is stripped of his armour and beaten half senseless by Apollo, and delivered over in this helpless state to Euphorbus and Hector; and Hector, in his turn, is cheated and beguiled to his death by Athene. In the chariot race which is described in the twenty-third book Athene wrecks the car of Eumelus to secure the victory for Diomede; and the same goddess interferes in the foot race on behalf of Odysseus, whom she loves like a mother. We have already remarked, in the Introduction to the *Odyssey*, that the only humorous scenes in the *Iliad* are those in which the gods play the chief or sole part. And, in fact, the want of dignity and decorum which we find in these mighty beings is simply astonishing. The battle of the gods, which is introduced with such pomp and parade, ends in the broadest farce. In the fifth book, Ares roars and bellows like a beast when he is wounded by the spear of Diomede, and Aphrodite, whose hand has been scratched, goes whimpering and whining to her mother for comfort. Only in a few passages do we find a great and worthy conception of the divine nature—as in the famous lines in the first book, when Zeus nods his immortal head confirming his oath to Thetis, and in the sublime description of Poseidon at the beginning of the thirteenth book.

At the head of the Olympian hierarchy stands Zeus the lord of the sky, who divides with his brothers, Hades and Poseidon, the empire of the universe. He is the highest in power and authority, and with him rests the final decision in all the disputes of Olympus. But this genial and patriarchal deity is not without his troubles: he rules over a disorderly household, and his purposes are constantly thwarted by the lesser powers who reign under him. In his heart of hearts he favours Priam and the Trojans, but he is a fond and indulgent father and husband, and Hera, his wife, and Athene, his daughter, cherish an implacable hatred against Troy and all things Trojan. The reason for this bitter animosity does not appear: for the judgment of Paris, which is the cause assigned by later legends, is only mentioned in one passage, of doubtful authenticity. Hera is described as a lady of shrewish and vixenish temper; she will never be satisfied, says Zeus, until she has gone down into Troy and eaten Priam and all his people raw! Her human counterpart is Hecuba, who would like, she says, to tear out the heart of Achilles, and devour it. On the side of the Trojans are Apollo, Artemis, Hephæstus, the river-god Scamander, and Leto.

Such are the gods of Homer, and such the national divinities of Greece. For the poems of Homer and Hesiod, as Herodotus informs us, are the chief sources of the popular theology. Small wonder, then, that the more earnest minds of a later age were much occupied by the endeavour to raise and purify the accepted mythology, or that Plato excludes Homer, "the great magician," from his scheme of reformed education.

III. THE HUMAN CHARACTERS

Of Achilles and Odysseus we have already spoken at

some length, so that we have only to notice briefly the other chief characters. At the head of the Greek army stands Agamemnon, whose authority rests on his personal prowess, his vast wealth, and the extent of his dominions. In the absence of Achilles he shares with Ajax and Diomede the highest place among the warriors of Greece. A certain strain of weakness runs through his character. He is jealous of his authority, and somewhat covetous, and at moments of crisis and peril he is always foremost in the counsels of despair. Next to him in rank comes Menelaus, his brother, an amiable but somewhat feeble prince, to whom the poet shows a certain playful tenderness, such as is felt by chivalrous natures towards a woman or a child.

The most knightly figure on the Greek side is the young Diomede, whose wonderful exploits fill so large a space in the earlier part of the poem. His gallant and buoyant spirit shines brightest when the fortunes of the Greeks are at their lowest ebb; and the beautiful episode of his meeting with Glaucus on the battlefield is a rare exception to the savage ferocity of Homeric warfare.

After Achilles, the mightiest champion of Greece is the great Telamonian Ajax. He is a giant in stature and strength, and is the chief bulwark of the Greeks against the impetuous valour of Hector. In character, he is modest and unassuming; he lacks the brilliant qualities of Achilles, though equal to him in sheer physical force. He is the type of the rugged soldier, such as we find among the Spartans of a later date, loyal to his prince, a faithful comrade, ever at the post of danger, ever prompt to help where the need is sorest. His plain, frank nature views with contempt the fantastic pride of Achilles, whose frightful egoism, and indifference to the sufferings of his countrymen, revolt and disgust him.

This list may fitly be closed with the name of Nestor, "the clear-voiced orator, from whose lips flowed eloquence sweeter than honey." As becomes his age, he assumes the office of peacemaker between Agamemnon and Achilles; in spite of his eighty years, he still takes the field and fights in the van, though his arm is now of less value than his head. With regard to his eloquence, it can hardly be said, judging by the specimen preserved, that he is quite worthy of his reputation. He is, in fact, garrulous, rambling, and tedious—though in these qualities he is even surpassed by the aged Phœnix, who has played the part of male nurse to Achilles, and excels in a style of oratory dear to the professional guardians of childhood.

The great champion of the Trojans is Hector, the son of Priam and Hecuba. His character is, in every respect, a contrast to that of Achilles. With him the claims of king and country ever come first, though he is not indifferent to personal distinction. He falls very far short of the ideal knight—without fear and without reproach. In these qualities he seems to be eclipsed by Glaucus and Sarpedon, the princes of Lycia, whose beautiful friendship finds its most illustrious record in the immortal lines of the twelfth book, the finest exposition in the world of the principle involved in the words *noblesse oblige*. Hector, on the other hand, is full of weakness: at one time he is faint-hearted, and has to be recalled to the duties of his great position by the reproaches of those who serve under him; at another time he is overbold, and his rashness brings upon the Trojans overwhelming disaster. Yet with all this, his character is full of interest. In his greater moments he rises to sublime heights of heroism. He does not shrink from the consequences of his actions, but goes to certain death with the spirit of a patriot and martyr. He is the mirror of knightly courtesy, kind and gentle even to the guilty and the fallen; and his last meeting with Andromache is hardly to be matched for beauty and pathos in all literature.

A bare mention must suffice for Priam, the white-haired King, and the most tragic figure in the poem; Paris, the curled darling of Aphrodite, a mere beautiful animal, without soul or conscience, and the lovely passion-stricken Helen, whose strange story seems to have a closer affinity with mediæval romance than with classical antiquity.

IV. THE SIMILES

One word must be added on the frequent comparisons, or similes, which form one of the most characteristic features of the poem. At least half the *Iliad* is occupied with descriptions of battle, and Homeric warfare is exceedingly simple and uniform, consisting almost entirely of single combats between individual chieftains, or wholesale slaughter wrought by some puissant arm on the promiscuous herd of soldiers. To render so unpromising a theme interesting and attractive must have taxed the skill and invention of the poet to their utmost limit; and his principal resources for attaining this end is in the lavish use of the simile. In those parts of the poem where much is to be told in little space this ornament occurs rarely, or not at all. In the first book, which is crowded with incidents, not a single simile is used. But where the action is to be delayed or elaborated, and especially in the battle pieces, the similes are flung broadcast, shining like stars among the racing clouds of a stormy sky. Every corner of nature, and every province of human life, are ransacked to furnish illustrations of the eternal drama of «battle, and murder, and sudden death.» In a moment we are rapt by the magic of the poet from the steam and squalor of slaughter to some busy scene of human industry, or some living picture, grand, lovely, or terrible, drawn from the great panorama of nature. Nothing is too great, nothing too little, to furnish material for this splendid treasury of poetry. It would be easy to discourse for pages on this fascinating subject; but we must content ourselves with the above brief hint, and will conclude our remarks by declaring our full agreement with those who regard the similes in the *Iliad* as the chief glory and beauty in the first and greatest of epic poems.

TALES FROM THE ILIAD

1

THE QUARREL

I

THE SCENE OF our story is laid in the north-western corner of Asia Minor, where the blue waters of the Hellespont mingle with the waves of the Ægæan. The whole coast is lined with a multitude of war galleys, drawn up, row behind row, for a space of several miles; and behind them are thousands and thousands of wooden huts, affording shelter to a whole nation of warriors, with their slaves and followers. For nine years the Greeks have lain here encamped, striving in vain to sack the ancient city of Troy, whose towers and battlements, some five miles distant, can be seen from the elevated parts of the camp. The whole surrounding country has been laid waste, and town after town has been visited by all the horrors of war; but the walls of Troy still stand firm against all assault, and the end seems as far off as ever.

The chiefs are assembled in council, and in their midst sits Agamemnon, the mightiest prince in Greece, whose nod a hundred thousand warriors obey. Suddenly, a voice is heard on the outskirts of the crowd which surrounds the circle of elders, and an aged man, clad in the long flowing robes of a priest, is led into the royal presence. In his hand he carries a rod, adorned with studs of gold, and wreathed with olive leaves. "A boon, great king, a boon!" he cries, lifting the rod on high. "Speak," answers Agamemnon. "What wouldst thou have of me?" "Give me back my child, my daughter Chryseis," answers the priest. "Thou hast sacked my city, thou hast burnt my home; restore unto me my child, and leave me not altogether desolate in mine old age."

Dark was the brow of Agamemnon when he heard these words, and short and stern was his answer. "Let me not find thee," he said, "lingering here in the camp, and come not hither again on such an errand. Thy daughter thou shall not see again; she is mine, the captive of my bow and of my spear, and shall be my slave until the day of her death." In vain the old man urged him with entreaty, and offered a rich ransom to redeem his child from bondage. "Talk not to me of ransom," answered Agamemnon: "not all the gold of thy temple shall purchase liberty for the maiden, for she hath found favour in my sight. Get thee gone at once, and provoke me no further."

Then the priest, whose name was Chryses, feared for his own life, and fled from the angry face of the King. Down to the margin of the sea he went, and gazing with tear-dimmed eyes over the heaving waters, thus he prayed to Apollo, his protector and lord: "Hear me, god of the silver bow, whose altar steams day and night with offerings from the choicest of the flock. Remember my faithful service, and let thine arrows avenge my tears on the Greeks."

So he prayed, and Apollo heard him, and down from the peaks of Olympus he sped. In his hand he bare his mighty bow, and the arrows in his quiver made an angry rattling as he swooped down on the Grecian camp, swift and sudden as the southern night. He took his stand on a hill, and loosed an arrow from the string; and dire was the twang of the silver bow. First, he sent his shafts among the dogs and mules; then he changed his aim, and rained destruction among the men; and the whole place was filled with the smoke of funeral pyres.

For nine days the deadly shower fell without ceasing; but on the tenth, Achilles summoned a general gathering of the host, to inquire into the causes of the calamity which had fallen on his countrymen. The chiefs met in full conclave, and about them were gathered the meaner sort in their tens of thousands. When the clamorous cries of the multitude were stilled, Achilles rose in his place, and addressing himself directly to Agamemnon said: "Son of Atreus, how long wilt thou suffer thy people to perish? Is it not enough that our blood is poured forth every day in battle with thy foes, but must pestilence also make havoc among our ranks? This is Apollo's work, and it is time to ask some priest or soothsayer how we have offended the god, that we may appease his anger with the fat of goats and lambs, and save ourselves from further harm."

Among the elders sat Calchas, the chief seer of the Greeks; who knew all things—what was, and had been, and was to come—and was the chosen leader of the army in matters of religion. Seeing all eyes turned upon him he stood up and answered the challenge of Achilles, though with manifest reluctance and constraint.

"Illustrious chieftain," he said, "thou hast asked the cause of Apollo's anger, and I know that thou lookest to me for an answer. But swear unto me first that thou wilt defend me in word and in deed; for I fear that, by revealing the counsels of the god whom I serve, I shall offend one who is the greatest and mightiest among us."

"Tell us what thou knowest, and fear nothing," answered Achilles; "while I live no one shall lift his hand against thee, no, not Agamemnon himself."

Thus encouraged, Calchas spoke out, and declared that the only means of staying the pestilence was by sending back Chryseis to her father, without price or ransom, and offering a costly sacrifice of atonement to Apollo in his temple at Chrysa. It was not without reason that the prudent seer had appealed to Achilles for protection; for no sooner had his words been uttered than Agamemnon sprang from his seat, with fury in his looks, and overwhelmed the prophet with a torrent of reproaches. "Ill fare thy prophecies, thou prophet of ill!" he cried. "Not one good word have I ever heard from thy lips; but this is the worst that ever thou hast spoken. Hard and bitter is the charge which thou hast laid upon me, bidding me restore this maiden, fairer and dearer to me than Clytæmnestra, my wedded wife. Nevertheless I will send her back, if I cannot save my people otherwise; but look ye to it, princes and councillors of Greece, that I find fit recompense for my loss; for she was a choice prize of war, set apart for me as a gift of privilege and honour."

"And thinkest thou," said Achilles, roused at once to opposition by this unwarrantable claim, "that it befits thine honour as a king to be covetous of thy people's goods? Be generous; let thy prize go, and when next we divide the spoil of a captured town we will repay thee threefold and fourfold for thy loss."

"Payment I will have, and that right speedily," answered Agamemnon, with darkening brow. "See that ye find means to fill the place of this maiden, or one of you shall yield up his prize to me, whether it be Ajax, or Odysseus, or thou Achilles, who art so bold of speech, that thou mayest learn that I am king indeed. But concerning this we can speak again hereafter; our present task is to restore Chryseis to her father, and appease the god with sacrifice."

Agamemnon thought perhaps by his last words to avert the anger of the fiery young prince, whose eyes flashed fire when he heard the King's threat. But if such was his purpose it failed altogether. No sooner had he ended than the full tempest of Achilles' wrath fell upon his head. "Thou soul of avarice!" he cried, "clad in shamelessness as with a garment, was it for thee that we crossed all those weary leagues of water to make war on the men of Troy? I have no quarrel with the Trojans; they have not lifted my cattle, or driven off my horses, for my home is far beyond their reach, divided from Asia by shadowy mountains and sounding seas. For thee, thou dog, and for thy brother have I toiled, and in the division of the spoil 'tis but little that I win as the price of my sweat and my blood; and thou seekest to rob me of that little, to add to thine own monstrous hoard. I will go back forthwith to my native land of Phthia, for I have no mind to abide here in dishonour and heap up treasure for thee."

"Go when thou wilt," answered Agamemnon, in scornful tones. "Heaven forbid that I should hinder thee! Most hateful to me art thou of all the chivalry of Greece, for thou hast a heart full of hatred and malice. Go and lord it over thine own tribe; I am the master here, and as sure as I am a crowned and anointed king I will take thy prize, even the maiden Briseis, and lead her to my tent, that thou mayest learn to curb thy saucy tongue in the presence of thy lord."

Thus publicly insulted and defied, Achilles sat speechless with rage, fighting against the passion which shook his mighty frame. At last it seemed that he had resolved to let his fury have full scope; slowly he drew his sword from its scabbard, his mouth was opened for the battle cry, and in another moment the haughty King would have lain weltering in his blood; but in the very act of springing on his foe he felt himself restrained from behind, and turning to confront this new assailant he stood face to face with the goddess Athene. Unseen and unheard by the rest, the grey-eyed goddess spoke, bidding him to desist from his murderous purpose. "Put up thy sword," she said; "speak daggers to him, if thou wilt, but use none. Thine honour is safe in the hands of Zeus, and the day of reckoning shall come, when that proud head shall be humbled to the very dust before thee."

To those who were looking on it seemed that Achilles had fallen into a sudden trance of thought, from which he started abruptly, and, thrusting back his sword into its sheath, resumed the war of words with Agamemnon. "Thou drunkard," he cried, "with eye of dog and heart of deer, foremost in the revel and last in the fray! Thou of the itching palm, who lovest the chink of stolen gold, but turnest pale at the clash of steel! False shepherd, that devourest thy flock! Cowardly master of cowardly sheep! Now by this sceptre I swear, by this symbol of justice which the elders hold in their hands when they give judgment before the people, the day is not far distant when all this host shall be filled with longing for me, to save them from Hector's destroying arm, when their bravest and their strongest are falling beneath his spear. Then shalt thou learn thy folly too late, and drink to the dregs the bitter cup which thou hast filled for me."

With that he flung the sceptre at Agamemnon's feet, and sat down again in his place. Then arose Nestor, the clear-voiced orator of Pylos, from whose lips flowed eloquence sweeter than honey. Two generations of men had lived and died since his birth, and he still dwelt in kingly honour among the third. And thus he spake, striving to make peace between the two angry chieftains: "Alas! what sorrow has come upon the sons of Greece!—sorrow to us, but joy unto Priam and the sons of Priam, when they hear of the feud which hath arisen between ye twain. Be guided by me; I am older than ye, and before ye were born I moved as an equal among heroes mightier than ye, and was second to none in council and in fight. Hearken therefore to me, even as they did. Seek not, Agamemnon, to take from Achilles his prize of honour; and thou, Achilles, provoke not the King to anger by thy bitter words, for as thou art our bulwark in war, so he sits higher than thou in sceptred majesty."

"Thou sayest well," answered Agamemnon, "but this man's insolence is not to be borne. Because he is a stout spearman he thinks that he can lord it over us all. But there are some here who will not brook his tyranny."

"There is one here," retorted Achilles, "who refuses to be thy slave. But enough of this—I will waste no more words on thee. Come and take away my prize, if those who stand here suffer thee to do this wrong; but touch not aught else of my possessions, or thy blood shall pay the price."

With these words the stormy debate, so fruitful in disaster to the Greeks, came to an end.

II

Agamemnon's first task, when he returned to his tent, was to send back Chryseis, under the charge of Odysseus, to her father. This done, he at once took steps to secure possession of Briseis, the captive maiden who had been bestowed on Achilles as his prize of honour. Talthybius and Eurybates, the royal heralds, were sent to the quarters of Achilles to demand the surrender of Briseis. "And if he will not give her up to you," added the King, "I will come myself and take her by force." So they went with slow and reluctant steps on their thankless errand; and they found Achilles sitting alone by his ship, where it was drawn up on the beach. Awestruck and silent they stood in the presence of that great chief, unable to utter a sound; but he knew full well why they had come, and greeted them with courtesy and kindness. "Draw near," he said, "and fear nothing from me. I respect your office, and impute not to you your master's guilt. Patroclus my comrade shall deliver unto you the maiden, and be ye my witnesses in this matter, when it is asked why I threw down my sword and refused to fight any longer in Agamemnon's cause."

So saying he summoned Patroclus, and bade him bring forth Briseis from the tent; and Patroclus went, and presently returned, leading the weeping maiden by the hand, and gave her in charge of the heralds. When they were gone, Achilles wandered away by the margin of the sea, nursing his wounded spirit, and full of angry and bitter thoughts. Presently he came to a stand, and, stretching out his hands towards the sea, cried like a child in pain to Thetis, his mother: "Short is the term of years which Fate has vouchsafed to me, and therefore thou hast promised me honour from the hands of Zeus. But now is mine honour turned to infamy, and I am become a very scorn of men, and an outcast among the people." His words were broken by sobs and tears, for he was but a boy in years, and was smarting with an agony of wounded pride. And his mother heard him where she sat in her crystal cave in the depths of the sea; for she was a goddess, and daughter of the sea-god, Nereus. Swiftly she rose, "like an exhalation," to the surface of the sea, and came and stood by her young hero's side. "Why weepest thou, my child?" she asked, with a tender caress. "Tell thy mother all thy pain, that she may bear the burden with thee."

"Thou knowest full well," replied Achilles, with a groan; "what boots it to repeat to thee the story of my shame?" Nevertheless he went on to pour out all the tale of injury and outrage; for sorrow grows lighter in the telling. "Thou alone," he added, when he had finished the recital, "canst heal this deadly hurt to mine honour. I have often heard thee boast of an old service rendered to Zeus, when the other Olympians rose up in revolt against him, and he was in sore straits. Go, therefore, to Olympus, and remind him of the debt which he owes unto thee, and ask him in requital to lend aid to the Trojans, that the Greeks may be hurled back in rout upon their ships, and Agamemnon may learn what it means to deal despitefully with the best warrior in his camp."

"It shall be done as thou sayest," answered Thetis; "Leave everything in my hands, and thou shalt have atonement in full measure. Until twelve days are passed I can do nothing, for Zeus has gone on a far journey, to partake of a banquet in the land of the Ethiopians. When he returns I will lay thy case before him; and meanwhile sit thou idle here, and go not into battle, but leave me to champion thy cause." With this promise she left him, and he sat down to digest his anger, and wait for the day of redress.

III

On the dawn of the twelfth day Thetis rose again from her cavern into mid-air, and was borne by the breezes unto Olympus. She found the lord of heaven sitting apart on the topmost peak of the mountain, and kneeling before him she preferred her request. When Zeus heard what she desired he fell into a muse, and answered not a word; but Thetis remained kneeling at his feet, and, clinging to him with both hands, repeated her prayer. Being urged thus with importunity, at last the sire opened his mouth, and answered in heavy tones: "Thou wilt put enmity between me and Hera, my wife; already she upbraids me for showing favour to the Trojans, and thou askest me to take sides openly with them against the Greeks. But go to, what care I for the wrath of Hera? Nevertheless, get thee gone speedily, lest she find us together. Howbeit, thou shalt have thy wish; behold, I swear it, and confirm it with my nod, and whatsoever I have thus confirmed cannot be annulled or unfulfilled."

Thereupon the monarch of the sky bowed his immortal head, with all its dark and waving locks, and shook the mountain to its base.

Having thus attained her purpose, Thetis departed, and as soon as she was gone Zeus joined the assembly of the gods in the high palace of Olympus. All the gods rose from their seats to pay him homage as he entered and took his place on the royal throne. But the sharp eyes of Hera had spied out his conference with Thetis, and forthwith she assailed her indulgent lord in mocking tones: "What plot hast thou been hatching now, thou god of craft? I know that thou art keeping some mischief from me, thy lawful wife."

"Daughter of Cronos," answered Zeus, avoiding her piercing glance, "thou canst not expect that I should share all my counsels with thee. Whatever it is meet for thee to know thou shall learn; but I have some secrets which are not for thy ear."

"Thou must keep thy secrets more carefully," said Hera, with a bitter smile, "if thou wouldst deceive me. Listen, ye gods, while I tell you this fine secret! Zeus has promised Thetis that the Greeks shall suffer defeat, to avenge the insult put upon her son."

"And if such be my will, who shall say me nay?" replied Zeus, with a stern look. "I warn thee not to thwart my purpose, or all the gods who sit here shall not save thee from chastisement."

Then fear fell upon Hera, and she sat biting her lips, venturing no reply. And all the gods sat silent, glancing anxiously at one another, when they heard the angry tones of the Olympian sire.

At last Hephæstus, the lame god of fire, came to his mother's relief. Rising from his seat, he took a goblet of nectar from the hands of Hebe, who was serving drink to the gods, and went hobbling to the place where Hera sat. "Mother mine," said, he, as he offered her the cup, "I counsel thee to give way, and not provoke our father to anger. Shall we, the sons and daughters of heaven, brawl over our cups for the sake of miserable mortals? Let Zeus have his way—for what can we do against him? Hast thou forgotten how he served me when I presumed to stand between thee and his ire?—how he caught me by the foot, and flung me forth from the open portals of Olympus, as a boy slings a stone? From morn till eve I fell, and at the setting of the sun I struck on Lemnos, the Ægæan isle."

Hera smiled at her ungainly son; and when she had drunk of the nectar he took the cup, and went limping round the circle of the gods, offering them to drink. And all the immortals laughed loud and long, to see the huge, hairy god engaged in the office of the lovely Hebe. Then music and song came to crown the banquet, as Apollo led the choir of the Muses on his golden harp.

2

THE DREAM:
The Muster of Greeks

I

Agamemnon lay sleeping in his tent, and in a dream he saw Nestor, the son of Neleus, who addressed him in these words: "Sleepest thou, son of Atreus? It is not meet that thou, on whom lies the weight of a mighty monarchy, shouldst slumber all night long. Hearken now to my words: I am the bearer of a message from Zeus, who bids thee summon the whole host of Greeks, and lead them against Troy. Her hour is come at last, and the gods with one consent have decided that she shall fall."

Agamemnon awoke, and behold it was a dream. But the words had sunk deep into his heart, and he deemed that the vision had spoken truth. In that vain belief he arose from his couch, clothed himself in a fair linen tunic and a woollen robe, and, taking his sceptre in his hand, went to rouse Nestor and tell him his dream. Then the whole body of the chiefs met in council, and the heralds were sent round to proclaim a general assembly of the army. The people came flocking at the summons, numberless as bees which hover round the flowers in spring; and nine heralds went about among the multitude, marshalling the clamorous commons in their places, and commanding silence, that the counsel of the King might be heard.

As this was a great occasion, it had been resolved, in the private meeting of the elders, to try the temper of the people before disclosing to them the real purpose of their leaders. Accordingly, when silence had been obtained, Agamemnon rose up in his place, holding in his hand his ancestral sceptre, the symbol of his great office, which had descended from father to son since the days of Pelops, the founder of the royal house of Argos. Planting the sceptre firmly before him, and leaning upon it, thus spake the King, to prove the heart of his people.

"Friends and comrades in war, I have heavy news to tell you. Zeus brought us hither under a solemn promise that in the end we should take the sacred city of Priam. But now he hath revoked his promise, and bids us sail back to Greece, for all our toil is vain. Shame and dishonour must be our portion, now and hereafter, when our sons' sons shall hear how we, the embattled host of Greece, outnumbering the citizens of Troy by ten to one, fought against them for nine long years, and then departed, as beaten and broken men. But such is the will of Zeus, and none can gainsay it. Therefore I bid you hoist sail and away, for we are not destined to take the town of Troy."

At these words of the King there arose a wild commotion among his hearers, and the vast multitude swayed to and fro like the waves of the Ægæan driven this way and that by shifting gusts of wind. Then, as a wide field of corn bends down before the strong breath of the west, the whole host turned seaward, and with a mighty shout they rushed downward to the shore, and began to launch their ships.

Agamemnon, and those who were in his confidence, were thunderstruck by the tremendous effect of his speech, and stood helpless and amazed in the midst of this scene of tumult. The first to recover himself was Odysseus, the wisest and the firmest spirit among all the chieftains. Flinging off his mantle he went to Agamemnon, and took from his hand the royal sceptre. Armed with this symbol of authority he hurried hither and thither among the excited throng, urging each man by threats or entreaties to return to the place of assembly, and wait there for further instructions from the recognised leaders of the host.

To those of rank and character he spoke courteously, urging them to use their influence among their followers, and check the general flight; while with the baser sort he used rougher means of persuasion, striking them with the sceptre and rebuking them fiercely. Others among the chiefs followed his example, and at length the tumult was stayed, and the fickle mob swept back into the camp with a roar like the billows breaking on a long line of rocky shore.

At length that vast audience was seated, and waiting attentively to hear the counsels of the King. But one unruly knave remained standing, and poured out a torrent of abuse against Agamemnon and the other chiefs. This fellow's name was Thersites, and of all the Greeks who came up against Troy he was the foulest, both in aspect and in speech. His huge misshapen head, sparsely covered with thin, downy hair, sat awry on his stooping shoulders. He was bandy-legged, and lame of one foot. And he was the sworn enemy of the valiant, the noble, and the wise. This low-born railer now began to shriek out insults in a hideous voice against Agamemnon, his sovereign lord. "Son of Atreus," he bawled, "what lackest thou yet? Thy tents are full of gold, and crowded with slaves, which we have won for thee with our swords and our spears. Lustest thou yet after more gold, the ransom of Trojan captives? Or dost thou want more Trojan dames to be thy handmaids? Up, sirs, let us be gone, lest we be called women, and not men, if we remain here to heap up riches for this greedy tyrant. Have we not seen him put public dishonour on our bravest warrior, taking from him his lawful prize? Surely Achilles lacks gall to make oppression bitter, seeing that he has suffered this bitter wrong to go unavenged. Were he of like mind with me, the ruffian king would not have survived to commit further outrages."

A stern voice here broke in upon the seditious harangue, and Thersites perceived with alarm that Odysseus was standing by him, staff in hand. "Peace, saucy knave!" said the Prince of Ithaca, in threatening tones. "How darest thou, the very scum and refuse of the army, to hold such language against our exalted leader? If I find thee uttering thy mad folly again, may my head be smitten from my shoulders, and may I never more be called the father of Telemachus, if I do not strip thee naked and drive thee forth from among the people with blows like this." And suiting the action to the word he laid the heavy staff with no gentle hand across the deformed shoulders of Thersites. The wretch shrank beneath the blow with a cry of pain, and the golden staff left its print in a crimson weal on his back. So he sat huddled together, with distorted face, wiping away his tears, and spoke not another word.

Having thus silenced that loose tongue, Odysseus mounted a platform, whence he could be seen and heard of all the host, and lifting up his mighty voice he began to rebuke the people for their weakness and want of faith. "Must I speak to you," he said, "as to homesick women and children, or as to veteran warriors bound by an oath to follow their great captain for weal or for woe? Not that I blame you overmuch, for indeed your service has been both long and hard. For nine long years we have toiled in vain, and the cordage of our ships is rotten, and their timbers are warped. Nevertheless, endure yet a little while, until we have learnt whether the son of Cronos is a true prophet or no. Ye cannot have forgotten the day when our ships were assembled at Aulis, or the portents vouchsafed us there at a solemn sacrifice to the gods. The altar was raised in the shadow of a goodly plane-tree, near a running water; and in the tree was a nest of sparrows, a mother with eight young, cheeping and cowering beneath the leaves. Just as we were kindling the altar fire, a great serpent, with blood-red back, darted up from the altar into the tree and pounced upon the sparrows' nest. The mother-bird fluttered anxiously around, uttering piteous cries to see the monster devouring her young; and the serpent, when he had swallowed up the nestlings, caught their mother by the wing as she hovered near, and swallowed her also. Then we beheld a wonder: for the serpent, when he came down from the tree, was turned into a stone. And while we stood amazed Calchas declared unto us the meaning of that omen: "Why stand ye thus amazed, ye warriors of Greece? That which ye have seen is a sign from Zeus, and this is the interpretation thereof: the nine birds are the nine years, during which we shall lay siege to Troy, and the serpent is the tenth year, in which Troy shall fall! Therefore abide steadfast, my comrades, for the nine years are passed, and we are nearing the end of our labours."

Odysseus ended, and a great roar of acclamation went up from a hundred thousand throats, and rolled like thunder along the hollow shore. The next speaker was Nestor, who addressed Agamemnon, and bade him command an immediate muster of the whole army, and lead a general attack upon the Trojans. "Let the people," said he, "be ordered according to their several tribes and clans, that thou mayest distinguish the faint-hearted from the loyal and valiant. Thus shall thou learn, if disaster befalleth thee, to whom it is due—whether to adverse heaven, or to the cowardice and weakness of thine allies."

"Thou speakest ever to the purpose," answered Agamemnon; "and would that I had ten such counsellers as thee! Then would Priam's royal city soon bow her head, sunk in the dust beneath our victorious hands. But the son of Cronos hath sown division among us, and put enmity between me and my bravest champion. But to our task: let the people now get their morning meal, and then prepare for battle. Let every man whet his spear, and look to the fastenings of his shield; let every steed be fed, and every chariot set in order, that we may fight all day till the going down of the sun. There shall be no rest or respite till darkness puts an end to the fray. Many a shield strap shall drip with sweat, and many a hand ache with holding the spear, and the steeds shall droop with weariness, ere the day be done. And if I find any man skulking among the ships, I will give his flesh to feed the dogs and vultures."

Then the people arose and scattered among their tents, and soon the smoke of a thousand fires went eddying up into the still morning air. And every warrior lifted up his heart in prayer to heaven, that he might return safe and sound from the great perils which lay before him.

Agamemnon slaughtered an ox five years old, and summoned the noblest of the chiefs, among whom were Nestor, Idomeneus, the two princes named Ajax, Diomede, and Odysseus, to take their meal with him. In those days every meal was a sacrifice, and this was the manner in which it was performed: the company stood round the ox, holding in their hands a portion of barleymeal. Then the giver of the feast addressed a prayer to Zeus, the meal was sprinkled between the horns of the victim, and after that the beast was slaughtered and flayed. Portions of the meat were then cut off from the carcass, wrapped in a double layer of fat, and burnt as an offering to the gods. When all religious rites had been duly paid, the choicer parts of the meat were broiled in thin slices over the fire, and eaten with wheat or barley bread. The flesh of beeves and swine, or less commonly of sheep and goats, with bread and wine, formed almost the sole diet of the Homeric heroes.

When they had finished a copious repast, Nestor, who, despite his eighty years, was as keen and alert as the youngest soldier, sprang from his seat, and cried: "To arms, comrades, to arms! Agamemnon, bid the heralds summon the host to the field."

The King gave the order required, and forthwith the heralds, who were chosen for the power and reach of their voices, went about in the camp, and called the people to arms. Then every captain called his company together, and led them to the place appointed for the general array. And by degrees a strange fire spread from rank to rank, kindling in every breast a fierce longing for battle. All softer emotions, all homesick longings, were forgotten; for a mysterious influence was at work, due to the unseen presence of Athene, who was there with her wondrous, immortal shield, with its fringe of golden tassels. None beheld her, but all felt her power, and the boldest grew bolder, and the weakest were inspired with a valour not their own.

Like a fire blazing among the thickets high up on a mountainside, so blazed the sunlight on shield and helmet, as those countless thousands poured forth into the plain of Scamander, and the earth shook beneath the tramp of steeds and men. On and still on streamed the tide of warriors, unnumbered as the leaves in spring, or as flies that buzz round the milkpails on a sunny day, when the goats are milked by a hundred hands.

And as the shepherd numbers his sheep, for he knoweth them every one, so moved the captains with mastery, each among his own people, and marshalled them in their ranks. Conspicuous among all was seen the majestic form of Agamemnon, to whom it seemed that every god had on that day bestowed some peculiar grace, to make him the observed of all observers, and give the world assurance of a king.

But what tongue can count the myriads brought together by the word of power on Scamander's plain, or what memory can hold the names of the nations assembled there? All the chivalry of Greece had obeyed the summons of the monarch, sent forth nine years before, and they had come flocking in their thousands from the broad plains of Thessaly; from the mountain dells of Locris and of Phocis; from the fat fields of Bœotia; from Attica, with her thin soil and bright, pellucid air; from Salamis, the mother of heroes; from storied Argos and renowned Sparta; from the western islands, and from Creta, the cradle of gods. It would be a weary task to tell over all the heroic titles in that muster-roll of fame, but a few must be mentioned, as being the prime in valour and in worth.

From Locris came the lesser Ajax, son of Oileus. He was small of stature, but swift of foot, and the most skilful spearsman among all the Greeks. His greater namesake, Ajax, son of Telamon, and cousin to Achilles, came from Salamis; he was a giant in stature and in strength, and, next to Achilles, the greatest warrior in all the host.

The ancient city of Tiryns in Argos, with its massy walls, built by a mighty race in the very dawn of time, sent forth a goodly company in eighty ships; and these were commanded by Diomede, son of Tydeus, a gallant and youthful prince, whose deeds fill many a page in the tale of Troy divine. And from the neighbouring city of Mycenæ, the royal seat of the line of Pelops, came Agamemnon himself, at whose imperial nod whole nations flew to arms. His brother, Menelaus, the husband of Helen, on whose account the war had arisen, brought sixty ships, manned by the warriors of Sparta, of which city he was king. He was a mild and gentle prince, and a zealous leader, though in valour and prowess not of the first rank.

Ninety ships formed the contingent led by Nestor, the aged King of Pylos, the most venerable figure, and the wisest head, among all those who fought in the cause of Helen.

Of those who came from the islands the most famous were Odysseus, King of Ithaca, the hero of another famous story, mighty in word and in deed, and, after Nestor, the sagest counsellor in the Grecian camp; and Idomeneus of Crete, a grey-haired veteran who had proved his valour on many a hard-fought field.

Among others singled out for special mention are Nireus, renowned for his wonderful beauty, but otherwise a weakling; Philoctetes, now living in lonely exile on the island of Lemnos, where he had been left by the Greeks on account of a dreadful wound, which rendered his presence in the camp unbearable, and Protesilaus, who had been the first to leap on to the Trojan shore, and had been struck down by a Trojan in the very act.

These two were missing in the grand review of the forces which was now held in anticipation of a victorious march upon Troy, and their places were supplied by others. But there was one whose place none could fill, and whose absence was soon to make itself felt in dire and deadly fashion. Achilles sat idle in his tent, brooding over the insult which he had received two weeks before. His ponderous spear, which none but he could wield, was resting from slaughter, and his squires were polishing the armour which he was not to wear that day. He started when he heard the great shout of the Greeks, as the word was given to march, and his heart burned with longing for battle; but remembering his wrongs, he sank back in his seat, frowning darkly, and muttered the single word "Revenge!"

3

THE DUEL:
Greeks and Trojans
Face to Face

I

PRIAM WAS SITTING in council with all his elders before the doors of his palace, when a messenger rushed breathless up with the tidings that the Greeks were marching in full force against the city. Instantly the meeting broke up, and the Trojan leaders, with Hector at their head, set out with the whole body of native warriors and their allies to bar the way of the invader.

Halting before a solitary mound, the tomb of the Amazon Myrine, within sight of the walls of Troy, they drew up their forces in order of battle. The native Trojans, who fought under Hector, son of Priam, formed the flower of the army; but in numbers they were far exceeded by the troops which had assembled, at the call of Priam, from the adjacent provinces and coastlands of western Asia—from Lydia, Mysia, Paphlagonia, and far-off Lycia—from Sestos and Abydos and Thrace. After Hector, the most famous leaders were Æneas, son of Anchises and Aphrodite; Pandarus, unrivalled for his skill in archery; Paris, whose crime had brought all these woes on his country, and above all the two captains of the Lycians—Sarpedon, the son of Zeus, and Glaucus, the most knightly figure among all the heroes of Greece and Troy.

When the various members of that motley host had taken their appointed stations, the defenders of Troy advanced with clamour and with tumult, like flocks of cranes winging their way to the shores of the ocean stream to make war on the Pygmies. Presently the van of the Greeks came in sight, moving on in silence, like men with one mind and one heart.

Foremost among the Trojan champions was seen the gay and beautiful Paris. He was clad in a panther's skin, over which hung his bow and arrows, and besides these weapons, in the use of which he excelled, he was armed with two long spears and a sword. Menelaus marked him as he came on with long strides, and rejoiced in spirit, like a hungry lion when he catches sight of his prey; and leaping down from his car he advanced with uplifted spear to take vengeance on his treacherous foe. But when Paris saw him coming his guilty heart quailed within him, and he shrank back among the ranks of his comrades, like one who has trodden on a snake while walking in a mountain glen.

"Now curse on thy fair, false face!" cried Hector to his cowardly brother, "thou carpet-knight, thou foul deceiver! Better for thee to have died childless and unwed than thus to bring shame on thy father and all thy kinsfolk and people. Thou art a fit foe for women, whom thou beguilest with witchcraft of thy wit, and wicked gifts; but all thy gifts—thy curling locks, thy smooth, white brow, thy sweet voice, and cunning minstrelsy—avail thee naught when thou lookest upon the face of a man. Verily the Trojans are as dastardly as thyself, or long ere this thou wouldst have put on a doublet of stone[2] for all the ills that thou hast wrought."

"I have deserved thy rebuke," answered Paris. "Keen as the blade of an axe, which bites deep into the heart of an oak, when wielded by a sinewy arm, so is the keenness of thy spirit, and thou knowest not fear. Nevertheless, mock me not for the lovely gifts of Aphrodite, for the gifts of heaven are not to be despised. And if thou desirest me to take up this quarrel with Menelaus thou hast thy wish. I will fight against him hand to hand, and he who is victor shall be lord of Helen and all her possessions. So shall the long strife have an end, and peace shall dwell again within our borders."

When Hector heard his brother's bold words he was glad, and gave the word to make the Trojans sit down in their ranks. At first the Greeks did not understand what was happening, and pressed onward to the attack

---

2. That is, "Wouldst have been stoned to death."

with a shower of stones and arrows; but Agamemnon soon perceived that Hector had something to propose, and gave the signal for a general halt.

Then Hector, standing midway between the two armies, made known the offer of Paris, and asked for an armistice, that the two champions might try the issue between them. All eyes were now turned on Menelaus, who responded boldly to the challenge. "I am well content," said he, "that this quarrel should be decided by the hands of us twain; for it grieves my heart that so many should suffer for the sake of my private wrong. Let two lambs be brought—a white ram as an offering to the sun, and a black ram as an offering to the earth; and go some of you to fetch Priam, that he may preside at the treaty. His sons we may not trust, for they are hot-blooded and faithless; but an old man's head is cool, and his eye looks before and after."

Right pleased were both Greeks and Trojans when the order was sent round to dismount from their cars and pile their arms; for they thought that the end of their bitter feud was near. Two heralds were despatched to bring down Priam from the city, and Agamemnon sent another for a victim to be sacrificed on behalf of the Greeks.

II

Helen was sitting in her chamber, weaving a fair tapestry, on which were wrought the famous deeds done in her cause by Greek and Trojan heroes, when her task was interrupted by the sudden entrance of her kinswoman, Laodice, a daughter of Priam. "Make haste, dear sister," said the lady, "come with me, and see the wonderful thing which has been brought to pass. Greeks and Trojans are sitting down in amity together, and Paris and Menelaus are to fight with long spears for the mastery; and he that prevaileth shall call thee his wife."

When she heard that, a great longing came into the heart of Helen for her Spartan home and her former lord. With one tearful glance at the speaker she rose from her seat, veiled her face, and made her way to the high tower above the gate where Priam was sitting with the elders of Troy. The shrill, piping voices[3] of the old men struck upon her ears as she stepped out upon the turret; and when they saw her they put their heads together, and whispered their admiration of her wondrous loveliness. "How fair, how very fair she is!" murmured one white-bearded veteran. "Is she not worthy to be the arbitress of life and death to a whole generation of heroes! Nevertheless let her depart, and breed no further mischief to us and our children."

Then Priam called to her, and beckoned her with a courteous gesture to take her place by his side. "Come hither, dear daughter," he said, "where thou canst see thy former husband, and thy kinsfolk and friends. I blame thee not at all because of this war which the

---

3. Compared by Homer to grasshoppers.

gods have brought upon me in mine old age. Now tell me," he continued, pointing with his finger towards the Greek army, which lay in full view upon the plain, "who is that stately man to whom all the other chieftains seem to pay homage? Ne'er saw I one of so kingly a mien."

"I dread thy presence, father," answered Helen, glancing in the direction indicated, and then casting down her eyes. "I tremble before thee, kind as thou art, for I feel all the wrong which I have done unto thee and thine. And as touching him of whom thou askest, that is Agamemnon, son of Atreus, lord of a wide empire, a righteous king, and a valiant warrior. Once I called him brother," she added, with a sigh.

"'Tis then as I thought," rejoined Priam, "for there is sovereignty in his look. And who is he who stands next to Agamemnon, in stature less than he, but broader of shoulder and deeper of chest? Methinks he is like a stately ram, who stalks majestic before the flock as they go to pasture."

"That is Odysseus, son of Laertes," answered Helen, "bred in the rugged isle of Ithaca. All Greece cannot show his equal in wisdom and eloquence."

"Lady," said Antenor, an elder of high rank. "herein thou hast spoken the very truth. I entertained him of whom thou speakest as my guest when he came hither on an embassy with Menelaus, and I heard them both speaking before the assembly of the Trojans. When they stood up together Menelaus was by far the taller; but when they were seated there was greater dignity in Odysseus. Then as to eloquence, Odysseus bore away the palm from all—though Menelaus spoke both fluently and to the purpose. At first, when Odysseus rose to speak, we wondered to see how ungracefully he stood, leaning heavily on his sceptre, with eyes fixed upon the ground. He seemed a very churl, unskilled in all courtesy and the arts of civil life. But when he lifted up his mighty voice, and his words floated about us like the snowflakes of winter, we knew that we were listening to a divinely gifted man."

At Priam's request Helen named the other chieftains of the Greeks, Ajax and Idomeneus, and the rest; and when the recital was ended she remained gazing wistfully at the dense masses of fighting men who sat waiting on the plain. "I cannot see them," she murmured sadly: "they are not there." "Of whom speakest thou?" asked Priam. "Of Castor and Polydeuces," she answered, "the bold rider, and the stout boxer, my own brothers, born of the same mother with me. Perchance they sailed not in the fleet to Troy, or perchance they have remained behind in the camp, in sorrow for their sister's shame."

Ah! Helen, thy brothers are lying where shame and sorrow can reach them no more, sleeping in their quiet graves, in Lacedæmon, their native land.

III

While Priam was still conversing with Helen, a herald entered with the startling news that his presence was required in the field, to settle the conditions of the single combat between Paris and Menelaus. Some natural pangs he felt, when he heard of the danger which threatened his son. Nevertheless he set out at once, taking with him the victims required for the sacrifice. When he came to the open space between the two armies he found all things ready for the solemn rite. The chiefs stood waiting in a circle, and in their midst was Agamemnon, who acted as priest. The heralds mingled two portions of pure[4] wine in a bowl, and poured water over the hands of the chieftains. Then Agamemnon drew a sharp knife, which hung at his girdle by his ponderous sword, and cutting off a few hairs from the foreheads of the victims gave them to the heralds to distribute among the princes. When this was done, amidst a general hush he uttered this solemn prayer: "Father Zeus, Lord of Ida, most glorious, most mighty, ye rivers, and thou earth, and ye dread powers beneath, who take vengeance after death on all those who swear a false oath, be ye all the witnesses and guardians of our treaty. If Paris slays Menelaus he shall keep Helen for his wife, with all her goods; but should Paris fall Helen shall go back to Menelaus, her lawful lord. Let the war be decided by the issue of this combat, and

---

4. In sacrifices pure wine was used; wine for drinking was always mixed with water.

Heaven defend the right!" Therewith he cut the throats of the victims, and laid their quivering bodies on the ground. Then the drink-offering was poured, with this awful imprecation on those who should break the treaty: "If any man violate our sworn oath, may his brains be poured out, even as this wine, and may his wife and children be sold into bondage."

Priam now took his departure from the field, for he could not bear to see his son in deadly combat with Menelaus. When he was gone, Hector and Odysseus measured out the ground for the duel, and shook the lots in a helmet, to see who should be the first to cast his spear; and the lot fell on Paris. Meanwhile Paris was putting on his armour; for he had come lightly equipped as an archer into the field.

The two rivals took their stand on either side, clad in their brazen harness, and armed with sword and spear. And first Paris cast his spear, which struck upon the shield of Menelaus, and did him no harm. Then Menelaus lifted up his spear, and murmured a prayer to Zeus: "Grant me, O King, to take vengeance on him who brought dishonour on my home, where he dwelt as my honoured guest." As he spoke, he flung his good ashen spear, which clove its way through the shield of Paris, and tore his tunic close to his side; but Paris swerved aside and escaped a wound. Before he could recover himself Menelaus was upon him, sword in hand, and struck him with all his force upon the helmet; but once more fortune favoured the Trojan, for the blade was shivered on the ridge of the helmet, and Menelaus grasped a useless hilt. "Curse on thee, treacherous steel!" cried he, and, seizing Paris by the helmet, began to drag him towards the ranks of the Greeks. This time he would have succeeded, and taken his enemy captive, had not the strap which held the helmet given way under the strain, so that the brazen headpiece came away empty in his hand.

Menelaus flung the helmet towards his friends, and picking up his spear turned again upon his cowardly foe, with purpose to slay him. But Paris was nowhere to be seen: an invisible hand had caught him up, and carried him away from the righteous hand of the avenger. For Aphrodite, the soft goddess of love, had been hovering near to protect her favourite. She it was who had caused the helmet strap to break, and now she saved him a second time, and bore him swiftly to his house in Troy. There he was presently visited by the lovely Helen, who, though she scorned him in her heart, was drawn thither by a fatal spell which she could not resist; and in the sunshine of her smiles he soon forgot dishonour and defeat.

All this time Menelaus was raging about the field, like a tiger robbed of his prey, and calling upon the Trojans to surrender the recreant to his vengeance; and they would gladly have done so, if they had known where to find him, for they hated him worse than death. And Agamemnon, amid general applause, demanded the surrender of Helen, according to the terms of the treaty.

4

THE BREAKING
OF THE TRUCE

I

THE GODS WERE met in full assembly in their golden palace, pledging one another in full cups of nectar, and looking down upon the great drama which was being enacted on the plains of Troy. Then Zeus began to speak, casting a sly glance at his fair consort, Hera: "Menelaus has two stout backers among the gods, Hera, Queen of Argos, and Athene, strong to defend. But they seem to have renounced his cause, for they have suffered Aphrodite to steal away Paris when death stared him in the face. 'Tis well, then, Menelaus has the victory, and naught remains but to give back Helen, and put an end to the war."

At this most unwelcome proposal Athene frowned angrily at her father, but said nothing; Hera, however, could not contain her wrath, and raised her voice in indignant protest: "Out upon thee, son of Cronos, what a word hast thou spoken! Is this to be the end of all my toil and my sweat, when I travelled without ceasing, until my steeds were well-nigh foundered, to gather this host against Troy? Do as thou wilt; but know this, that, if thou doest this thing, not one of us shall praise thee, no, not one."

"What strange passion possesses thee?" answered Zeus, in tones of displeasure, "Why harbourest thou this deadly rancour against Priam and the sons of Priam? Methinks thou couldst find it in thy heart to go down into the city, and feast on the raw flesh of the men of Troy, until thou hadst devoured them all. Howbeit, let there be peace among us; I give thee leave to work thy will upon this king and his people; only remember that I have yielded to thee in this, and when I am minded to destroy some city which is dear to thee stand not thou in my way. For I love the towers of holy Ilios, and they that dwell therein, for they have paid me faithful worship, with meat-offering and with drink-offering, with reverence and with prayer."

"Take Argos," replied the impetuous Hera. "Take Sparta or Mycenæ, the three choicest jewels in my crown; burn, waste, and destroy them, if such be thy pleasure. Only grant me this boon, and let me wreak my fury upon Troy. If thou consentest to this, lay thy command upon thy daughter, Athene, that she may go down among the Greeks and Trojans, and make an end of this detested truce."

Zeus nodded in token of approval, and Athene, who was only waiting for the signal, shot down from

Olympus like a falling star, and alighted in the space between the two armies. Arrived there, she put on the form of Laodocus, a noble Trojan youth, and went in search of Pandarus, a famous bowman, and a favourite of the archer-god Apollo. And when she had found him, she spake unto him in this wise: "Bold son of Lycaon, art thou man enough to do a great deed, and win praise and reward from all the Trojans, but especially from Paris? If thou art, take thine arrows and thy bow, and aim a shaft at Menelaus, having first vowed a vow to Apollo that when thou returnest to thy home among the rich pastures of Ida, thou wilt offer him a sacrifice of lambs, the firstlings of the flock."

So spake Athene, tempting him; and he hearkened unto her in his folly, and began to take the cover from his bow. It was a powerful weapon, formed from the horns of a great ibex, which he himself had brought down by a skilful shot long ago. The horns, each sixteen palms in length, were set firmly in a solid bridge, and tipped at each end with gold. Resting the lower end of the bow against his foot, he leaned upon it, and strung it, and laying it down took off the lid of his quiver, and selected an arrow. Then he took up the bow again, and set the arrow on the string. His companions, who had been covering him with their shields while he was making his preparations, now stepped aside, and he, having made his vow to Apollo, lifted up his bow, drew the arrow to his ear, and shot. The bow twanged loud and clear, and the arrow leapt hissing towards the

Grecian ranks.

Then ill had it fared with thee, Menelaus, had not Athene been standing at thy side, to guard thee from fatal hurt. And as a mother brushes a fly from the face of her babe, lying in sweet slumber on her lap, so Athene suffered not the arrow to reach any vital part, but guided it to the place where the plates of his corslet met at his side. Through the girdle pierced the shaft, through the brazen corslet, and through the taslet which covered his loins; the point just grazed the surface of his flesh, and the red blood began to flow, staining his thighs, and trickling down to his ankles.

When Agamemnon saw his brother wounded and bleeding, he ran to his side, and taking him by the hand began to deplore the evil issue of their treaty. "Must thy life pay the forfeit for the perjured men of Troy, who have trampled our covenant underfoot? I know indeed that vengeance will overtake them in the end from the hands of Zeus, whose name they have taken in vain; yea, well I know that the day shall come when holy Ilios shall fall, involved with all her people in one common doom. But what will that avail, if I lose thee, my brother? My army will desert me, for they cannot fight without a cause, and thou art the cause which brought them hither. Troy's doom will be wrought by other hands, and I shall go back to Argos, a beaten man, leaving thy bones to rot in a foreign grave."

"Speak not so loud," said Menelaus, when Agamemnon paused at last; "thou wilt cause a panic in the army. There is no ground for alarm; the wound is not deep. Send for Machaon, the skilled leech, that he may draw out the arrow, and stanch the flow of blood."

Then Agamemnon was comforted, and sent Talthybius the herald to bring the leech, who was a son of Asclepius, the most famous physician of those times. After some delay, Machaon came to the place where Menelaus was standing, leaning on his brother's arm, and surrounded by an anxious group of his friends. With firm but gentle hand the leech drew out the arrow, and, removing the prince's armour, exposed the wound to view. Then he applied healing herbs, and bade the patient be of good cheer, for his hurt was but slight.

II

The truce having been broken by the treacherous act of Pandarus, both sides prepared for an immediate assault. Agamemnon, as soon as he was assured that his brother was in no danger, summoned his chariot, and, bidding the driver keep within call, went on foot up and down the ranks of the Greeks, encouraging those whom he saw pressing forward to the attack with promises of favour and reward, and upbraiding those who hung back with taunts and rebukes. His heart rejoiced when he saw the towering form of Ajax, who was hurrying to battle, followed close by a stout troop of spearsmen, with shield pressing on shield, and bristling spears.

Near him was Idomeneus, the grizzled captain of the Cretans, with his comrade, Meriones, at the head of a numerous and well-appointed troop. And after these he came to the men of Nestor, who were receiving instructions from their veteran leader how to bear themselves in the battle. "Keep your ranks," he was saying, "and fight shoulder to shoulder, the horsemen in the van, and the infantry ready to support them behind. And let no one be carried away by his zeal to engage singlehanded with the enemy, for union is strength, and weakness comes of division."

These were the foremost, but there were others, and among them some of the most valiant leaders in the army, whose station was more remote, and who had not yet heard of the breaking of the truce. One of these was Diomede, and when Agamemnon found him standing inactive, he rebuked him harshly, reminding him of his father's prowess, and calling him an unworthy son. The young chieftain deigned no answer to the unmerited reproach, but at once put his men in motion to join the encounter.

The whole army was now advancing, rank pressing on rank, and column on column, like the waves rushing landward along a wide-watered shore. The Greeks came on in silence, broken only by the short, sharp words of command; but the Trojans, whose army was made up of a motley throng of many nations, rushed to the onset with multitudinous cries, like ewes at milking-time in the folds of a wealthy sheep master, when they hear the voices of their lambs. On the Trojan side was Ares, and on the side of the Greeks stern-eyed Athene, with whom were seen Panic and Flight, and insatiable Strife, who is small of stature at the beginning of a fray, but grows and grows as the feud proceeds, until her head presses against the sky as she stalks along the earth.

Then the air was rent with a deafening crash, as the two armies met, and shield was dashed against shield, and brazen armour was dinted by spear and axe and sword. Shouts of triumph arose, and cries of anguish, as the wild *mêlée* swayed to and fro, and the ground ran with blood. As two torrents descending from copious springs high up in the mountains, and swollen high by winter rains, mingle their waters with a roar at a place where two glens meet—such was the roar which went up to heaven, at the conflict of those mailed hosts.

Among the many victims of that bloody day, some are singled out for especial mention. One of these was Simocisius, a tall and comely youth, so named because he was born on the banks of the Simocis, when his mother went to visit her parents on their farm. Ajax marked him as he came on, and smote him in the breast with his spear; and down he fell, like a tall poplar, which rears its stately height in a meadow by the riverside, until it is hewn down by a wheelwright to make a felly for a chariot; and there it lies seasoning on the banks of the stream. So lay the young Simocisius, and Ajax stripped him of his armour. While he was thus engaged, Antiphus, a son of Priam, flung a javelin at him, but, missing him, struck down Leucus, a comrade of Odysseus, who had laid hold of the corpse to hale it away. Odysseus was exceeding wroth at the fall of his comrade, and stepping forward he flung his spear, and smote Democoon, a natural son of Priam, in the temple. The Trojan champions fell back before him, and the Greeks rushed forward and gained possession of the dead. Apollo, who sat watching the battle from the citadel of Troy, was indignant when he saw the Trojans give ground, and shouted to them in a loud voice, crying: "Up, ye horsemen of Troy, and fly not from these Greeks, for their flesh is not of stone or of iron, to resist the thrust of your spears. Now is your time, while Achilles is absent, chewing the cud of his ire among the ships."

The Trojans rallied at the cry of the god, and the battle was resumed with fresh fury on both sides. It was no child's play, no holiday tilting, which was seen that morning on the Trojan plain, but the dire and dreadful game of war, with Ares and Athene for players, and the blood of heroes for the stakes.

5

THE EXPLOITS OF DIOMEDE

I

AGAMEMNON'S TAUNTS had sunk deep into the heart of Diomede, and he went into battle with a stern resolve to vindicate his manhood in the eyes of all Greece. A fierce light blazed from his helm and shield as he rushed, like a living engine of destruction, into the thickest of the fight. The first to feel the weight of his arm was a young Trojan named Phegeus, son of Dares, a priest of Hephæstus. Mounted on the same car with his brother Idæus, he drove furiously at Diomede, who was fighting on foot, and aimed a blow at him with his spear; but the weapon went wide of the mark, and the next moment he rolled from his car, pierced through the breast by the spear of Diomede. Idæus sprang to the ground and fled, leaving car and horses as a spoil to his brother's slayer.

While Diomede was disposing of his booty, the Greeks pursued their advantage, and there was not a chieftain of name among them who failed to slay his man. Then fell Scamandrius, a famous Trojan hunter, and the favourite of Artemis, pierced in the back by the spear of Menelaus, and Phericlus, whose father, Tecton, had built the fatal ships which bore Paris and his retinue to Greece, and many more, of whose names there is no record.

Back to the field came Diomede, sweeping all before him like a river in flood, which breaks down dyke and dam, and covers the smiling fields with ruin. So impetuous were his movements as he darted to and fro in pursuit of the flying Trojans, that it was hard to see on which side he fought; but, wherever he passed, his path was strewn with Trojan dead.

At last he received a check from Pandarus, the archer whose treacherous hand had broken the truce an hour or two before. Watching him from a safe distance, Pandarus shot an arrow, which pierced clean through Diomede's right shoulder, staining his corslet with blood. Loud was the joy of Pandarus when he saw the success of his archery: "Turn again," he shouted, "ye horsemen of Troy! Back to the fray, every one! The bravest of the Greeks is wounded unto death."

The boast of Pandarus was premature, for the wound was not severe, though sufficient to disable the hero's arm for the moment. Diomede drew back out of the press, and with the assistance of Sthenelus, his charioteer, drew out the arrow which was galling his shoulder. Then he stood apart and prayed to Athene, the patron goddess of his mighty father, Tydeus. And she heard him, and came and stood before him in all her divine majesty, and said: "Take heart, son of Tydeus, for I am ever near thee, and I have put into thy heart all the valour of thy sire. And I have taken from thine eyes the darkness which before lay upon them, that thou mayest look upon the gods and know them, face to face. If thou seest any of the other gods, avoid them, and presume not to fight against the children of heaven; but if Aphrodite, Jove's froward daughter, comes into the battle, have at her, and strike, and fear nothing."

Athene vanished as she spoke, but Diomede felt her influence working powerfully within him, and in an instant the flow of his blood was stanched, and he felt no more pain from his wound. Then like a lion who has been grazed by the shepherd's spear as he leaps into a lonely sheepfold, and is but provoked to new rage by that slight wound, so that he falls upon the helpless flock, and gluts himself with carnage, while the shepherd cowers away in terror—so Diomede returned with new fury to the slaughter, and drove the Trojans in rout before him. Like hammer on anvil, so rained his strokes among the ranks of the foe. With one blow he sent his spear through the breast of a tall Trojan; with the next his keen falchion shore oft the arm and shoulder of another. Leaving these where they lay, he went in pursuit of Abas and Polyidus, the sons of Eurydamas, a famous seer and interpreter of dreams. Often had they listened to their father's lore, and brought their dreams to him to expound unto them. But the worst dream they ever had now came upon them; and when they awoke they were on the banks of the Styx. Yet another Trojan father had cause to mourn that day—Phænops, a man of wealth, who sent two sons, the children of his old age, to the war. But never again did his aged eyes brighten to behold the face of his children, and all his wealth was divided among strangers.

When Æneas observed the havoc which was wrought by the arm of Diomede he went to Pandarus, and said to him: "Where is thy boasted skill in archery, that thou sufferest this man to hew down our ranks, and never liftest thy bow against him? Come, shoot me an arrow at the breast of Diomede, and first utter a prayer to Zeus, that we may know if the gods are indeed against us."

"If that be Diomede," answered Pandarus, "there is something divine in this frenzy of his; methinks he is some god, who has put on the likeness of Diomede. But now, I aimed an arrow at him, and struck him fairly in the right shoulder. I thought that he was already a passenger to Hades, but, lo! he comes forth stronger and more terrible than before. In an evil hour I took my bow from the wall, when I came to fight on the side of Priam; and I hearkened not to my father's words when he bade me fight like the rest with chariot and with horses, whereof he had goodly store. Twice have I drawn my bow this day against the noblest of the Greeks, Menelaus, and Diomede, and struck them fair, and made their blood to flow; but it hath naught availed. If ever I get safely home again, I will offer my head to be severed from my shoulders by the meanest churl, if I do not break this accursed bow of mine in pieces, and burn it with fire."

"This is idle talk," answered Æneas. "We must meet this man face to face and hand to hand if we would stay his fury. Come, mount my car with me, that thou mayest see of what mettle are these steeds of mine, unrivalled in flight or in pursuit. If thou wilt, take the reins, and I will stand by thy side to wield the spear; or if thou preferrest it, I will drive and thou shalt fight."

"Drive thou," replied Pandarus, mounting by the side of Æneas, "so that if there be need of hasty flight, the steeds may not fail us, knowing their master's hand." "Thou sayest well," said Æneas, and, lashing the horses to a gallop, drove rapidly towards the place where Diomede was fighting.

"Back, Diomede!" shouted Sthenelus, in alarm, when he saw them approaching. "I see two mighty men coming against us—Pandarus, son of Lycaon, and Æneas, whose mother is the goddess Aphrodite. Mount the car, and let us retreat."

"How darest thou name retreat to me," answered Diomede sternly, "I scorn thy counsels, and will go to meet these champions even as I am, on foot; both of them shall not return alive. And now mark my words, and do as I shall bid thee: if these twain fall beneath my spear, leave thou the horses which thou art driving, and, having mounted the car of Æneas, drive with all speed to the rear. For these steeds are of blood divine, descended from those which Zeus gave unto Tros as a recompense for the loss of Ganymede his son. If we can capture them it will be a splendid prize."

So saying, he turned to meet the Trojan chieftains, who were now close at hand. Pandarus held his weapon ready poised, and when he came within throwing distance he cast his lance, crying: "Take that, bold son of Tydeus! Perchance I shall have better luck with the spear." The weighty spear, thrown by no feeble hand, pierced through the shield of Diomede, and struck against his breastplate, but there stopped short, without inflicting a wound. "Thou hast no luck to-day, Sir Pandarus," said Diomede, smiling grimly. "Now see how thou likest the taste of Grecian steel," and as he spoke he hurled with all his force, right in the face of Pandarus. The keen point struck him just beneath the eye, and passing downwards clove through his tongue at the root, and came out under his chin; and the false Trojan fell with a crash on the plain, and died as he fell.

Æneas had now but one thought—to save his comrade›s body from outrage at the hands of the Greeks; for it was the cruel custom of those days to mutilate the bodies of slaughtered enemies. Valiantly he took his stand, bestriding the fallen Pandarus, holding his shield before him, and armed with two spears. But Diomede picked up a huge stone, and flung it at Æneas; and the jagged missile struck him on the hip, just at the socket of the thigh, bruising the sinews and lacerating the flesh. Æneas sank down on one knee, sick and giddy with the pain of that dreadful blow; and that would have been his last hour had not his goddess mother perceived his evil plight, and come to her son›s relief. Swiftly she flew to the place where he lay, and, throwing her white arms about him, bore him from the field, covered by the folds of her robe.

Sthenelus had not forgotten his friend's command, and as soon as he saw the car of Æneas deserted he made fast the reins of his own steeds to the chariot rim, and mounting the Trojan car drove at a gallop towards the rear. Meeting a comrade he gave the captured chariot into his charge, and returned with all speed to the support of Diomede, who was in hot pursuit of the tender goddess and her wounded son. Presently he caught her in the midst of the press, and, thrusting with his spear, wounded her on the hand, in the thick part of the thumb. The ichor[5] flowed forth in a purple stream, and stained her immortal vestments, wrought for her by the Graces; and with a loud shriek she let fall her son, who was picked up and borne to a place of safety by Apollo.

"Hast thou had enough of war, daughter of Zeus?" shouted Diomede as she fled; "go and make war on cowardly women—they are thy proper prey."

---

5.   The blood of the gods was so called.

II

The beautiful, tender goddess of love, who was a stranger to wounds and pain, was found by Iris wandering about the battlefield in a distracted state, with livid face and shaking limbs. Iris took her by the hand, and brought her to the place where Ares was sitting, outside the roar and tumult of battle. When she saw her brother, Aphrodite fell on her knees before him, and begged him to lend her his car, and Ares having readily consented, she mounted the golden chariot with Iris, and was driven through the air till she came to Olympus. There she sought her mother Dione, who received her with sweet words of comfort, and asked who had handled her so roughly? "It was that unmannerly Greek, the son of Tydeus," answered Aphrodite pettishly, "for the Greeks have left off butchering the Trojans, and are making war on the gods."

"Take heart, my child," said Dione, "and be not overmuch dismayed, for many of us, the children of heaven, have suffered at the hands of mortals, for whose sake we afflict one another. Ares was bound and held captive by the giant sons of Aloeus, and would have perished in his bonds, had not Hermes stolen him away. Hera was wounded in the breast with an arrow by Hercules; and Hades came groaning to Olympus, hurt in the shoulder by the same presumptuous hand. And thou hast suffered through the spite of Athene, who set on the son of Tydeus to assail thee. Rash fool!

He knows not that he who fights with gods is doomed to an early grave. Let him take heed lest the young wife whom he left at home in Argos be made a widow untimely, and rouse her household at dead of night, weeping and wailing for her fallen lord."

Then she laid a healing finger on her daughter's wound, and the hand was made whole, and the bitter pangs were stilled. Athene had been watching the scene, and now she said mockingly to her father: "Be not wroth, dread sire, at what I shall say! Surely Aphrodite hath been seeking to beguile some Grecian dame on behalf of her darling Trojans, and amidst her soft caresses has scratched her slender hand on the pin of the lady's brooch."

Zeus smiled at his daughter's words, and calling Aphrodite to him he took her in his fatherly arms and said: "Not for thee, my child, are wars and fightings; leave these to Ares and Athene, and keep to thine own province of love and marriage."

III

When Diomede saw his prey snatched from him a second time he was very wroth, and followed close on Apollo, who was bearing Æneas towards the city. Three times he sprang upon the god, and three times Apollo hurled him back; and he was preparing to make a fourth assault, when Apollo rebuked him sternly, and bade him stand off. Remembering the words of Athene, who had warned him not to meddle with any other god save Aphrodite, Diomede drew back, and Æneas was carried in safety to the shelter of the citadel.

Apollo was highly incensed at the presumption of Diomede, and leaving Æneas in good hands he hastened back to the battlefield, and roused Ares to take up the cause of insulted heaven, and chastise the impious man who twice that day had pointed his weapon against the person of a god. Ares readily took up the challenge, and putting on the likeness of a Trojan he flung himself in the path of the panic-stricken fugitives, shouting: "Where are the sons of Priam, and why suffer they the people to be slaughtered like sheep?"

"Hearest thou what he saith?" cried Sarpedon, the giant leader of the Lycians, to Hector, who had been dismayed, like the rest, by the prowess of Diomede. "What art thou doing, thou and thy brethren, that ye leave the brunt of battle to be borne by your allies? Have we not left home and country, our wives and our little ones, to pour out our blood in defence of thy city?—and wilt thou not play thy part, when honour and duty call thee—when the very stones of thy streets cry aloud to thee to be the first in the onset, the last to retreat?"

Stung by Sarpedon's reproaches, Hector leapt from his car, and exerted all his authority to rally the flying Trojans. By his efforts the flight was checked, and the Trojans wheeled their chariots and returned to the charge. The ranks of the Greeks grew white from the clouds of dust thrown up by their chariot wheels as they came on like a whirlwind, with Ares in their van. Presently, to the equal delight and amazement of the Trojans, the princely form of Æneas was seen glittering among the foremost champions; and his step was as light, and his arm as firm, as when the fight began. They would have learnt, if they had asked, that this was the work of Apollo; but they had no time to question him, for by this time the storm of battle was raging with redoubled fury.

Like clouds which lie heavy on the mountain-tops, when all the winds are sleeping, so steadfast stood the Greeks to abide the shock of that charge. And Agamemnon strode up and down the armed files, crying as he passed: "Stand firm, and play the man! Before you lies the path of honour, but behind is shame and defeat."

Long the contest swayed to and fro with doubtful issue, and many a Greek, and many a Trojan, named or unnamed, received the wages of the sword. At last Diomede, whose vision had been purged by Athene, recognised Ares under his disguise; then even he began to lose heart, and cried out to the Greeks: "We must retreat! Ares is fighting against us. Fall back upon the ships, keeping your faces to the foe." And slowly, step by step, disputing every inch of ground, the Greeks began to retire.

Hitherto Hera and Athene had remained inactive spectators of the struggle: but when they saw that the tide of battle had turned they resolved to make a vigorous stand against the victorious career of Ares. With her own hand Hera harnessed the steeds to her royal car, which was the work of no mortal artist, with its brazen wheels and axle of iron. The body of the car was cunningly wrought with bands of gold and silver; the pole was a solid bar of silver, and the yoke was of gold. Meanwhile Athene was arming herself for the conflict. First she put on a coat of mail, not to be pierced by any mortal weapon; on her head she placed a helmet, glittering with symbols of war and death; then she grasped her shield, the immortal ægis, of "ethereal temper, massy, large, and round," on which were pictured Panic and Strife, Defence and Pursuit, and all the dread powers whose realm is the battlefield; and in the midst glared the Gorgon's head, with its awful eyes, which freeze the blood and paralyse the limbs.

Having asked and obtained permission of Zeus, they mounted the car, Hera guiding the fiery coursers of heaven, and Athene standing, spear in hand, at her side. In another moment they drew up before the cloudy portals of Olympus, which are given in charge of the mystic Daughters of Time, to open and to shut. Wide flew the gates, with muttered roar, at the summons of the queen of heaven; and forth they leapt into the void and cavernous vault of air. Far as a man can see into the dim distance, when he stands on some skyey peak and gazes across the purple sea—so wide is the space traversed by the heavenly steeds at a single stride.

When they came to the place where Simoeis and Scamander mingle their waters in one stream, they drew up their car, and dismounted, leaving the steeds in charge of the river-god Simoeis, whose banks put forth ambrosial herbs for them to feed upon. Then, walking delicately, like a pair of doves,[6] but with no tender thoughts in their breasts, they went and joined the ranks of the Greeks, where they stood at bay round Diomede, like boars or lions hard pressed by the hunters. Standing in their midst, Hera took the form and the voice of Stentor, whose shout was as the shout of fifty men. "Shame on you, ye Greeks!" she thundered. "As long as Achilles fought among you, the Trojans never ventured beyond their gates; but now they are fighting at the very confines of your camp."

Diomede had drawn back from the fighting-line, for his arm was lamed by the wound which he had received from Pandarus, which now began to stiffen and grow painful. In this state he was found by Athene, just as he was lifting up his shield strap to wipe away the blood from his shoulder. Laying her hand on the yoke of his car she said: "The son of Tydeus is most unlike his sire, who was little of stature, but mighty of heart. With him I needed the curb to restrain his fiery spirit, which prompted him to fight against any odds. But thy sluggish nature ever wants the goad. Say, art thou weary, or art thou afraid?"

---

6. I have preserved the language of the original, which seems to have a touch of irony.

"It is not fear that has made me shrink," answered Diomede. "I am but obeying thy behest, when thou forbadest me to resist any god, save only Aphrodite. And thou seest Ares is lending aid to the Greeks."

"Fear neither Ares, nor any other god," replied Athene. "Mount thou thy car with me, and thou shalt see whether this turncoat, this fickle, furious, blood-thirsty god of war, will brook thy onset when I am by thy side.

Thereupon she thrust down Sthenelus from the chariot, and taking his place beckoned to Diomede to mount with her. Diomede obeyed, and the beechen axle groaned beneath the weight of the hero and the goddess. Athene plied the lash, and drove straight at Ares, who was stooping to strip off the armour of a Greek champion whom he had just slain with his own hand. The goddess had put on the helmet of Hades, which made her invisible to the eyes of Ares; and he, when he saw Diomede coming against him, left off stripping the corpse, and charged with levelled spear. But Athene caught the weapon by the shaft, and turned the point aside. Then Diomede thrust at Ares with his spear, Athene aiding him, and wounded him in the side. And as the roar of ten thousand men in the full fury of battle, so was the roar of Ares when he felt that wound.

Like a heavy thundercloud, which hangs black and threatening when heaven is overcast, and a storm is brewing on a sultry day, such appeared the giant form of Ares as he fled darkling across the sky to Olympus; and when he reached the seat of the gods he sat down near Zeus, his father, and showed him the immortal blood flowing from his wound. "What thinkest thou," he said, speaking in a pitiful voice, "of these deeds of violence? Thou art the author of this wound; for it is thy weak indulgence which makes thy daughter, Athene, so violent and unruly. Nothing but the speed of my feet saved me from worse outrage."

But the injured Ares found scant sympathy from his father. "Come not to me," he said sternly, "with thy whining complaints. Blame thy mother for what thou hast suffered; for to her thou owest the froward temper which makes thee the most hateful to me of all my children. Nevertheless I will not leave thee in pain, for thou art my son, the child of my wedded love. Were it not so, I would have found thee a place in the dungeons where the Titans groan." Then he laid his commands upon Pæan, the god of healing, who sprinkled powerful remedies on the wound, which gave instant relief. Swift as is the action of the fig-juice when it falls with eager droppings[7] into milk, and turns it to curd, so quickly closed the wound under the skilful hands of Pæan. And when he had bathed, Ares sat down, hale and whole, by his father's side.

---

7. Used as rennet. "Eager droppings" is from Hamlet.

6

THE BATTLE CONTINUED: Hector and Andromache

I

HAVING DRIVEN Ares from the field, Hera and Athene returned to Olympus, leaving the battle to be decided by human strength and valour. Soon the numbers and prowess of the Greeks began to prevail, and the Trojans were gradually forced back towards their walls. At this critical moment Hector, who hitherto had played but a secondary part in the battle, was suddenly inspired with almost superhuman courage and energy, and by his example the Trojans were saved from a general rout. Having allayed the panic, he left the other leaders to make head against the enemy, and went himself into the city, with the purpose of ordering a general sacrifice and supplication, to avert the anger of Athene.

Both armies were growing weary of the long struggle, and during Hector's absence the work of slaughter ceased for a time by mutual consent. Diomede alone kept the field, and stalked about in the space between the two armies, eyeing the ranks of the Trojans, and seeking for a foeman worthy of his steel. Glaucus, the Lycian captain, marked his defiant attitude, and strode forward undaunted to the encounter. When they were met in the middle of the plain, Diomede accosted him with haughty mien, and said: "Who art thou, bold sir, that hast dared to match thyself with me? Unhappy are the parents whose sons affront my might.[8] If thou be a god, I will not meddle with thee, for I fear to lift my hand again to fight with the sons of heaven. But if thou art of the race of men, that live by bread, come on, and I will give thee to thy doom. But first tell me thy name and thy race."

"Valiant son of Tydeus," answered Glaucus, "why askest thou my race? As the leaves which clothe the woods in spring, to be scattered by autumn winds, such are the generations of men: one riseth up, and another is passing away. Nevertheless, if thou desirest to know my race, know that I am sprung from the line of Sisyphus, through my grandsire Bellerophon, who came as an exile to Lycia, banished from his native Corinth by a woman's spite. For, while he was dwelling as a guest in the house of Prœtus, King of Corinth, the Queen Anteia poisoned her husband's ears against him, because

---

8. "And with their darkness durst *affront* his light.» — Milton, *P.L.* i.

he had refused to be her partner in crime, and Prœtus believed her lying tale, and sought opportunity to destroy Bellerophon. So he sent him on an embassy to the King of Lycia, the father of Anteia, and gave him a sealed packet to take with him. Bellerophon set sail, and after a fair voyage he landed in Lycia, and went up to the palace of the King. Then for nine days the King made good cheer, and invited the highest in the land to meet his noble guest; and on the tenth day he asked concerning the business which had brought him to Lycia. Bellerophon gave him the packet, and he opened it privately, and found within it a folded tablet, whereon were written these words: *Bellerophon is a traitor, and hath sought to bring dishonour on our house: he must die.*

"When he had read the message from his son-in-law the King was wroth, and devised means to compass Bellerophon's death. First, he bade him slay the Chimæra, a dreadful monster, with the head of a lion, the body of a goat, and a long coiling tail like a vast serpent. The gods helped Bellerophon to slay this monster, and the King then sent him to fight against the Solymi, a fierce and warlike tribe. But neither they nor the Amazons, with whom also the King bade him fight, could work any mischief on that valiant champion. Yet a fourth time the King tried to take his life, and sent an ambush of picked men to slay him by treachery on his way back to Lycia; and Bellerophon killed them all.

"Being now assured that his guest was the favourite of heaven, the King retained him in his house as an honoured guest, and gave him his daughter to wife; and he received a fair appanage of cornland and vineyard, and three children were born to him, one of whom, Hippolochus, is my father. Thus have I told thee my lineage and my race."

Diomede had listened with deep attention to the Lycian chieftain's story, and when he had heard him to the end he came forward with outstretched hands and cordial words of greeting: "Thou art a friend," he said, "of my father's house, for Œneus, my grandsire, long ago welcomed Bellerophon as his guest, and entertained him for many days. I have still among my treasures a golden cup which Bellerophon gave to his host as a parting gift. Therefore let us remember the ancient tie which connects our families, and avoid each other's spears when we meet in the press of battle. And let us now change armour, that all these may know that we are friends, both we and our fathers."

So for a while that knightly pair stood with hand clasped in hand, and gazed into each other's faces with eyes of kindness, joined for a few brief moments by an ancient tie of amity, but soon to be parted by national feud. Then Glaucus took off his golden armour, and gave it to Diomede, without grudging, though he received in exchange armour of brass.

II

WE MUST NOW follow Hector on his errand of piety to

the town. As he entered the gates, an anxious crowd of Trojan women pressed round him, with eager questions about brothers, husbands, or sons. He put them gently aside, bidding them pray to the gods, and made his way through the streets until he came to the vast pile of the royal palace, where dwelt Priam and his fifty sons and twelve daughters, with their wives and husbands. Hecuba, his mother, saw him coming, and hastened to meet him, taking with her Laodice, the fairest of her daughters. "What has brought thee hither, my son?" said she, holding his hand, "is it that the Trojans are hard pressed by the Greeks, and thy spirit moved thee to go up to Jove's holy temple and pray? Wait awhile, till I bring thee a cup of wine, that thou mayest pour a drink-offering and then take a comfortable draught, to refresh thee after thy sore toils."

"I will drink no wine, mother," answered Hector, "lest I dull my spirit, and unnerve mine arm. Neither may I pour a drink-offering with hands defiled by blood and the soil of battle. But go thou to the temple of Athene, thou and the venerable mothers of Troy, and take with thee a robe, the largest and the most precious which thou hast, that thou mayest lay it on the knees of the goddess, as an offering meet for her. Do this, and vow a sacrifice of twelve yearling heifers that have never felt the goad, if so be that she will take pity on us and our wives and little ones, and save us from the fury of Diomede. As for me, I go to find Paris, and rouse him to play a man's part among the defenders of Troy."

Having despatched his mother on that bootless errand, Hector went to visit Paris in his luxurious home, which was built on the same hill where stood the palace of Priam. Clad in all his brazen mail, and carrying in his hand a spear eleven cubits long, he crossed the threshold, and passed on to Helen's bower, where Paris was sitting, with his armour strewn around him, fitting new feathers to his arrows. The great warrior stood awhile, gazing in silence at his unworthy brother; then smiling bitterly he said: "I perceive that thou art wroth with thy poor countrymen seeing that thou leavest them to perish, while thou art dallying here. Rouse thee, Paris," he added, changing his tone; "the flames of war, which thou hast kindled, are blazing round our walls. Shake off this unmanly sloth, and play the man for once."

"Hector, I feel the justice of thy reproaches," answered Paris. "But it was sorrow, not anger, that kept me in my chamber. But away with regrets! My turn will come, and I am resolved to go back to the battle, urged thereto both by Helen's entreaties and by thy biting words. Wait while I don my armour—or go thou first, and I will overtake thee."

Hector turned to go, without answering a word; but Helen, who was present with her handmaids, laid her hand upon his arm, and said: "Leave me not thus, dear brother! Kill me not by thine accusing silence! Unhappy that I am, the sport and victim of evil powers, given over to perdition from my birth! And if I needs must sin, could I not at least have sinned for a man, and not have wrecked my life for a caitiff like this, without conscience, without heart? But sit thee down, Hector, and rest awhile, for on thee lies heaviest the burden which has been laid upon thy city for my sake, and for the sake of Paris, an ill-starred pair, whose evil fate shall be a theme of song in days to come."

"Seek not to detain me, Helen," answered Hector gently; "my duty calls me hence, and I must join my faithful comrades, whom I left in the toil and heat of the fray. Thither am I bound, when I have taken one look—it may be for the very last time—at my house, and my wife, and my little child. Look thou that Paris keeps his word, and joins me before I quit the town."

With hasty step Hector left the house, and went to his own home, which was close by. Learning there from a handmaid that Andromache had gone with her child and his nurse to watch the battle from the tower of the citadel, he went back to look for her there. As he ascended the steep path which led to the tower, the quick ear of Andromache recognised his footstep, and she ran to meet him, followed by the nurse, who carried the little Astyanax, a lovely boy, fair as the morning star, the sweet pledge of their wedded love. She clasped her husband's hand, and said, with a look of fond reproach in her tearful eyes: "Rash man, it will be thine undoing, this hardy spirit of thine! At thee every spear is pointed, when thou goest into battle, and soon, very soon, the Greeks will take thy life. Then who shall be my defender, and who shall guard thy child, when thou art gone? I shall be left alone in the world, for all my kith and kin have perished. My father, Eëtion, was slain by Achilles, when he sacked my native city, the stately town of Thebes; and his tomb lies in the shadow of a fair grove of elms, planted there by the nymphs to do him honour. Seven brothers I had, who grew up with me in my home; and they were slain by Achilles in a cattle raid, and one grave received them all. My mother Achilles released for gold, and she went back to her father's house; but she also is no more, slain by the gentle shafts of Artemis.

"Hector, thou art my father, my mother, my brother, my husband, my life, my all! Leave me not to perish in lonely widowhood with a fatherless child. Call the people within the walls, and fight no more in the open plain. Why wilt thou hazard thy life against such fearful odds?"

"Dear love, it cannot be," answered Hector sadly; "what would my brethren say, if I bade them skulk like cowards behind their walls? No; I must go where honour calls me, though I know that Troy is doomed with all her sons. Yea, the day shall dawn when temple and tower shall go down, and these streets shall run with Trojan blood. Then many a noble dame shall be led away captive, and among them—bitter, bitter thought!—thou shalt go, to eat the hard bread of bondage, and do menial service under a haughty mistress. Methinks I see thee, stooping under thy burden, as thou bearest water from some Grecian spring, while men point the finger at thee, and cry in scorn: 'Hail, Andromache, wife of Hector, Troy's bravest champion!' May death overtake me, and hide me deep in darkness and the grave, before ever I see thee dragged into slavery by ruffian hands."

A long silence followed, broken only by the sobs of Andromache, who was overpowered by the dreadful picture conjured up by her husband's words. At last Hector beckoned to the nurse, who had been standing a little apart, to bring him the child, and stretched out his arms to receive him; but the little one clung crying to his nurse's breast, affrighted by the brazen helmet and its nodding plume. His father and mother exchanged a loving smile, and Hector removed his helmet, and, laying it on the ground, took the boy in his arms, kissed him, and fondled him, and then put up this prayer to heaven: "Father Zeus, and all ye gods, grant that this, my child, may be strong and valiant in fight, even as I am, and win him honour among the Trojans; and may his mother's heart be glad when he comes back from the war laden with the spoils of the foe."

Then he gave the child to his mother, who pressed him to her bosom with a tearful smile. "Now I must leave thee," he said, with a tender gesture: "and mourn not overmuch for me. I shall not die before my day: every man has his appointed time, be he noble or base. Thou hast thy tasks, I mine; let us both play our part bravely, and leave the rest to heaven."

With many a pause and many a backward glance Andromache left him, and went back to her house, with her heart full of sad foreboding. When she was gone, Hector remained standing for awhile, lost in sorrowful thought. He was about to turn away when he heard the clatter of hurrying feet, and Paris came running up, glittering in his new-burnished armour, and tossing his plume, like some wanton, stall-fed steed. For he was a stout fellow, though a coward at heart, and was full of vigour and animal spirits after his long rest. "Who is the laggard now?" cried the gay holiday soldier, with a loud laugh. "Art thou ready to go, or shall I wait for thee awhile?"

"Forget my harsh words," answered Hector mildly. "I was vexed on thy account, when I saw thee hanging back, and heard the Trojans speak evil of thee. Let us forget our quarrels, and fight side by side for hearth and home; perhaps we may yet live to see happier days."

7

SECOND BATTLE:
Repulse of the Greeks

I

THE RESULT OF THE first day's fighting had been all in favour of the Greeks, but, as many had fallen on both sides, a truce was made by mutual consent for the next day, to enable both armies to bury their dead. By the advice of Nestor the Greeks dug a trench and threw up a rampart for the defence of their camp, and by the zealous labour of that vast multitude the work was finished on the same night.

Zeus had not forgotten his promise to Thetis, and on the morning of the third day he summoned all the gods to council, and thus declared his will: "Hear me, all ye gods and goddesses, and let none dare to cross my purpose. I forbid any among you to take part in the battle to-day, and if any disobey me I will take him and fling him into Tartarus, the black and gloomy pit, as far beneath Hades as heaven is above the earth. Then shall ye learn how much mightier am I than ye all together."

Without waiting for question or reply, the lord of Olympus mounted his car, and swept along his airy road until he came to the mountain-range of Ida, overlooking the Trojan plain. There he halted and took his station on Mount Gargarus, the highest peak of Ida, from which he had a complete view of Troy and the Grecian camp.

Forth sallied the rival hosts, and soon the clash of arms rang through the cool morning air, as Greek grappled with Trojan in deadly conflict. All through the long hours, until noon, the issue remained doubtful; but when the sun stood at the zenith Zeus lifted a pair of golden scales, and weighed the fates of Greeks and Trojans; and the scale which held the fate of the Greeks sank down, heavy with defeat and disaster. Then Zeus thundered with a mighty peal from Ida, and hurled his bolt among the thronging ranks of the Greeks; and they were sore amazed, and pale Fear gat hold of them. Not one among them dared to stand his ground, neither Ajax, nor Idomeneus, nor Agamemnon himself. Only Nestor lagged behind, for he was hindered by the fall of one of his horses, which had been pierced through the brain by Paris with an arrow. Nestor sprang down, and began cutting through the traces with his sword; and while he was thus engaged, Hector came thundering past in hot pursuit of the Greeks, and seeing Nestor's plight turned aside to slay him. Diomede saw the old man's danger, and lashing his horses to a gallop drove instantly to his aid. "Mount, mount," he cried, "with me, and leave to my squires these sorry steeds of thine. Take thou the reins, and we will see if we can check the onset of the Trojans, and arrest Hector's destroying arm."

Nestor was not slow to obey the summons, and mounting by the side of Diomede he drove straight at Hector. Then Diomede flung his spear, and struck down Hector's charioteer, and, pursuing his advantage, he fell fiercely on the broken columns of the Trojans, scattered in wild pursuit of the enemy. Already the Greeks were beginning to rally, when Zeus hurled a second bolt, which crashed down before the feet of the horses of Diomede. "We must fly," said Nestor; "heaven is against us," and wheeling the affrighted steeds he followed the main body of the Greeks, who were now in full retreat towards the ships. That was a bitter moment for the gallant Diomede, when he heard the exulting voice of Hector, calling him coward, minion, woman. But peal after peal came from the frowning peak of Ida, now wrapped in black clouds; and that proud spirit was forced to bow to a higher power.

"On, Trojans, on!" shouted Hector, pushing on at full speed to head the pursuit. "Zeus favours our cause, and the Greeks are doomed. Neither walls, nor moat, nor all their sorry devices, shall stay our fury, but we will burn their ships and cut them off to a man." So on they sped, driving the Greeks before them across the plain, even to the very gates of the camp. Here the leaders turned at bay, and Agamemnon succeeded by desperate efforts in restoring some order in the panic-stricken host. Foremost among the defenders of the camp were Ajax, the greater and the less, Idomeneus and his comrade, Meriones, Diomede, and Teucer the half-brother of the greater Ajax. Teucer especially, who was a famous archer, did splendid service to the Greeks in that dreadful strait. Crouched behind the vast orb of his mighty kinsman's shield he watched his opportunity, and shot down man after man as the Trojans came rushing to the assault.

"Well done, brave bowman!" cried Agamemnon, who was standing near, as the eighth victim to Teucer's skill bit the dust. "Now aim an arrow at yonder mad dog"; and he pointed at Hector, who was leading the attack. Again the bow twanged, but this time he missed his mark, and instead of Hector struck another son of Priam, who was fighting by his brother's side. And as droops the poppyflower in a fair garden plot, heavy with its seed-pod, and drenched with the summer rains, so drooped that comely head, oppressed by the weight of its helmet.

"Nine have I slain," cried Teucer, in triumph. "Now let me see if my tenth arrow will bring down this noble quarry"; and once more he pointed a shaft at Hector's breast. But a second time the arrow went amiss, and pierced through the heart of Hector's charioteer. Cebriones, Hector's brother, succeeded to this dangerous office, thus twice left vacant on one day; while Hector himself sprang to the ground, and picking up a stone hurled it at Teucer, who was just fitting another arrow to his bowstring. The stone struck Teucer on the collar-bone, breaking the bowstring, and paralysing his arm. Ajax sprang forward to cover his injured brother, who was carried, groaning with pain, to the shelter of the ships.

The fall of Teucer struck fresh dismay into the Greeks, who now shrank back behind their defences, Hector following them close, and cutting down the stragglers, like a hound hanging on the flanks of a wild boar. When the last man had passed the barriers the gates were shut, and Hector was left outside, glaring with baffled rage.

II

Deep was the wrath of Hera when she saw her darling Greeks driven like sheep before the exultant Trojans, and huddled in wild disorder behind their ramparts. As the voice of Hector rang out above the din, like a trumpet sounding the charge, she rocked herself with fury in her seat, and at last, being able to contain herself no longer, she cried to Athene: "I will not endure it! Come what may, I will save my Greeks from perishing by the hands of that mad Trojan."

"It is the hand of Zeus," answered Athene, "that hath brought these foul deeds to pass, in fulfilment of the promise which he made to Thetis, when she clasped his knees, and besought him to honour her son. Graceless, thankless god! Did I not serve him day and night, when I watched like a mother over Heracles, his favourite son, and saved him from a thousand perils? And this is my reward, to be crossed in all my designs, and robbed of my just revenge, by him, my false father, who fools me with his caresses, and calls me his dear, grey-eyed maid! But go thou and harness our steeds, while I put on my armour, and we will try whether Hector will blench or not when he sees my spear flashing among the dykes of war,[9] and the Trojans falling thick and fast, to glut the dogs and vultures with their fat and their flesh."

Not a minute elapsed before the rebellious goddesses were equipped for battle, and ready to swoop like eagles on the heads of the hated Trojans. But Zeus had been watching their movements, and summoning Iris he sent her with a stern, imperious message to his mutinous wife and child. Prompt at his command, Iris sped on her rainbow wings to Olympus, and met the angry pair as they were issuing from the gates. "Are ye mad?" she said, confronting them with warning looks. "Listen to my message, and get ye back the way ye came. Thus saith the son of Cronos, and his words shall surely come to pass: he will maim the swift steeds which draw your car, and blast you with his lightnings, and shatter your chariot wheels, and for ten long years ye shall not be healed of the wounds from those corrosive fires. Then shall thou learn, thou grey-eyed maid,

---

9.   The armed columns, which keep back the *flood* of battle.

what it means to fight with thy sire."

Both Hera and Athene knew full well how far they might presume on the indulgence of Zeus, and without another word they turned back to Olympus, unyoked their steeds, and with quaking hearts joined the company of the gods. Soon after, the monarch of Olympus entered, and took his seat on his exalted throne; for he had returned from Ida when his business for the day was ended. Not a word, not a look, did he receive in greeting from his wife and daughter; but he knew their thoughts, and said: "Why sit ye thus dismayed, Hera and Athene? It cannot be that ye are wearied from doing battle with the Trojans, against whom ye have so dire a grudge, for ye were seized with trembling before ever ye had looked into the face of war. And well for you that it was so!—or your warring should have had a fearful end."

Athene remained cowed and silent, but the shrewish Hera, though she too was scared by her husband's anger, could not hold her peace, but muttered a few words of complaint and remonstrance, of which only the words "faithful Greeks" and "unmerited disaster" were audible. But Zeus was in no mood for contradiction, and he cut her short with this peremptory announcement of his purpose: "To-morrow, if thou wilt, thou shalt see thy 'faithful Greeks' plunged yet deeper in 'unmerited disaster.' They shall have no respite from slaughter and defeat until the swift-footed son of Peleus shall once more be roused to arms. Go then, and fill heaven and earth with thy rage and thy fury—go down to Tartarus, if thou choosest, and tell thy wrongs to the demons who dwell in that sunless den."

III

Night fell at last, bringing relief to the sore-stricken Greeks, and compelling the reluctant Trojans to suspend their attack on the camp. Hector drew off his forces, and pitched his camp by the riverside. This was a sign of great confidence on the part of the Trojans, who hitherto had rarely ventured outside their walls, and had always returned to the city at nightfall. But now the besiegers had become the besieged, and active preparations were made for a campaign in the open field. Orders were sent to the city for supplies of corn and wine and cattle to victual the camp, and the elders of Troy were warned to keep a vigilant watch during the night, to guard against surprise.

When these measures of prudence were completed, Hector, who had been the leading spirit through all this eventful day, summoned the Trojan chieftains to a council of war. High and proud was his glance, as he stood leaning on his tall spear, with its point of tempered bronze and its socket of gold; for he dreamt of nothing less than the total rout and discomfiture of the Greeks. And he found ready hearers in the leaders of the Trojans and their allies, who read in his looks an augury of triumph and victory. "This day," he said, "I thought to have destroyed the Grecian fleet and army, and to have offered thanks to the gods of our country in the Trojan citadel. For this time night has saved them from utter ruin; but the blow is only delayed, not averted, and to-morrow we will set the finish to this glorious work. Let every man now get to his supper with good heart and hope, and look ye to it that numerous fires be lighted in the camp, sufficient to illuminate all the country round, as far as to the fleet. For I fear that these hounds will try to escape under cover of night, and I would not that they should leave us without some token of our loving-kindness—some deep mark in their flesh from Trojan arrow or spear to remember us by when they reach their homes in Greece. If they abide here till to-morrow, the better for us, and the worse for them! Then shall Diomede, the mighty son of Tydeus, pay the price of the lives which he has taken, and to-morrow's sun shall behold him lying stiff and stark, with all his comrades heaped in slaughter around him."

Having listened to the words of their great captain, the leaders dispersed to their several quarters to carry out his orders. And the swift southern night came down, wrapping sea and land in shadow. But soon the realm of darkness was invaded by the flame of a thousand fires. Thick as are the stars which cluster round the moon on a windless summer night, gladdening the shepherd's heart as he keeps his lonely vigil among the hills, so thick shone the fires of the Trojans in the space between the river and the ships. By every fire sat fifty men, and their horses stood near at hand, tethered to the cars, cropping their barley and waiting for the dawn.

8

THE EMBASSY TO ACHILLES

I

So the Trojans held their bivouac, and whiled away the time with drinking, and music, and song. Far other were the feelings of the cowed and beaten Greeks. Many a warrior lay sleepless on his uneasy couch, tossed on a troubled sea of anxiety and dread. Among the leaders there was no thought of rest, and they soon received a hasty summons to attend a council in Agamemnon's quarters. Small comfort had they to receive from the lips of their king, who was utterly broken and cast down, and had nothing to advise but instant flight. A long silence followed his despairing words, and the first to speak was Diomede, whose young and elastic spirit made him a bright exception amid the general despondency of his comrades. Indignantly rejecting the cowardly counsels of Agamemnon, he avowed his intention of remaining and carrying on the war with his single troop, if all the rest of the Greeks deserted their posts. His bold words rekindled the courage of the rest, and they all joined their voices in a fixed resolution to remain and fight out their quarrel to the last.

"'Tis well," said Nestor, who was the next to speak. "Thou art a proper youth, young son of Tydeus, worthy to take the lead in council and in fight. But now listen to an old man's advice. The Trojans are holding their leaguer within sight of our gates, and may make an onfall at any moment; therefore let a watch be set by the moat outside the camp, and let this charge be given to the young men. We, the elders, have a graver matter to consider—how we may end the lamentable feud which has brought division among us, and made us an easy prey to our enemies."

The matter thus obscurely hinted at by Nestor was, of course, the quarrel between Achilles and Agamemnon; and as soon as the watch was set, and left under the charge of Antilochus, Nestor's eldest son, the old King of Pylos reopened the debate with these words: "To thee, mighty son of Atreus, I will address myself, for thou art the vicegerent of Zeus, and holdest the sceptre of righteousness which thou hast received from his hands. Great is thy place, and high the trust imposed in thee—even the lives and fortunes of all this people. Therefore will I speak roundly with thee, concealing nothing which is in my heart. Thou hast erred, great sovereign, thou hast erred grievously, in putting public dishonour on the bravest and most illustrious champion in all thy host. It is thine act which hath brought us to this pass; and it is for thee to make restitution, that he may cease from his sore anger, and incline his heart unto us again."

Far from showing any resentment at Nestor's plain speaking, Agamemnon freely confessed his fault. "I have sinned," he said, "yea, I have sinned grievously, in the great blindness of my heart. But, thanks be to heaven! I am both able and willing to atone for the wrong which I have done. Attend, while I declare unto you the ransom which I will pay unto Achilles to wipe out the stain upon his honour. Vessels of silver will I give him, and vessels of bronze, ten talents of gold, and twelve steeds, all prizewinners, which have won me much wealth by the speed of their feet. Also I will give him seven women, my bondservants, skilled in all manner of needlework, whom I won at the sack of Lesbos; and with them shall go Briseis, who, since I took her from him, has lived in all honour with the ladies of my retinue. And if ever the gods grant us to capture the city of Priam he shall have a shipload of treasure, and twenty Trojan ladies, the noblest and the fairest, as his share of the spoil. Moreover, when we return home from the war, he shall be as a son of my house, and I will give him one of my daughters in marriage, without money and without price,[10] and will add a rich dower besides. And he shall be a prince of my land, and lord of seven fair cities, honoured and obeyed as a god by those that dwell therein. Surely, if he hath a human heart, he cannot turn away from me, his monarch, and

---

10. In Homeric times wives were bought by their husbands.

his elder, when I come to him with full hands, beseeching him to forgive."

The King's magnificent offer drew warm words of praise from the chiefs, and nothing now remained but to choose those who were to be entrusted with this important embassy. At the suggestion of Nestor it was decided to send Phœnix, an aged noble, who was connected with Achilles by close ties of early affection, Odysseus, and the greater Ajax. After a few words of warning and counsel from Nestor, they were despatched forthwith to the tent of Achilles, and with them went two heralds, to give greater solemnity to their mission.

II

So together they passed along the level sand, with many a prayer to Poseidon, lord of the sea, that they might easily persuade the mighty heart of Æacides.[11] And when they came to the tents and ships of the Myrmidons, they found Achilles sitting at the door of his tent, and soothing his troubled spirit with song, and the clear music of a harp, which he had taken among the spoil of Eëtion's city. Opposite to him sat Patroclus, the most beloved of his comrades, waiting until Achilles should have finished his lay, whose theme was the deeds of famous men. And they came and stood before him, with Odysseus at their head. When Achilles saw them he gave a cry of surprise, and sprang from his

---

11. Grandson of Æacus, the father of Peleus.

seat, harp in hand; and Patroclus rose up with him. Then, greeting them with a courteous gesture, he said: "Welcome, dear friends! Most welcome are ye of all the Greeks, even in this hour of my displeasure. Be seated. I know why ye have come hither—sore indeed is the need." So saying, he led the way into the tent, and as soon as they were seated he called to Patroclus, saying: "Set forth the largest bowl, and open the oldest cask of wine, to do honour to the dear guests who have come under my roof."

Therewith he placed a table, in the light of the fire, and on it he laid the loin of a sheep and another of a fat goat, and the chine of a hog. Automedon, his squire, held the meat, and Achilles with his own hands cut it into slices, spitted it, and roasted it over the glowing embers. When all was ready, they feasted sumptuously, and drank of the rich wine which Achilles poured out without stint. The banquet being ended, Ajax made a sign to Phœnix; but Odysseus took the word from him, and, rising with a full cup in his hand, pledged Achilles, and said: "I drink to thee, son of Peleus, and thank thee for thy good cheer. Never have I tasted choicer fare, not even in the tent of Agamemnon himself. But, alas! my noble host, we have little heart for feasting and making merry, for we stand on the very brink of ruin, and thou alone canst save us. The Trojans have pitched their camp before our very gates, and it will not be long before they sweep us into the sea. Zeus hath openly taken sides with our foes, and affrights us with thunders and with lightnings; and Hector, full of mad presumption, is breathing out threatenings and slaughter against us. I fear—yea, I fear exceedingly—that the god will accomplish his threats, and that we are indeed doomed to perish in the land of Troy, far from our native Argos. Up, then, and gird thee to the fight, if thou art minded to save the sons of Greece, even in the eleventh hour. If thou wait longer the mischief will be done, and thou wilt repent of thy stubbornness too late. Remember the words of thy father, Peleus, when he sent thee to the war: 'My son, thou art very strong, but this good gift thou owest to heaven. Do thou curb thy haughty spirit, and turn thee to thoughts of kindness, if thou wouldst be honoured of old and young.' Thou hast forgotten the good words of thy father, and given place to malice and uncharitableness. Quit this froward mood, and mark while I tell thee the brave gifts which Agamemnon offers as the price of thy good will."

Accordingly Odysseus went on to recite the whole tale of the royal bounty, and when the list was complete he wound up his speech by appealing at once to the humanity, the pride, and the ambition of Achilles. "If thou despisest Agamemnon and his gifts, take pity on thy poor countrymen, who will honour thee as a god, and glorify thee as their preserver. And now thou mayest slay Hector, for assuredly he will not refrain from thee in the frenzy which possesseth him, boasting that there is none to match him among all the Greeks who sailed to Troy."

Odysseus resumed his seat, and amidst a breathless silence Achilles rose up and began to speak, calmly at first, but rising in passion as he proceeded. "Most noble son of Laertes, I will answer thee bluntly and to the purpose, that ye may know my mind, and may not come hither on this errand again. For hateful to me, even as the gates of death, is the man who hides one thing in his heart, and speaks another. Hear, then, what I have to say. Neither Agamemnon, nor all the Greeks together, shall turn me from my purpose. I have fought—thou knowest how I have fought—against the common foe; and what my reward hath been thou knowest also. Like a mother bird, who flies to and fro, never weary, never resting, carrying morsels to her nestlings, while she remains empty herself, so have I passed my days in war and bloodshed, and my nights in sleepless watchings, putting my life in jeopardy, for the sake of another man's wife. Twelve cities have I sacked, sailing the sea in my ships, and eleven on land, within the realm of Troy. First the toil, which was mine, and after that the spoil, which was his. I brought it all, and laid it at his feet, and he kept the greater part by far, giving me back a little—a very little—for all my pains. And that little he hath taken away. Let him keep it, and joy go with it! I loved the maid Briseis, yea, dearly I loved her! Thinketh he that he alone and his brother love their wives? She was my prize, my bride: he hath torn her from mine arms, and that foul deed I will never forgive.

"And as to the gifts which he offers, let him know that I came here to fight for honour, not for pelf. He hath denied mine honour, and now he would bribe me to erase that dark record with a purse of gold. But I will not be bribed. Away with his gifts! I value them not a straw. Not though he offered me ten times and twenty times as much—all the wealth that he hath, or ever shall have—not for all the riches of Egyptian Thebes, which sends forth ten thousand warriors, with chariots, and with horses, from its hundred gates—no, not for treasures unnumbered as the sands and dust of the earth—could he buy pardon of me, until he hath suffered the full penalty of the outrage which devours my heart.

"Long ago my mother gave me the choice of two diverse fates—short life with honour, or long life without a name. Mine honour is lost—therefore I will cling to my life, and live it out to the end. Thy miser king holds that men's lives are to be bought and sold, as the lives of sheep and oxen; but herein he is mistaken again. Wealth may be won, and lost, and won back again, seized by the strong hand, or heaped up slowly by plodding industry; but the breath of our life cannot be called back again, when once it hath passed the door of our lips. Therefore I am determined to end my days in peace and quietness among my own people, and quit these brawls, which concern not me. And I counsel all the rest to do the same, for it is clear that Troy's overthrow is not to be wrought by you.

"Ye have heard my answer; go tell it to the chiefs, and bid them be assured that they have naught to hope from me."

Deep was the disappointment of the three envoys, as they followed the wild eloquence of that fierce and implacable man. For a long time not a word was spoken, for it seemed vain to argue against such passion and pride. At last the venerable Phœnix rose feebly from his place, and in a voice broken with sobs and tears began a discourse of immense length, full of tender personal reminiscence and old-world legend. This old man had a curious history. Born to wealth and power, he became an exile in his youth, having been cursed by his father, whom he had bitterly provoked in the course of a family feud. In consequence of the curse he remained a childless man, and, finding a new home in the land of Peleus, he lavished more than a father's tenderness on Achilles, Peleus' infant son.

These incidents from his own life, which he dwelt on with the fond garrulity of an old nurse, furnished a copious theme to Phœnix in the first part of his harangue. "I little thought," he said, "when I set thee on my knee, a little, helpless babe, and fed thee with choice morsels of meat, and held the cup to thy lips, and thou wouldst spill the wine over my gown in thy childish weakness—I little thought to see thee grow up to be so pitiless and inflexible, more hard to move than the gods themselves, whom we approach with prayer and sacrifice, and with bended knees. Beware of the vengeance which waits upon a stubborn and unforgiving heart. Swift and strong is the dread goddess Ate, who prompts man to give and take offence; but Penitence is an old and wrinkled goddess, who goes halting behind her, to heal the mischief; and if he who is wronged will not listen to her voice he himself becomes the offender, and the whole guilt of the quarrel rests on his head. Hearken thou, therefore, to her gentle pleading, and receive the bountiful gifts of Agamemnon, or the day will come when thou wilt take thy sword perforce, and fight the battles of the Greeks without reward."

Achilles listened with manifest impatience to the rambling appeals of Phœnix; and when at length the old man had finished, he replied briefly: "I seek no reward but the favour of Zeus, which I have, and shall not cease to have as long as the breath of life is in me. Vex me no more with thy vain repinings; my purpose is fixed, and it is for thee to choose whether thou wilt be friends with Agamemnon or with me. If thou art on my side remain here for the night, and to-morrow we will consider whether we will go or stay."

The conference was brought to a close by a few words from Ajax, whose frank and soldierly heart was hot with indignation at the vindictive temper of Achilles. Turning to Odysseus, he said: "Noble son of Laertes, let us be going. Words are wasted on this fierce and froward man. Surely he has a heart of stone, which no kindly thought, no gentle memory of ancient comradeship, can soften. All the homage of his countrymen, all the loving-kindness of his friends, are as dirt beneath his feet. Many a man hath accepted a price for the blood of a son or brother slain, and suffered the slayer to remain unharmed in the land; but thou, Achilles, hast scorned the most princely offers for the sake of one captive maid. O yet at last be moved! Bring not scorn upon us, thy guests, thy friends, but give us a gentle answer to take back to our countrymen in their dire need."

These manly and moving words had some effect on Achilles, half maddened as he was by wounded pride. Yet still he would not yield, though his answer showed that he had not been in earnest when he spoke of abandoning the war. "Thou hast spoken well, Ajax," he said, "and there is much reason in what thou sayest. But my heart boils with rage when I think of the contumely which was heaped upon me before the eyes of all Greece, as though I were some beggared and nameless outcast; and I will not put on mine armour again, until I see the smoke arising from the Grecian ships, and Hector drawing near to my galleys with sword and fire. Then, methinks, his career of victory will end."

After this final declaration of his purpose by Achilles, Ajax and Odysseus took their leave, and returned to the assembled chieftains, who still sat anxiously awaiting the result of the mission. Phœnix remained behind, having resolved to cast in his lot with Achilles.

9

THE NIGHT RAID ON THE TROJAN CAMP

I

UNEASY LAY THE head of Agamemnon the King that night, and, thick as lightnings which herald the storm, thronging cares shot through his brain, forbidding all repose. As often as he opened his eyes he saw the red gleam of the Trojan watchfires; and the hum of the armed multitude, mingled with the strains of flute and pipe, filled his ears. After an hour of weary tossing he left his couch, and wandered out into the camp, until he came to the quarters of Menelaus, and, finding him also afoot, he sent him to call up Ajax and Idomeneus, and went himself to summon Nestor, intending to hold a midnight council, and devise some plan of relief in this hour of general depression and dismay.

On the way he was joined by Diomede and Odysseus, and when they all met it was resolved to pay a visit to the sentinels and see if they were faithful to their trust. When they came to the place where the pickets were stationed, outside the barriers, they found the whole troop keeping watch and ward with sleepless vigilance, like dogs in charge of a sheep-fold when they hear a lion prowling without. Every man was on the alert, with his face towards the Trojan leaguer, as if expecting an instant attack. Nestor's long experience of war now enabled him to make a suggestion which led to one of the most famous adventures in the whole course of the war. "Is there one among you bold enough," he said, "to go and spy out the movements of the Trojans in their camp, and bring back a report of what they design against us? 'Twould be a noble enterprise, and would bring both fame and profit to him who should accomplish it."

There was a short pause, and then Diomede declared himself willing to undertake this perilous adventure, "But will not one of you go with me?" he asked. "Two heads are better than one, and I may find myself in a strait in which I should need a comrade's help and advice."

Six of the leaders at once offered to accompany Diomede, and among these were Menelaus, Odysseus, and Antilochus, the captain of the outpost, who was especially eager to go. "Choose him whom thou thinkest best fitted for the task, without respect to rank or birth," said Agamemnon, in fear lest he should name Menelaus for his companion. "Well, then," answered Diomede, "I choose Odysseus, the hardiest and the shrewdest spirit among us all, and the darling of Athene. With him at my side I will go through fire and water without scathe."

"A truce to thy praises," said Odysseus, "and let us away, for the night is far spent, and the day is at hand."

II

Lightly armed and equipped, the stout-hearted pair passed out of the light of the watchfires, and set their faces towards the Trojan camp. Just as they were starting they heard the cry of a heron flying on the right, and Odysseus was glad, for he knew it was a sign sent by Athene, promising success to their journey. Murmuring a prayer, they stepped forward boldly, like two lions bound on a midnight foray, and crossed the battlefield of yesterday, over corpses and broken armour and pools of blood. Suddenly Odysseus came to a halt, and laying his hand on Diomede's arm whispered: "I hear a footstep as of one coming this way, whether to spy out our camp, or to plunder the dead, I know not. Let us allow him to go by us, and then spring upon him as he passes."

Crouching down among the heaps of slain, they waited until the man had passed in the direction of the ships, and then leapt from their ambush and gave chase.

When he heard them he hesitated a moment, doubting whether they were friends or foes; then, recognising them as Greeks, he bounded away at full speed, Odysseus and Diomede following hard behind, like two hounds on the track of a doe or hare. But the fellow was a fleet runner, and would have been fairly driven into the hands of the Greek sentinels, if Diomede had not raised his spear, and sent it whizzing close to the ear of the fugitive, crying as he did so: "Halt! whoever thou art, or my next cast shall bring thee down."

Then the wretch was afraid, and stood still, in obedience to the summons, with knees knocking together and chattering teeth; and the two Greeks ran up, panting for breath, and seized him by the arms. Weeping with terror he began to beg for his life. "Make me your prisoner," he faltered, "and I will pay you a heavy ransom, for my father's house is full of silver and gold, and vessels of iron,[12] choicely wrought, and he will pay you a heavy price when he hears that I am alive."

"Have no fears for thy life," said Odysseus; "only answer me truly, and thou art safe. Why art thou wandering here in the dead of night? Art thou on an adventure of thine own, or did Hector send thee to spy out the Grecian camp?"

"It was Hector who beguiled me to commit this folly," answered the captive, whose name was Dolon; "for he bribed me with a great bribe, promising to give me the steeds of Peleus' haughty son, if I would go

---

12. Iron was scarce and highly prized among the Homeric Greeks.

down to the fleet, and bring back information whether you were preparing to fly from our shores in the night."

"Thou art ambitious, I see," replied Odysseus, smiling. "Bold must be thy heart, and firm thy hand, if thou wouldst drive the steeds of Æacides, which are of no mortal breed. But tell me now, and answer me truly, where is Hector stationed in the Trojan camp, and in what order have the others pitched their tents?"

"Hector and the chiefs," answered Dolon, still shaking with mortal dread, "have their quarters by the tomb of Ilus, and round them lie the native Trojans, keeping good watch. The allies are encamped about them, in no fixed order, and they are all asleep. On the very outskirts of the camp lie the Thracians, and Rhesus their king; and if ye are minded to make an onfall on their leaguer ye may do it in safety, and win a rare prize. For Rhesus hath a pair of milk-white coursers, unmatched in strength and speed, and a car richly adorned with silver and gold. Likewise he hath a suit of golden armour, fit for the gods to wear. And all this ye may win without a blow. Now leave me in the custody of your comrades, or bind me fast here, that ye may know when ye return whether I have spoken the truth."

But that night was to afford a second instance of broken faith, hardly less infamous than the first. Having tempted this poor caitiff to betray his comrades by promising him his life, they now gave him the traitor's wage. "Thou must die, Dolon," said Diomede coldly, "for all thy good news. Thou art a foe, delivered into

our hands, and thou shalt never spy upon us or fight
with us again." Dolon clung to him with cries of anguished entreaty, pleading for his life; but Diomede,
with one downward stroke of his sword, swept off his
head, which rolled, with lips still moving, in the dust.
Then stripping off his armour, he hung it in a tamarisk
tree, and, having marked the place, went forward with
Odysseus in the direction of the Thracian camp.

When they came to the quarters of Rhesus, they
found him lying in the midst of his men, with his famous steeds standing near, tethered to their car. All the
troop was sleeping heavily, for they were newly arrived
at Troy, and had travelled far and fast the day before.
"There he is," whispered Odysseus, "and these are his
steeds, a glorious pair! Now to work! Slay me a score of
these sluggards while I loose the steeds."

Thereupon Diomede drew his sword, and struck
right and left like a headsman, until he had slain some
dozen of the sleeping Thracians; and, as he proceeded,
Odysseus dragged the slaughtered men out of the way,
to make a path for the horses, which were young, and
unused to such sights. Diomede's last victim was the
giant Rhesus, who was breathing heavily, and dreaming of his home; but a Grecian blade cut short his
dreams, and his fleet coursers now found a new master.
While Diomede was thus busy, Odysseus untethered
the steeds, and coupling them together by their harness
drove them out of the camp, striking them with a bow
which he carried; for he had forgotten to take up the

whip. Diomede still lingered, meditating some final act of daring, to crown the night's adventure. Beneath him lay the corpse of Rhesus, and his golden armour, and he was hesitating whether to take these, or slay a few more Thracians, when Odysseus gave a low whistle, warning him that it was time to be going. The next moment he heard the sound of hurrying footsteps, and, perceiving that the alarm had been given, he joined Odysseus, and mounting one of the horses seized the other by the bridle, and rode at a rapid trot towards the sea. Odysseus ran by his side, holding on by the harness, for he was no rider,[13] but a swift and enduring runner.

They had no sooner departed than a wild commotion arose behind them in the awakened Thracian camp, but increasing their pace they soon reached the spot where they had left the unhappy Dolon, and, having paused for a moment to take up his armour, they hurried forward, and before long they were within hail of the Grecian outposts, where the whole company of the leaders was still assembled, anxiously awaiting their return.

Nestor was the first to hear the sound of the horses' feet, and thinking that the Trojans were attacking he ran to raise the alarm. But he was soon reassured when he heard the voice of Diomede, followed a moment later by the arrival of the hardy adventurers with their splendid booty. Joyful were the greetings on both sides, and when the story of that great exploit had been brief-

---

13. Riding was little practised among the Homeric heroes.

ly told they all dispersed to their quarters, to snatch a few hours of sleep before the toils of the coming day.

10

THE BRAVE DEEDS OF AGAMEMNON: Reverses of the Greeks

I

IN THE STILL hours of the dawn the Greeks were startled from their slumbers by a loud and fearful cry, which came from no mortal lips, but from Eris, the dread goddess of strife, who had been sent down by Zeus to give the signal for battle. The first to obey that awful summons was Agamemnon; for this was to be his great day, and his heart was aflame with the lust of slaughter. Springing from his couch he began to don his armour. First he put on his greaves, which were made of pliant white metal, with ankle pieces of silver. Then he took up his corslet, with a glance of pride, for it was of choice and costly workmanship, cunningly fashioned of thin strips or courses of metal. Ten courses were of blue steel, and ten of gold, and twenty of tin; and round about the corslet wound three serpents, wrought in divers colours, like the rainbow, with their heads meeting where the corslet narrowed at the neck. His sword glittered with golden ornaments, and the scabbard was of silver, and the baldric of gold. On his shield, which had ten circles of brass, were twenty bosses of white tin, and in the centre a boss of blue steel; and it bore an image of the Gorgon's head and the dreadful faces of Rout and Panic. Attached to it was a silver strap, bearing the device of a serpent with three heads.

Glittering in this gorgeous panoply, brandishing two spears, and raising his battle cry, Agamemnon rushed to the gates of the camp, and placed himself at the head of his bravest champions, who were mustering there with the flower of the Greek army, prepared for the expected attack. They had not long to wait; hardly had they set their ranks in order, when the Trojans appeared on the summit of the slope which ran down to the shore. And like a star which appears and disappears on a stormy night, when the sky is covered with scudding clouds, so glittered the mailed form of Hector, as he ranged in and out among the advancing columns, marshalling his men to the fight.

Then like two lines of reapers working together on opposite sides of a deep field of wheat or barley, so met Greeks and Trojans on the plain before the camp, and war's dread harvest began. None of the gods were present, save only Eris, whose savage heart was glad when she smelt the smell of blood. And Zeus sat apart on a lonely peak, looking down upon Troy and the Grecian fleet and the two warring nations in the space between.

Until the hour of noon the battle was waged with equal fortune on both sides. But just at the time when a woodman in some mountain glen breaks off his labour to prepare his midday meal, having wearied his hands with holding the axe, the Greeks made a vigorous charge, and broke through the Trojan line. Agamemnon fought in advance of all the rest, and recognising among the enemy two sons of Priam, who had formerly been taken captive by Achilles and let go for a ransom, he slew them both, and stripped off their armour. And as a lion slays two hapless fawns, while their dam, who is feeding near, flies sweating with terror from the onslaught of the mighty beast, so the Trojans saw their young princes slain, but were helpless to aid them, being themselves hard pressed by the victorious Greeks.

Like a famished lion who has broken into a sheepfold, and ravages the flock, so fell Agamemnon on the huddled masses of the Trojans, striking about him with sword and spear. Presently he had an opportunity of gratifying his private revenge; for right before him, impeded by the press, he saw the two sons of Antimachus, a Trojan who was bribed with gold by Paris to oppose the restoration of Helen. There they stood helpless, both together in one car, holding out their hands in supplication, and begging him to spare their lives.

"There is no mercy for such as you," cried Agamemnon fiercely. "Did not your father, in the hearing of all the people, advise the murder of my brother, Menelaus, when he came on an embassy to Troy? Die, and pay for your father's treachery." With that he thrust down one of them with his spear, and the other, who turned to fly, he slew with his sword, lopping off head and arms, and spurning the trunk with his foot, so that it rolled like a log along the ground. Then, raising his battle cry, he plunged into the thick of the fight, where the main body of the Trojans were flying before the Greeks, horse and foot mingled together in headlong rout. And as a fire sweeps through the dry brushwood, borne onward by the wind, and leaving a black waste behind, so thick and fast fell the Trojans before Agamemnon; and many an empty car went rattling over the field, borne hither and thither by its affrighted steeds, whose master was lying where he fell, until the vultures assembled to the banquet at eventide.

Across the plain they sped, past the tomb of Ilus and the wild fig-tree, making straight for the city, and as they came to the gates they turned at bay, and waited for those who were still flying before Agamemnon and the Greeks.

"Now haste thee, swift Iris!" said Zeus to the maiden messenger of heaven, "and bear this message to Hector. As long as he sees Agamemnon foremost in the slaughter, let him hold back, and leave the others to stem the tide of war; but when Agamemnon receives a wound, as he shall do soon, then let Hector take the lead again, and drive the Greeks back upon their ships."

Hector duly received the message, as he was rallying his men to defend their gates; and in obedience to the command of Zeus he retired from the front, and waited for the promised relief. He had not long to wait. Presently Agamemnon was assailed by Iphidamas, a son of Antenor, one of the chief men of Troy, who charged at him, spear in hand, and thrusting with all his force struck him full on the breastplate. But the spear point was turned on the tempered metal, and Agamemnon, seizing the shaft, dragged the weapon from his hands, and smote down the tall champion with a blow of his sword. But as he was stooping to strip the armour from the corpse, Coön, the brother of Iphidamas, crept up to his side, and drove his spear clean through Agamemnon's forearm.

Though grievously hurt Agamemnon turned on his assailant, and cut him down; and having thus avenged himself he still fought on, dealing havoc among the Trojans with his spear and his sword, and with heavy stones. But presently his blood ceased to flow, and his arm grew stiff, as the wound began to close. Being now in dreadful pain, he could fight no longer, and summoning his chariot he left the field, and drove at full speed back to the camp.

II

"Forward, men of Troy!" shouted Hector, rushing to the front. "Agamemnon is sorely wounded, and Zeus has promised us the victory." And as a hunter cheers on his hounds against a lion or wild boar, so Hector encouraged his Trojans, by word and by action, to assail the Greeks; and like a black squall which leaps suddenly on the Ægæan, he himself led the assault, strong in the support of Zeus, and confident of victory.

Diomede marked him as he moved his way through the Grecian ranks, and stood to oppose him, poising his spear. The weapon flew, and struck him on the helmet, but rebounded from the massive brazen ridge, and dropped on the ground. Hector, though unwounded, was hurled back by that ponderous stroke, and sank, half-stunned, on one knee, leaning on his hand. Following up his advantage, Diomede rushed forward to regain his spear; but meanwhile Hector had recovered from his faintness, and escaped in his chariot to the rear. "Again thou hast avoided death at my hands, thou dog!" shouted Diomede after him. "But I will slay thee yet." And he stooped to take the armour from a Trojan whom he had killed.

Leaning against a stone pillar, the monument of Ilus, an ancient King of Troy, stood the gay archer Paris; and when he saw Diomede kneeling by the fallen Trojan he took steady aim, and launched an arrow, which pierced through Diomede's right foot, and pinned him to the ground. "Thou art hit," he cried, springing from his ambush with a loud laugh. "Would that my shaft had cloven thy very heart! So should I have given a breathing space to the Trojans, who cower before thee like bleating goats before a lion."

"Out on thee, cowardly bowman!" answered Diomede, with scorn. "Thou fightest thy battles from a safe distance, and shunnest the push of sword or spear. And now thou art boasting aloud over this pinprick, which harms me not at all. There is no force in the blow from a coward's arm. But the touch of my weapon means death, and they who feel it need no second stroke. Their last bed is the bare, cold ground, and vultures perform their obsequies."

Notwithstanding these bold words, the wound was severe, and as soon as Odysseus, who ran to aid his friend, had drawn out the shaft, Diomede was obliged to retire from the battlefield.

As Odysseus was about to join the ranks of the retreating Greeks he found himself hemmed in by a party of Trojan spearsmen, who surrounded him with a circle of bristling points. Then as a wild boar issues from his shady lair, foaming and champing his teeth, and charges down upon the hounds and hunters who have beset the covert, so sprang Odysseus on his assailants, and in a moment four of them lay writhing at his feet. The last of these, a young noble named Charops, found an avenger in Socus, his brother, who thrust so vigorously at Odysseus with his spear that the point clave through shield and corslet, and made a long ragged wound in his side. Socus, in his turn, who fled as soon as the blow was struck, was gored in the back, between the shoulders, by the spear of Odysseus. But that sage and valiant warrior was now in deadly peril; for when the Trojans saw his blood flowing, as he drew out the lance from his corslet and shield, they fell upon him like one man, with wild cries of triumph. Slowly he gave back before them, shouting aloud to his friends to come to his rescue. Three times he cried, and his voice reached the ears of Menelaus, who hurried to his relief, bringing with him the mighty Ajax, son of Telamon.

They came not a moment too soon, for Odysseus was hard beset by his clamorous foes, who crowded round him, like jackals round a tall antlered stag which has been wounded with an arrow, and has fled to the shelter of the woods: but while the jackals are yelping about him, up comes a great bearded lion, and scatters the jackals, and makes the stag his prey. So when the towering form of Ajax appeared, as he advanced with his huge orbed shield, the Trojans abandoned their intended victim, and fled in dismay. Menelaus took the wounded man by the hand, and led him to the place where his chariot was waiting, leaving Ajax occupied with a fresh column of Trojans, who came pouring to the attack when they saw their friends routed. Then mightily raged the sword of Ajax, falling like a flail on the heads of his foes, and man and horse went down before him.

All this time Hector had been fighting in another part of the field, at the extreme left of the line of battle, where the Greeks were led by Nestor and Idomeneus. A lucky shot from the bow of Paris disabled Machaon, who, besides being a stout fighter, was the most skilful leech in the Greek army. "We must save him at any cost," said Idomeneus to Nestor. "A skilful physician is worth a whole troop of spearsmen. Mount thou thy car, and carry him with all speed to the camp." Nestor did as he was advised, and Idomeneus was thus left to bear the brunt alone.

Just at this moment Cebriones, Hector's charioteer, came galloping up with the news that the main body of the Trojans was suffering severely from the attack led by Ajax. As the departure of Nestor and Machaon had left him little to do in this part of the field, Hector at once mounted his chariot, and directed his course towards the spot where Ajax was fighting. Right between the warring lines he drove, trampling over corpses, helmets, and shields; and steeds and car were spattered with blood. Soon he was joined by a strong troop of Trojan warriors, and Ajax found himself assailed by a storm of missiles. Then even that mighty man felt a touch of fear, and throwing his shield behind him he began slowly to retire, halting at every step, and striking down some too daring assailant. Like a lion who has been driven off from a herdsman's steading with javelins, and with stones, and with burning brands, yet will not leave the place, but prowls near all night, lust-ing after the flesh of the fat beeves—so Ajax, though hard beset, drew back reluctantly, inch by inch, before the clamour and fury of his foes. Dogged he was, and hard to stir from his place, like some big greedy ass who has found his way into a deep field of corn, and will not budge till he has filled his belly, though assailed by a laughing crowd of children, who rain blows on his back and ribs,—even so the blows rained upon Ajax, who was encumbered by the weight of the spears which had pierced his shield. At last, the Greeks advanced to his succour in close array, and joining their ranks he wheeled once more and faced the thronging Trojans.

III

The tide of battle had thus turned again, and the Greeks were being driven steadily back upon their camp. The roar of the conflict reached the ears of Achilles, who was standing near his ship, peering out eagerly over the Trojan plain; and at the same moment he saw Nestor driving past in his chariot, bringing with him the wounded Machaon. Then he called to Patroclus, and bade him go and inquire who the injured man was. "I think," he added, "that it was Machaon; but the car passed me in a flash, and I saw not his face. Methinks the hour of my revenge is near, for the Greeks are in a sore strait." Ah! son of Peleus, thy revenge is indeed near, but thou little dreamest how dearly thou wilt pay for that bitter morsel.

When Patroclus reached the tent of Nestor he found the venerable King of Pylos sitting with Machaon, waiting while a handmaid prepared for them a slight refection. The woman drew a table before them, and on it she placed a brazen dish, with onions, and honeycomb, and barley cakes. Then she took a massive cup, embossed with gold, resting on a double base, and having four golden handles, each one of which was wrought in the form of two doves, which seemed to be feeding from the cup. In this vessel she prepared a posset, pouring in a rich red wine, into which she sprinkled cheese of goats' milk and white barley meal. And when the posset was ready she set it on the table, and bade them drink.

The cup was very weighty, and a strong hand was needed to lift it to the lips; but Nestor raised it easily, old as he was, and was about to take a draught, when, looking up, he saw Patroclus standing at the door of the tent. Replacing the goblet on the table, Nestor rose to greet him, and taking him by the hand invited him to enter. But Patroclus hesitated, wishing to return at once with the required information to his friend, whose impatient and exacting mood he knew and feared. "I was sent," he said, "to ask the name of the wounded man, and I see that it is Machaon. Achilles waits for an answer, and I dare not keep him waiting." Nevertheless, he lingered awhile, and listened to the long harangue of that "old man eloquent," who soon wandered, according to his wont, into a long story of his youthful prowess, when he lived as the sole survivor of twelve sons in the house of his father Neleus. "But why," he asked, when that theme was exhausted—"why should Achilles inquire about one wounded Greek? He knows not the extent of our mischances, nor how much cause we have to mourn. Diomede, the valiant son of Tydeus, is stricken with an arrow, Agamemnon also is wounded, and likewise Odysseus. Will Achilles now be satisfied, or is he waiting until our ships are consumed with fire, and all of us put to the sword? Would that this arm of mine were as of yore, when I was the bulwark of my father's house, and of all my people. But Achilles puts forth his might and his valour only for his own honour and glory, and cares not though his country perish. Canst thou do nothing with him? Remember the charge which Menœtius, thy father, gave thee, when we were sojourning, I and Odysseus, in the house of Peleus. We came thither to summon thee and Achilles to the war, and ye were both fain to go. And these were the parting words of Menœtius to thee: "My son, Achilles, is far mightier than thou, but thou art the elder, and it is for thee to guide him, and counsel him for his good. Be wise, and be kind, and he will obey thee."

"Ah! take those words to heart, and reason with that wilful youth. If he is obeying some oracle from Zeus, which forbids him to go into battle, at least let him send thee to lead the Myrmidons in his stead, and let him lend thee his armour, that the Trojans may be affrighted when they see thee, thinking that Achilles has arisen. Thus, at least, we shall get a little respite, and gain time to breathe."

Pondering deeply on the last words of Nestor, which were to prove so fatal to himself, Patroclus hastened back on the way to his own quarters. But he was to be delayed a second time: for as he was passing the tent of Odysseus he met Eurypylus, one of the bravest of the Greeks, who came limping towards him, being wounded in the thigh by an arrow. He was a pitiful sight, begrimed with dust and sweat, and bleeding copiously from his wound. And Patroclus groaned in spirit when he saw him, for he was cut to the heart to find so many of his comrades disabled. "Woe is me!" he said, with a glance of pity, "to see thee thus. But tell me, how goes the day?"

"We can keep the field no longer," answered Eurypylus. "The Greeks must retire behind their barriers. But thou seest how grievously I am hurt; take me with thee to thy tent, and cut the arrow out of my thigh, and when thou hast washed my wound with warm water, lay thereon some of the powerful simples which Achilles received from the wise centaur, Chiron. For of the two leeches of the army one, Machaon, is in need of a physician himself, and Podalirius, the other, is fighting in the front."

"I am in haste," said Patroclus, "howbeit, I will not leave thee in this state"; and, supporting the wounded man in his arms, he guided him slowly to his tent, and seating him on a couch of bulls' hides played the part of physician with such skill and success that the blood was stanched, and the sharp pain allayed.

11

THE ATTACK ON THE GRECIAN CAMP

THE GREEKS WERE now driven back upon their defences, and a furious struggle ensued for the possession of the walls. The battle was no longer a succession of duels, such as we have witnessed hitherto, but a desperate contest for life and death, in which high and low, nobles and commons, had to take their share. As before, Hector took the lead, and tried to force his way across the moat, and up the steep slope on the other side, which was topped by a wall of stone, and a stiff fence of palisades. Again and again he rushed at the yawning moat in his car, but each time his horses refused the leap, and stood neighing and trembling, with their hoofs planted at the brink.

At last, perceiving that he was wasting his strength to no purpose, he changed his method of attack, and leaving his car in charge of a squire prepared to lead the assault on foot. Some time was lost while he was collecting a picked body of men to follow him, and instructing them how to proceed; and while he was taking his measures, Asius, a captain of the allies, made a bold attempt to carry the Greek position at a single blow. Disregarding Hector's orders, he remained in his chariot, called to his troop to keep close behind him, and drove rapidly round the line of the wall, looking for a weak point where he might hope to force an entrance. He succeeded beyond his hopes; for on the extreme left of the camp he found a gate which was still open to admit any stragglers who might have been left behind in the flight of the Greeks. With a shout of triumph he drove straight at the open gateway, with all his company following pell-mell. But just as he was about to cross the portals he found himself confronted by a pair of gigantic brothers, who stood like two mighty oaks deep-rooted on a mountain top, ready to dispute the way. They were well supported by the defenders who lined the walls, and a hail of stones and javelins rattled down on the shields of Asius and his men, who were driven back with loss and compelled to retire out of range. The gates were then closed and barred, and for this time the camp was saved.

Meanwhile the Trojans under Hector's command were still hesitating on the brink of the moat. For a strange portent had occurred, which gave them pause, just as they were rushing to the assault. On the left hand of the army they saw an eagle soaring high in the air, holding a huge serpent in his talons, which writhed and struggled to escape. And indeed the eagle had met his match, for suddenly the serpent drew back his head, and darting forward bit his captor in the breast. The eagle gave a scream of pain, and dropping the serpent, which fell in the midst of the Trojans, flew swiftly away.

All stood amazed, and doubt and fear crept into their hearts when they saw the monster writhing at their feet. At last Polydamas, a warrior who was famed for his skill in augury, turned to Hector, and said: "My prince, the sign is against us; and as the eagle was stricken, when he strove to carry the dappled snake to his young, so shall we also be stricken, if we persist in our assault on the Grecian stronghold. Let us draw off our men, lest we be found fighting against the gods, and bring upon ourselves rout and disaster."

"Polydamas," answered Hector, with bended brows, "if thou hast no better counsel than this thou hadst better hold thy peace, for the gods have marred thy wit. Vain man! knowest thou not that we came hither under a sure promise from Zeus? Are we to obey his voice, or shall we be cowed by the flapping of a wing? What care I for any fowl that flies east or west, while I stand under the favour of heaven's high lord? To the patriot all omens are good, when his country summons him to her defence. A truce to thine idle prate! Thou hast naught to fear, whether we fight or fly, for thou art never seen on the perilous edge of battle. But keep thy cold counsels for thine own coward heart, or I will find means to lock thy lips for ever."

Thereupon he sprang forward towards the wall, and all his men followed, raising a deafening shout. And from the glens of Ida there came a rushing mighty wind, which bore a blinding cloud of dust into the faces of the Greeks, and hindered them in the work of defence. The Trojans had now crossed the moat, and were striving with all their force to break down the wall. Some tugged at the battlements, and tried to pull them down, while others brought levers to overthrow the projecting buttresses. On the other side the Greeks fought stubbornly, making a fence with their shields along the line of the wall, and keeping up a shower of javelins and stones.

Foremost in the defence were the greater and lesser Ajax, who hurried up and down the battlements, encouraging, rebuking, and threatening. "Stand fast!" they cried. "This is no time for flinching. Let every man do his part, whether he be weak or strong. Your lives are in your own hands."

As on a winter day, when Zeus has lulled the winds to sleep, and all the air is thick with flying snowflakes, until mountain top and jutting promontory, green field and black ploughland, level shore and rocky bay, are all hidden under the same dazzling mantle, whose fringe touches the cold, grey sea—so thick flew the missiles on either side, rattling down uninterruptedly on battlement and helmet and shield.

Conspicuous among the allies of the Trojans were Glaucus and Sarpedon, the leaders of the Lycians. They were bosom friends, of one heart and one mind; and the night before they had discoursed earnestly together on the duties and privileges of their rank. The words of Sarpedon on this occasion are ever memorable. "I need not tell thee, Glaucus," he said, "why we twain are honoured above all the rest with the highest seats, the costliest fare, and cups ever full, and why a fair domain of corn-land and olive ground and vineyard was set apart for us on the banks of Xanthus. As we have received freely, so freely must we give, sparing not even our heart's blood in the service of those to whom we owe all we have. Let us be no sluggard kings, first in the feast and last in the fray, but, as we are foremost in privilege, so let us be foremost in peril. Man walketh as a vain shadow, and all his steps are encompassed by death; die he must, ere many days are passed—herein he hath no choice—but, unless he hath the soul of a slave, he will choose death with honour."

Acting in the spirit of these noble words, Sarpedon, with Glaucus at his side, and all the chivalry of Lycia at his back, now made a determined attack on the part of the wall where Menestheus, the captain of the Athenians, was directing the defence. Menestheus, feeling that he was ill provided to sustain the onset of these two famous captains, raised his voice to summon Ajax to his succour; but his cry was drowned by the tremendous din of the battle which was raging around him, and the thundering blows which the Trojans were now raining upon the gates. So he sent an urgent message by a herald, begging Ajax to come to his relief. Ajax responded promptly to the call, and joined the men under Menestheus, bringing with him Teucer, his half-brother, who was now sufficiently recovered from his wound to take part in the defence.

On came the storming party, with Sarpedon at their head, and they were already beginning to swarm up the battlements, when the arrival of Teucer and Ajax gave them a check. Lifting up a ponderous stone, which he found lying loose by the wall, Ajax dashed out the brains of a stout Lycian, whose knee was already on the rampart, and down he toppled, plunging head-foremost, like a diver, into the moat; and at the same moment a lucky shot from Teucer's bow struck Glaucus in the arm. Incensed to see his comrade wounded, Sarpedon redoubled his efforts, and grasping one of the battlements with both hands he wrenched it from its place, and sent it crashing to the ground. But, being fiercely attacked by Ajax and Teucer together, he was compelled to draw back a little, and wait for support. "On, Lycians!" he shouted. "Why loiter ye behind? I cannot win the wall alone."

The Lycians rallied to the voice of their prince, and the battle was renewed with fresh fury on both sides. Up the steep bank they swarmed again, and strove with all their might to drive back the defenders from their battlements. But the Greeks would not yield an inch, and besiegers and besieged held their ground stubbornly in that grim controversy, like two farmers who stand, with measuring-lines in their hands, disputing hotly about a few inches of ground, on the boundaries of their fields—or like an honest labouring woman, who holds the scale in even balance, weighing the wool which she has spun to win a scanty wage wherewith to buy her children bread.[14] So in even balance hung the fray, and many were the wounds given and received in back or in breast, until the battlements ran with blood.

But the chief honour of the day was reserved for Hector, who was the first to set foot within the fortress of the Greeks. While the battle was still raging on the wall, he made his way to the main entrance of the camp, which was defended by stout oaken gates, fast closed with massy bolt and bar. In front of the gates lay a huge stone, such as two men could hardly lift in these less heroic days. Lifting the mighty boulder, he carried it, easily as a shepherd carries a fleece, close up to the gates. Then, planting his feet firmly, he heaved that ponderous mass above his head, and flung. Like a thunderbolt flew the enormous missile, dashing through panel and bolt and bar. The gates, torn from their hinges, fell inward, and over the ruins sprang Hector, with brow black as night, and death in his glance. Terribly gleamed his brazen armour as he leapt upon the foe, with a lance in each hand. None save the gods could have dared to face him in that hour of triumph and victory. The Trojans poured in behind him, or leapt down from the wall, now deserted by the

---

14. The yarn is weighed to show that none of the raw wool has been stolen.

panic-stricken Greeks, who fled with one accord to the shelter of their ships.

12

POSEIDON AIDS
THE GREEKS

I

THE PROMISE which Zeus had made to Thetis seemed now on the point of being fulfilled, and accordingly Zeus, by whose direct interference alone the Trojans had been able to work such havoc among the Greeks, relaxed his attention, and left the rival armies to fight out the issue between them, never dreaming that any of the gods would venture to act against his express command.

But Poseidon, his brother, and second only to Zeus himself in power, was a staunch ally of the Greeks, and was bitterly indignant that they should suffer defeat at the hands of the hated and despised Trojans. As long as the eye of Zeus was on the battlefield he dared not interfere; but as soon as he saw his great brother engaged elsewhere he left his seat on the island of Samothrace, where he had been overlooking the battle, and sped on his way to Ægæ, his sacred city on the shores of the

Gulf of Corinth. The mountains bowed their heads, and the trees vailed[15] their high tops, beneath the immortal feet of Poseidon, the King. In three steps he reached his goal, and entered his shining, golden palace, built in the cool depths of that glassy bay. There he bade harness his brazen-footed steeds, and mounting the car drove it across the waters. The charmed billows parted to make him a path, and round him played the dolphins, and other huge children of the deep, as his wheels passed unwetted over that heaving, liquid floor. So on they bounded, until they reached the shores of Troy.

The Greeks were still flying before the victorious Trojans, who pressed them hard, with furious uproar, when suddenly there appeared among them one like unto Calchas, the prophet, in form and in voice. "Take heart, comrades!" said he, addressing himself to Ajax, who, with his namesake, was still heading the defence; "we shall beat them yet, if only we can quench the fury of that madman, Hector, who bears himself like a son of Zeus. Have at them, and thrust them back from the ships!"

His words were common, but they were uttered by a god, and breathed a mysterious influence, which was aided by a light touch from the staff which he bore. Instantly a strange lightness and vigour entered into their limbs, and when the pretended Calchas vanished

---

15. "*Vailing* [stooping] her high top lower than her ribs."—Shakespeare: *Merchant of Venice*.

as abruptly as he came, they knew that the words which they had heard were spoken by no mortal lips.

Without pausing for a moment, Poseidon continued the work which he had begun. From rank to rank, from leader to leader, he flew, inspiring, encouraging, entreating; and wherever he passed a new fire was kindled in every breast, so that they who but a moment before had given up all for lost now thought with shame of their faintheartedness, and rallied to the call of their leaders, resolved to conquer or die.

Where Ajax and his namesake fought were mustered the choicest troops in the Greek army. Shoulder to shoulder, and knee to knee, they stood, making a firm fence with shield overlapping shield, and bristling with a forest of spears. "Stand fast!" shouted Ajax, as Hector came on with headlong rush, like some huge rock, which hangs threatening on a steep mountain-side, until it is undermined by a winter torrent, and thunders down the slope until it has spent its force and lies motionless on the plain. So Hector hurled himself with fury against the solid phalanx of the Greeks, but spent his fury in vain on that hedge of iron, and could not break through it, for all his rage.

II

Idomeneus, the leader of the Cretans, had been absent some time from the battle, attending to a wounded comrade, and when he left him he went to his tent, to replace part of his armour, which had been damaged in the fight. On reaching his quarters he was met by Meriones, his second in command, who had gone to fetch a fresh spear, having broken his own on a Trojan shield. "What doest thou here, Meriones?" he asked. "Art thou wounded, or bringest thou some message to me?"

"I came to fetch a spear," answered Meriones; "my own was broken in the fight." "Spears there are in plenty in my tent," said Idomeneus, "and helmets, and shields, and burnished corslets—the spoils of many a vanquished Trojan." "And in mine too there is no lack of such," replied Meriones. "But thy tent was nearer. Thou knowest best whether I do my devoir on the field of honour or not."

"I have seen thee prove thy manly worth," said Idomeneus. "Thou needst not remind me. I have noted thy bearing in the long cold hours of the night, when thou wast one of a picked company lying in ambush, and waiting for the dawn. This is the sternest, sharpest test of valour and endurance. Mark then the coward, how he flushes, and then pales, shifting uneasily from one foot to another, as he cowers in his place, with chattering teeth and wildly beating heart, and mark the hero, crouched, like a good hound, motionless and silent, ready to spring at his enemy's throat. None ever passed through that sharp ordeal with more honour than thou. And in open battle thy face is ever to the foe, and thy scars are all in front. But enough of this: here stand we bragging of our prowess, while our comrades are encompassed by the flames of war. Let us away, and show our manhood by deeds, not words."

Like murderous Ares when he arms him for battle in the savage land of Thrace, and by his side goes Terror, his son, whose fierce eyes appal the stoutest heart, so rushed Idomeneus back to the field, with Meriones, his trusty friend. "Let us make for the left of the fighting line," cried Idomeneus. "On the right the Trojans are weaker, and in the centre fights Telamonian Ajax, a pillar of strength, the equal of Achilles in all save speed of foot. On the left the need is sorest, with most room for a leader of note."

As on a wild and gusty day, when two clouds of dust are whirled together by conflicting winds, so met the Greek and Trojan columns, with clash of shield and glitter of spear, when Idomeneus and his comrade returned to the field. Not in vain had Idomeneus boasted of his deeds of war. Many a Trojan went down that day before his spear; and the first of them was Othryoneus, who was lately come to Troy, and was a suitor for the hand of Cassandra, the fairest of Priam's daughters. Great was the price which he had promised to pay for his bride. "Give me thy daughter," he said, "and I will drive these Greeks out of the land." But the lance of Idomeneus cut short his wooing, and down he fell with a sounding crash. "Is it thou, gallant bridegroom?" shouted Idomeneus, as his helmet fell off, exposing his face. "How wilt thou keep thy bargain with Priam now? That wager is lost, but come with me, and we will find thee a fair partner yet. Thou shalt have the fairest of Agamemnon's daughters, if thou wilt aid us to sack the stately city of Troy. How likest thou the terms?"

Thus insulting his fallen foe, Idomeneus began to drag him away by the foot, intending to spoil him of his armour. While thus employed, he was confronted by Asius, who came on foot against him, his squire following close with the chariot, so that he felt the hot breath of the horses on his shoulders. But Idomeneus was too quick for him, and pierced him, as he stood with weapon poised, in the throat, driving the point clean through his neck. Like an oak, or poplar, or tall pine, hewn down on a mountainside to make a ship's timber, so fell that proud champion, and lay in his blood at his horse's feet, moaning and clutching at the dust. The charioteer was dumfoundered by his master's fall, and dropped the reins in his terror; and while he stood thus, with staring eyes and gaping mouth, Antilochus thrust him through with his spear, and leaping into the car drove off with his prize.

Idomeneus was now fiercely assailed by a formidable antagonist, in the person of Deiphobus, a brother of Hector, and one of the bravest of the Trojans. Idomeneus crouched low as he saw him coming with brandished spear; and the weapon passed over him, just grazing the rim of his shield, but found a victim in another Greek, who was advancing to his support, and received the point in his breast. Down he went, and Deiphobus cried exultingly: "Not unavenged falls

Asius, but I have given him a companion on his journey to the shades."

Thus saved from his peril, the stout old Cretan glared about him, looking for another mark for his spear; and he found one in the young Alcathous, who was married to a daughter of Anchises, and was thus closely related to Æneas. The youthful prince, being new to the work of war, was bewildered by the roar and tumult of the struggle which was raging around him, and stood, overpowered by sudden panic, within close range of the Cretan captain's lance. "Sleepest thou, pretty lad!" shouted the grim veteran, "I will wake thee from thy slumber." And he clove him through the breast with his spear, which stilled the last beatings of his heart.

"Three Trojans for one Greek!" shouted Idomeneus. "Art thou content, Deiphobus? Come hither, and I will add a fourth. It will be glory enough for thee to die by the hand of Idomeneus, whose grandsire was Minos, the very son of Zeus."

Deiphobus deemed it prudent to decline the challenge, and he went in search of Æneas, to inform him of his kinsman's fall. Æneas was loitering in the rear, for he had a grudge against Priam, which chilled his ardour for the battle. But when he heard that Alcathous was slain his heart burned to avenge him, and he hurried to the front, where he was joined by Paris and a strong band of Trojans. Idomeneus, on his part, was reinforced by the arrival of Meriones, Antilochus, and Ascalaphus, a son of Ares, with their followers; and so the fight raged on, and many a stout warrior went down to swell the muster-roll of death.

There fought Helenus, the prophetic son of Priam, armed with bow and arrows, and wielding a mighty falchion, tempered in a Thracian forge. With one blow of that trenchant blade he shattered the helmet of a Greek warrior, a friend of Menelaus, and laid him at his feet, stunned and bleeding. Menelaus sprang to his friend's relief, and flung his spear at Helenus; and at the same moment Helenus shot an arrow, which struck the prince on the breastplate, but rebounded as beans or pulse rebound from the winnower's shovel, while the spear of Menelaus pierced him through the left hand, pinning it to the bow. Helenus retired, trailing the spear after him, until a comrade drew it out, and bound up the wounded hand with a woollen sling, which he took from his squire.

Menelaus was now attacked by another Trojan chieftain, who, after making an abortive thrust with his spear, took in his hand an axe, which hung inside his shield, and, swinging the weapon over his head by its long shaft of olive-wood, leapt upon him with a fierce cry. But before the blow could descend he received a fearful wound in the forehead, from the sword of the Spartan king, and fell backwards in the dust. "So may all the Trojans perish!" cried Menelaus, setting his foot on the breast of his prostrate foe. "Ye have robbed me of my wife; ye have plundered my treasure, after receiving generous welcome under my roof. And now ye come hither to burn our fleet, and butcher us in our camp. Great sire of heaven, men praise thy righteousness, and call thee wise above all gods and men: how then canst thou lend thy countenance to these bloodthirsty robbers, whose pastime is murder, whose joy is to betray?"

Carried away by his eloquence, Menelaus failed to observe that he was threatened by a new assailant. This was Harpalion, son of the King of Paphlagonia, who charged at him, lance in hand. Menelaus was just in time to receive the blow on his shield, and before Harpalion could recover his weapon he was transfixed by the spear of Meriones, and lay writhing like a worm on the ground, until he was borne, groaning, from the field by his attendants, followed by his weeping father.

Paris was wroth at the fall of the Paphlagonian prince, who was his friend and guest, and he drew his bow at a venture, and slew Euchenor, the son of a famous seer, who dwelt in Corinth. Often his father had prophesied to him that he was destined to die either by a wasting disease, or on the battlefield at Troy. He chose a warrior's death, and found it on that day, by the hand of Paris.

III

In the other part of the camp, near the main gate, where Hector had first effected an entrance, the Greeks were still fighting with indomitable spirit under Telamonian Ajax, and his namesake, the son of Oileus. These two held together, and battled side by side, like two stout oxen yoked to the same plough, and toiling from dawn till sunset, while the sweat streams without ceasing from the roots of their horns: so stood they side by side, and bore the brunt, all through that long and bitter fray. And behind them were arrayed the bowmen and slingers of Locris, whose captain was the lesser Ajax, and kept up such a shower of arrows and leaden bullets that the Trojans at length began to waver, and broke their ranks.

When Polydamas, the wisest head among the Trojans, saw that the great assault, which had begun so boldly, was beginning to flag, he called Hector aside, and said to him: "Hector, thou art strong of hand, but weak of head. Seest thou not that we are wasting our valour, by fighting thus in scattered parties, with no settled plan of attack? Now, hearken to me, and do as I shall say, if thou wouldst not have us driven back in shameful rout upon the town. Gather all our parties into one strong phalanx, and charge with them all at once on one point in the Grecian line. Thus, and thus only, may we hope to prevail, outnumbered as we are by two to one."

Hector saw that the advice was good, and, leaving Polydamas to hold the Greeks in check, he went in search of Asius, Deiphobus, and the rest, who were fighting on the left. Sore were the gaps which now appeared in that gallant company, and many a hero, whom he called by name, was lying cold in death. Gathering such as remained, he formed them into one body with those whom he had left in the charge of Deiphobus, and with the powerful column thus formed made repeated charges, which were sustained with undaunted firmness by Ajax and his men.

13

ZEUS IS BEGUILED BY HERA

I

WHILE THE BATTLE swayed to and fro, and the Greeks were enabled by Poseidon's aid to hold their own against the Trojans, Zeus was sitting on a lonely peak of Ida, wrapped in a high celestial reverie. Hera saw the uxorious king from her place of outlook on Olympus, and, noting his abstracted mood, she resolved to play him a trick. So she went to her chamber, which her son Hephæstus had made for her, and opened the door with a private key, which she always kept by her, so that none might invade her apartment in her absence. Having locked herself in, she began to make her toilet with peculiar care. First, she washed her person with ambrosia, and anointed herself with a fragrant oil, so rich and rare that, when she lifted the lid of the casket in which it was stored, a divine perfume filled earth and heaven with sweetness. Then she dressed her lustrous hair, and put on a wondrous robe, which Athene's own hands had wrought for her, clasping it to her bosom with golden brooches. A rich girdle confined her robe at the waist, and in her ears she hung earrings of costly pearl; and when she had put on her sandals, and thrown a glittering veil over her head, she went forth smiling in triumphant beauty, like a bride adorned for her husband.

Having thus prepared the whole battery of her charms, she went in search of Aphrodite, and when she had found her she drew her apart from the other gods, and said: "Wilt thou grant me a boon, dear child, or wilt thou deny me in anger, because I favour thine enemies, the Greeks?" "Name thy request, great queen of heaven," answered Aphrodite, "and I will grant it, if I can."

Concealing her real purpose, the cunning Hera replied: "I am bound on a journey to the ends of the earth, to visit the ancient deity Oceanus, and Tethys, his wife, who have long been parted by a bitter quarrel. If I can bring them together in love and kindness I shall do a good deed, and repay part of the great debt of gratitude which I owe them. Therefore, lend me, I pray thee, the mighty talisman which thou hast, whereof neither man nor god can resist the powerful spell."

"It becomes me not," answered Aphrodite, "to deny thee in this, for thou art the consort of high Jove." And therewith she took from her bosom an amulet, in which there was a mysterious virtue, able to soften the hardest heart, and turn it to thoughts of love and tenderness. There dwelt persuasion and sweet endearment, the eloquence of silence and the witchery of sighs. "Take it," she said, "and hide it in the folds of thy robe. Armed with this, thou wilt accomplish all thy desire."

Hera smiled her thanks, and taking the amulet sped away on her errand, which carried her, not, as she had pretended, to the distant dwelling of Oceanus, but to Lemnos, the Ægæan isle, the home of sleep. Arrived there, she sought out the drowsy god, and found him nodding in his shadowy cave. "Monarch of men and gods," she began, "Immortal Sleep, thou hast done me good service in the past, and I think thou wilt not fail me now. I would have thee lock fast the eyes of Zeus in slumber deep and long. Ask me not why, but do it, and I will give thee a golden throne, wrought, with a foot-stool, by Hephæstus, my son, whereon thou mayest sit in state like the Olympian king himself."

"Ask me aught else," answered Sleep, lifting his heavy eyes with a look of fear, "only ask me not to lay Zeus in slumber against his will. Hast thou forgotten what wild work he made when, at thy entreaty, I shed my power upon him, and lulled his wits in a deep trance, that thou mightest wreak thy malice on his favourite, Heracles? Then didst thou raise a storm, which drove Heracles far out of his course, when he was on his voyage from Troy. But when thy lord awoke, and saw what thou hadst done, he fell to buffeting all the gods in Olympus, who had hidden me from his sight. And soon they must have delivered me to his vengeance, and I should have been undone, but an ancient and venerable deity, even Night herself, came to my aid, and besought him to pardon me; and so he did, for he would not offend the august goddess, primeval Night."

"Go to," said Hera. "This is a far smaller thing than that of which thou speakest. All I desire is an hour of respite for mine afflicted Greeks. Come, do as I bid thee, and thou shalt have Pasiphaë, one of the Graces, for thy wife, and so fulfil the dearest of thy desires."

Then Sleep was glad, and answering said: "Swear to me, by the inviolable waters of Styx—placing one hand on the earth, and the other on the sea, that all the nether gods may be our witnesses—swear that thou wilt give me Pasiphaë for my bride."

Hera took the oath required, calling by name all the Titans that dwell in Tartarus. Then together they flew across the sea to Troyland, and paused not till they reached the wooded hills of Ida. Upwards then they soared, over the forest-clad slopes, and there was the sound of a going in the tree tops as they passed. And when they came to the peak where Zeus was sitting, Sleep disguised himself in the form of a swift, and hid himself in the branches of a tall fir-tree. But Hera went and stood in the presence of her lord.

As soon as the god saw her he was struck with wonder at her surpassing beauty, and his heart over-flowed with tenderness, as in the old days when first he made her his bride. And the little swift shot down from the tree, and come flitting round the monarch's head. "Dear lady of my love," said he, "sit down by me awhile, and let us hold sweet converse together." So down she sat by his side, and took his hand, and beguiled him with her false blandishments. Like two simple lovers they seemed, caught in sly Cupid's silver net—he the sovereign of earth and heaven, and she, his imperious queen. And swiftly the subtle influence of Sleep came over him, and down he sank overpowered, couched on a soft bed of crocus and hyacinth and violet, which the earth put forth to bear up his sacred person; and on him rested a canopy of golden cloud, that he might slumber unobserved.

II

Safe now from the observation of Zeus, Hera descended swiftly to bear the news to Poseidon, and urge him to redouble his efforts on behalf of the Greeks. Having brought her message, she returned to Ida, and remained watching by the side of Zeus, ready to give warning when he awoke.

Poseidon was not slow to seize the occasion thus offered. Suddenly, as the Greeks were preparing to receive a furious charge from the enemy, there appeared in their van a gigantic warrior, clad from head to foot in mail of proof, and wielding a sword which flashed and burned with an awful light. "On, Greeks, on!" he shouted; and his voice was as the sound of many waters. "Down with them, even unto the ground, that Hector may know that there is more than one Achilles among us." And the two armies met, with a crash which was echoed by all the caverns of Ida, and recoiled again, each solid phalanx reeling from that tremendous shock.

Into the space thus left sprang Hector, and hurled his spear at Ajax, who was stepping forth to meet him. The weapon struck him on the breast, just at the point where the shield strap, heavily studded with metal, was crossed by the baldric of his sword; and this double barrier, backed by the corslet, proved an effectual defence. Hector fell back, vexed at his ill-fortune, and, as he was retiring, Ajax picked up one of the stones which were lying around, to serve as props for the ships, and flinging it struck him on the back of the neck, just above the rim of his shield. It was no maiden's hand which had aimed that blow, and Hector was sent spinning like a top. And as an oak reels and staggers when struck by the bolt of Zeus, and topples headlong to earth, a blackened and shattered trunk, so fell the mighty Hector, crushed under the weight of his shield, which was pressed down upon him by the ponderous stone.

When they saw him fall, the Greeks rushed forward, hoping to make him their prisoner. But the bravest of the Trojans and their allies—Sarpedon, Æneas, Glaucus, and Polydamas—interposed their shields, giving time for the others to lift him up and carry him to the place where his car and horses were waiting. Carefully they placed his senseless body on the chariot, and drove him towards the city, until they came to the ford of Scamander. There they halted, and, laying him on the bank, dashed water in his face. Presently he looked up, and leaning forward on his hands began to vomit blood. Then darkness came over his eyes, and he fell back again in a swoon.

Now that Hector was down, the Trojans had no course left to them but to retreat. They still fought valiantly, and the Greeks had to pay dear for their success. But slowly and surely they were being driven back from the camp.

14

THE LAST BATTLE
BY THE SHIPS

HERA WAS WATCHING the action with such eagerness that she had forgotten her charge, and was startled by the angry voice of Zeus, who had awakened suddenly, and was looking down upon her with lowering brows. "This is thy work," he said sternly, pointing to the Trojan plain, where Hector lay senseless, and his comrades were beginning to fly. "Wilt thou never be schooled to obedience, or what harder lesson lackest thou yet? Dost thou remember the time when I hung thee in chains in the cold vault of ether, with two anvils at thy feet, and all the gods together were powerless to relieve thee? This was thy reward for thy evil devices against my son, Heracles; but that shall be mirth and laughter compared with the rod which thou shall feel if thou cease not from thy mutiny against my sovereign will."

Then Hera was sore afraid, and she answered submissively: "I swear by earth and heaven, and by the down-falling waters of Styx, the greatest and most awful thing by which a god may swear—yea, by thy sacred head I swear it, and by the holy bond which unites us—it was not by my devices that Poseidon first began to aid the Greeks, but he was led thereto by the thoughts of his own heart. And, by my advice, he will give way to thee."

Somewhat appeased by her humility, Zeus replied: "If that be so, and thou art willing to heal the mischief thou hast done, go and send hither Iris and Apollo, that they may receive my commands. And understand me once for all—I will not cease from my rage and my fury against the Greeks, nor suffer any of the gods to aid them, until the vengeance of Pelides is accomplished, and the oath fulfilled which I sware unto his mother, Thetis, when she touched my knees and besought me to honour her son."

Swift as is the glance of the mind when some great traveller revolves all his wanderings in thought, and murmurs to himself: "Would that I were in this place or that!" naming some distant scene which he hath visited, so swiftly flew Hera with her lord's message. When she reached Olympus she found all the gods seated together, drinking their nectar from golden cups. Smiling with her lips, but bending her dark brows in a gloomy frown, she said, as she eyed that festal gathering: "Ye are making good cheer, I see! And ye will be cheered the more when I tell you what Zeus intends. Ay, drink deep!" she continued, turning to Ares, who was just draining a full cup, "thou hast need of comfort, for thy son is slain." And she named a Greek, Ascalaphus, son of Ares, who had been slain by Deiphobus in the battle.

When he heard that, the god of war groaned with grief and anger, and crying: "I will avenge him!" rushed to seize his arms. But Athene hastened after him, and finding him already equipped for battle she snatched the spear from his hand, and took the helmet from his head, saying: "Madman, wilt thou undo us all? Go back to thy place, lest the wrath of Zeus descend upon the whole company of the gods, and on thee the first. Better men have fallen than this son of thine, and we must look to our own safety, and leave mortals to their fate."

While Athene was occupied in restraining the frenzy of Ares, Hera despatched Iris and Apollo to receive the commands of Zeus. So they went forthwith to Ida, and found Zeus sitting in the place where he had slept, with the golden cloud still hanging above his head. Zeus was well content that his wilful consort had been so prompt in his business, and he commanded Iris to go down to the fleet, and warn Poseidon to leave the battlefield. "And thus and thus shalt thou say unto him," added Zeus, instructing her in the very words which she was to use.

Iris descended to earth, walking delicately along her rainbow bridge, and, having found Poseidon among the warring Greeks, she said to him: "Thus saith Zeus, our sovereign lord and king: 'Let Poseidon leave the battlefield, and depart to Olympus, or to his own watery realm. And if he will not obey me I will come myself, and fight against him, face to face. Let him avoid my hands, for he knoweth that I am far mightier than he, and higher in station and in dignity.'"

"What!" answered Poseidon, swelling with injured pride. "Am I my brother's slave, that he sends me this haughty summons? I am no subject of his, but his peer, holding a third part in our divided empire. For three sons were born unto Cronos—Zeus and Hades and myself. And when Cronos ceased to reign we cast lots between us, and Zeus obtained the throne of heaven, I of the sea, and Hades of the underworld; but the earth, and wide Olympus, were left common to us all. Therefore I bid him keep to his own domain, and not meddle with me, for I will not live under his laws, nor bow to his rod, which he may keep for his sons and daughters."

"Is this, then, the answer which I must carry back to Zeus?" asked Iris gravely. "Oh, reflect a little! Enter not into an unnatural feud with thine elder brother."

"'Tis wisely said," replied Poseidon. "Thou art a discreet messenger, and knowest how to season thy words with courtesy. 'Twere ill, as thou sayest, to stir up the demon of domestic strife among us. Therefore I will depart, and leave him to work his will. But, since he has used threats, let him hear this from me: if he seeks to avert the doom of Troy, he will find a cold welcome when he joins the circle of the gods in Olympus."

It was not without relief that Zeus heard of Poseidon's submission; for he had feared that he would be obliged to engage in a fearful struggle, which would have confounded earth and heaven. This danger being removed, he sent Apollo, armed with his own shield—the awful ægis, clothed with attributes of terror—commanding him to heal Hector of his hurt, and bring him back to battle. Like a falcon stooping on his quarry, Apollo shot down from Ida's peak, and alighted at the ford of Scamander, where Hector was still lying. By this time the stricken man had recovered from his swoon, and was gazing in bewilderment around him.

One touch from that potent hand, one word from those immortal lips, sufficed to banish all the effects of the fearful blow which had left Hector as weak as a child. Bounding to his feet, he cried: "Lead on, mighty god! I fear no perils with thee at my side," and like a gallant war horse, that smelleth the battle afar off, he ran at full speed to rejoin the Trojans, who were now flying tumultuously from the camp. And as when a troop of hunters with their hounds have started a royal stag, and chased him with wild halloo to the thick covert of a tangled wood; then suddenly they shrink back with cries of dismay, for they see a lion standing in the path: so panic fell upon the Greeks in the midst of their triumph, when they saw Hector returning to battle, full of vigour and courage, though they had already counted him among the dead.

On poured the Trojans, Hector and Apollo leading the van, and the Greeks gave ground before them, scared by the dread ægis, which Apollo shook in their faces, crying his terrible cry. At first they yielded slowly, keeping their ranks, and attempting some defence; but soon the retreat became a rout, and the moat was filled with a struggling multitude, seeking the shelter of the wall and the ships. "Kill, kill!" cried Hector fiercely. "Pause not to strip the dead, but slay the men, and burn their ships. Let me but see anyone skulking behind for plunder and he dies by my hand."

With that he lashed his horses, and drove straight across the moat, the Trojans following him in dense column. In front strode Apollo, trampling down the sides of the moat as he went, and making a path broad as the farthest cast of a spear. Then he hurled himself on the wall, and overthrew it, as easily as a child destroys with his feet a castle of sand which he has raised in sport on the margin of the sea.

Like a towering billow, which topples down upon a ship, crushing her bulwarks and flooding her with brine, so rushed the Trojans in a torrent over the wall, and fell upon the hindmost row of ships; and the Greeks on their side mounted the decks, and thrust at their assailants with long boarding-pikes, which lay ready to hand.

Foremost among the defenders was seen the giant form of Telamonian Ajax; and by his side fought Teucer, whose bow had already done such good service to the Greeks. But just as Teucer was aiming an arrow at Hector his bowstring snapped, and the arrow dropped harmless to the ground. "Fate is against us to-day," he cried; "it was a new string, the stoutest and the best I had, which I fitted to my bow this very morning."

"Go quickly," answered Ajax. "And arm thyself with shield and spear; there is no room here for thine archery to-day." And Teucer went and armed himself, and returned with all speed to his mighty brother's side.

Hector was overjoyed when he saw Teucer's mishap, which he hailed as the direct act of Zeus himself. "On, Trojans!" he shouted; "on, ye men of Lycia! Zeus is fighting on our side. Now is the great day of vengeance, after all the weary years when we were penned within our walls like sheep."

"Why flinch ye?" cried Ajax, in his turn, to the Greeks. "Know ye not that we must conquer or die to-day? Or will we reach home on foot, if ye suffer your ships to be burned? Come, join the wild dance to which Hector summons us. Fight, and we will drive out this rabble yet; but if ye falter we shall surely perish."

Again the Greeks rallied to the well-known voice of Ajax, and drew up in close order before the ships, barring Hector's way. But the finger of Apollo had touched him, filling his breast with a divine frenzy. Foaming and glaring with rage, he flung himself on the solid phalanx, and cut down a tall champion of Mycenæ, making a gap in the line. Before the Greeks could close their ranks the Trojans were among them, hewing them down as a woodman hews a path through the forest. Forward and still forward they pressed, driving the Greeks before them, and compelling them to retire from the first line of ships.

Then nothing but the tremendous valour of Ajax could have saved the Greek army from total rout and ruin. Active as a panther, in spite of his huge bulk, he sprang from deck to deck, wielding an enormous boarding-pike and striking down the Trojans, as they advanced with lighted torches to set fire to the ships. Like a practised rider, who yokes together four horses, and drives them at a gallop along a level highroad, leaping from one steed to another as he goes—so Ajax shifted his ground from one ship to another, dashing down Trojan after Trojan, and shouting to the Greeks to come to his support.

It was a grim and desperate struggle. There was no shooting of arrows, no casting of javelins now, but foot to foot, and hand to hand, they fought, with axe, and sword, and spear. At last Hector forced his way to a beautiful galley, which had brought Protesilaus to Troy, and laying his hand on the high, fanlike ornament of the stern he shouted: "Bring a torch, that I may be the first to kindle the fire which shall burn these accursed ships, which came here for our destruction, but shall now serve as a pyre for their crews."

15

ACHILLES SENDS PATROCLUS TO BATTLE

I

PATROCLUS HAD BEEN long detained by Eurypylus, whose wound was severe, and demanded all his skill. But when the roar of battle drew nearer and nearer, and he heard the voice of Hector calling for a torch, he would delay no longer, but sprang up and ran in headlong haste to the quarters of the Myrmidons. There he found Achilles still sitting before his tent, and listening to the mingled cries of triumph and dismay which came from the distant scene of conflict. When Patroclus saw him, he came and stood by his side, and lifted up his voice, and wept.

"Why weepest thou, Patroclus," asked Achilles, "like a little maid, who runs by her mother's side, plucking her by the gown, and looking into her face with tearful eyes, begging to be carried? What means this melting mood? Hast thou ill news of thy father, or of mine, or are these tears for the Greeks, now perishing by their own transgression?"

"Ah! son of Peleus," answered Patroclus, with a pitiful sigh, "take not my words amiss, but I am sore afflicted for the sake of my countrymen. Their best and noblest are grievously wounded, and the leeches are busy about them; and those that remain can no longer make head against the foe. Can nothing move thee? What avails all thy splendid manhood, if thou wilt sit idle here, until thine arm is palsied with age? Oh! yet at last relent, if thou art indeed the son of gentle Thetis, and not some savage changeling, born of the rocks, and nourished by the sea! If thou wilt not go to the field thyself, at least let me put on thine armour, and lead the Myrmidons to aid our friends in their dreadful strait."

For some time Achilles answered nothing, and it was evident that a sore struggle was passing in his breast. At last he looked up, and said with an effort: "Thou hast prevailed, son of Menœtius, though I vowed that I would never cease from mine anger until the fire had reached my own ships. When I think of the foul outrage—— But enough! Down, down, rebellious pride!" He paused, frowning, and grinding his teeth; for the fierce fit had come on him again. Then, mastering himself, he continued: "Thou shalt have my armour, and lead the Myrmidons to battle. But take heed to what I shall say, and let not thine ardour carry thee too far, but when thou hast driven the enemy out of the camp lead thy men back, and be not tempted to fight in the open field, lest thou rob me of mine honour, and leave naught for me to do. Remember this, and have a care for thyself, for they have a mighty ally on their side, even Apollo."

While they were thus conversing, Ajax was still keeping up an unequal struggle against an overpowering force. The Trojans surrounded the ship on which he was fighting, and plied him with a shower of missiles, which rattled on his helmet, and threatened every moment to bring him down. His left shoulder ached with holding his shield, which was thrust back upon him by a dozen spears at once. Yet still he fought on, with his breath coming in heavy gasps, and the sweat pouring from every limb. Then Hector aimed a blow with his sword, and cut off the head of the pike which Ajax was wielding. Thus left without a weapon, Ajax was compelled at last to retreat, and the Trojans rushed forward, and set fire to the ship.

Achilles saw the smoke rising, and cried: "Arm thee, Patroclus. Make haste! I will go and call up the Myrmidons." Patroclus hurried to the tent, and put on the armour of Achilles—the greaves and starry corslet, the helmet and vast orbed shield—and girded on his great comrade's sword. Only the spear of Achilles he took not, for no arm in all the host, save only the arm of Achilles, could wield that ponderous beam of ash, toughened by many a storm on the windy slopes of

Pelion, where it grew.

Meanwhile Automedon, Achilles' charioteer, was yoking to the car the two immortal steeds—Xanthus and Balius—offspring of the West Wind, and nourished on the meadows by the shores of Oceanus. And with them went as a trace horse the mortal courser, Pedasus, which Achilles had taken among the spoils when he sacked the city of Eëtion.

When the Myrmidons heard their leader's voice calling them to arms, they rushed forth from their tents, like thirsty wolves which have gorged themselves with the flesh of a tall stag, and now hasten, with bloodstained chaps and lolling tongues, to slake their thirst in a deep mountain pool. With like eagerness arose the hardy veterans, whose warlike spirit had been fed high by their long repose; and proud was the glance of Achilles, as he glanced down the armed files, marshalled under five famous captains, five times five hundred men. When all were standing silent at their posts he addressed them briefly, and said: "Now is the time to make good the threats which ye uttered against the Trojans, during all the long time of my wrath. Remember how ye murmured against me because I suffered you not to go unto battle. 'Hard-hearted son of Peleus,' ye would say, 'surely thy mother nourished thee with gall, and therefore art thou so ruthless to thy loving comrades, keeping them here in inglorious ease.' See that your deeds are as valiant as your words, and let the Trojans feel the weight of your arm this day."

Firm and close as blocks of stone, fitted together by a master-builder to be the wall of some great house, so stood the warriors in that invincible column, shield leaning on shield, and man on man; and in the van were seen the tall figures of Patroclus and Automedon, two leaders with one heart. Then Achilles went to his tent, and brought forth a golden goblet, a gift from his mother, and sacred to the service of Zeus. Having purified it with sulphur, and washed it with fresh water, he cleansed his own hands, and filling the bowl with wine returned to the open space before the tent. Then lifting up his eyes to heaven he poured the drink-offering, and prayed thus to the king and lord of Olympus: "O thou, whose ancient dwelling is in wintry Dodona, where thy chosen priests serve thee day and night with fasting and prayer, as thou hast lent thine ear to my former petition, and grievously afflicted the Greeks for my sake, so grant me once more my heart's desire. Let thine eyes rest with favour on my noble comrade, and give him honour in the battle. And when he hath driven the Trojans from the camp bring him back safe, with his armour, and all this company, to our tents."

So prayed he in his ignorance, having yet to learn that Zeus is a jealous god, dispensing his gifts with unequal hand, two evil for one good.

II

Like a swarm of wasps which have their nest by the

roadside, and being ever provoked by wanton children wreak their vengeance on some harmless wayfarer; so flew the Myrmidons to join the fray, and soon the Trojans felt their sting. "For Achilles and for honour!" shouted Patroclus, as he hurled his spear, and struck down Pyræchmes, the savage leader of a wild mountain tribe from northern Greece. The rude clansmen fled when they saw their leader fall, and soon the panic spread to the whole Trojan army, and they too fled, leaving the burning ship, the flames of which were soon quenched by a score of eager hands. Like a cloud which lies heavy on a mountain top, and is then suddenly rent and dispersed, revealing all the long range of countless hills, peak beyond peak, far away to the distant sea, with green glades between, and above the boundless chasm of sky, up to the dazzling zenith: so was dispersed that cloud of Trojans which had hung about the ships, and the Greeks saw the fair face of Hope again.

But the end of that long and bloody day was still far off. Outside the barriers the Trojans rallied again, and a fearful slaughter ensued. There the sword of Patroclus bit deep, making dire havoc among the ranks of the Lycians, until Sarpedon, their leader, incensed by the slaughter of his men, sprang from his car, and threw himself in the way, to arrest that destroying hand.

Like two vultures, which tear each other with beak and claw, fighting with loud screams on a lofty crag, so leapt the two champions, the Lycian and the Greek, upon each other, uttering loud their battle-cry.

When Zeus saw his son Sarpedon about to engage in deadly combat with Patroclus he was filled with pity, for he knew that the Lycian chieftain was going to his doom. "How sayest thou, Hera," he began, "shall I save him, and waft him away in a cloud to his fair domain in Lycia, or shall I leave him to his fate?"

"That must not be," answered Hera. "His thread is spun, and his life is forfeit; shouldst thou annul that decree it will be an evil example to the other gods, who will forthwith all seek to avert the stroke of fate from their sons, of whom many are fighting in the fields of Troy. If thou wouldst do him honour, send Death and gentle Sleep to bear him softly, after he has fallen, from the battlefield, and bring him to his kinsfolk in Lycia, that they may pay him the rites which are due to the mighty dead."

"Thou hast persuaded me," answered Zeus, bowing his immortal head in sorrow. And he caused a rain of blood to fall upon the earth, in sad tribute to the heroic spirit which was about to pass away.

While this debate was proceeding, the struggle had already begun. In the first cast of their spears both warriors missed their aim. Patroclus slew the comrade of Sarpedon, while Sarpedon's lance struck Pedasus, the mortal steed, in the shoulder, and he fell dead. His immortal companions plunged wildly, striving to break away from the yoke when they saw their comrade slain. But Automedon cut the traces by which the slaughtered steed was attached to the car; and, being rid of their sad burden, Xanthus and Balius were once more obedient to the rein.

Again the heroes flung their spears, and the weapon of Sarpedon flew over his antagonist's left shoulder. But the spear of Patroclus sank deep into Sarpedon's breast, and he fell, writhing in his death agony, and sending forth loud groans, like a bull when he feels the lion's claws tearing his flanks. So raged Sarpedon in the pangs of death, and rolling his eyes he sought the familiar face of his beloved Glaucus. "Friend of my heart!" he cried, "valiant Glaucus, companion of all my toils, now must thou prove thy manly worth. Rally round thee the stoutest of the Lycians, and let not thy foot go back, or thy hand cease from slaying, until thou hast saved my body from the Greeks. To thee I shall be a reproach, and a hanging of the head, even unto thy life's end, if thou leave me, a rifled and dishonoured corpse, in the hands of the foe."

Even as he spoke, death stopped his breath and darkened his eyes. And Patroclus set his foot on the corpse, and drew forth his spear, while the Myrmidons took possession of the empty car with its affrighted steeds.

Glaucus was in dire distress when he heard his dying comrade's voice. But he was disabled by the wound which he had received in scaling the wall. Nursing his injured arm, he prayed aloud to Apollo: "Hear me, O King, whether thou art now in Lycia or in Troy; for thine ear is ever open to the cry of need, however far away. My hand is maimed, and my arm is burning with sharp pains, so that I cannot wield my spear, though Sarpedon is fallen, and his father hath forsaken him. So forsake thou not me, but heal my wound, and give me back my strength, that I may save his body from outrage."

Apollo heard, and granted his prayer, and straightway the flow of his blood was stopped, and he felt in his body that he was healed of his hurt. Then Glaucus was glad, and he made all haste to do his comrade's bidding. First he called to the men of Lycia to do battle for their slaughtered captain, and then he went to rouse the Trojan leaders to do their duty by their great ally. Finding Hector engaged in another part of the field, he reproached him for his neglect. "Hast thou forgotten," he asked indignantly, "what thou owest to us, who have come on a far journey to shed our blood for thee and thy country? Cold lies Sarpedon, chief pillar of thine allies; come, friends, and help us to save his corpse, or ye will be shamed for ever."

This was bitter news for the Trojans, who reverenced Sarpedon as the chief corner-stone of their defence; and they rushed with one accord to avenge his death. Patroclus on his side summoned the bravest of the Greeks to his aid, and the whole fury of the struggle was now centred in the place where the dead Sarpedon lay.

The first who fell in this new battle was a friend of Patroclus, who years ago had found a new home in the house of Peleus, having been banished from his own country for the murder of his cousin. He was now struck down by a stone from the hand of Hector; and Patroclus, in his anger at his comrade's death, made so furious an assault that the Trojans gave way before him about the length of a spear's cast. Then Glaucus advanced again, and slew Bathycles, a man of high note among the Myrmidons; and Meriones on the other side killed Laogonus, the priest of Idæan Zeus. Æneas, ever famed for his piety, hurled his spear at Meriones, hoping to avenge the fall of that sacred head; but Meriones stooped low, and the spear flew over his head, and sunk deep in the ground, with quivering shaft, just behind him. "The Cretan can dance, I see!" shouted Æneas; "he comes from a land of dancers." "Thou shall dance to my piping, before thou hast done," answered Meriones derisively. "Thinkest thou that we owe thee a life for every cast of thy spear?" "Peace!" said Patroclus, rebuking him. "We must fight with our swords, not with our tongues, if we would do aught worthy here."

Thick and fast rained the blows, on shield and helmet and mailed breast, as the two armies closed again, and the sound was as of an army of woodmen plying their axes together in a deep mountain glade. In the midst lay the lifeless Sarpedon, covered from head to foot with javelins, and blood, and dust, so that his dearest friend could not have recognised his face. Like flies buzzing round a milk pail, so thronged the Greeks and Trojans round the body.

Zeus sat watching the battle, pondering in his heart
what measure of glory he should mete out to Patroclus before he laid him low by the arm of Hector. At
last, having taken his resolve, he caused a coward spirit to enter into Hector's heart, and the Trojan captain
wheeled his car, and fled towards the city. The panic
spread to the other Trojans, and the Lycians, and they
retreated, leaving the body of Sarpedon in the hands of
the Greeks, who despoiled it of its armour, and were
about to do it further dishonour when a higher power
intervened. In the very act of violating the dead, they
saw their lifeless victim snatched from them by an invisible hand; for Apollo had received the commands
of Zeus, and bore away the soiled and blackened body
to the riverside, where he washed it clean, anointed it
with ambrosia, and gave it, robed in immortal raiment,
into the charge of Sleep and Death, for safe and speedy
conveyance to Lycia.

III

High dreams of triumph arose in the heart of Patroclus
when he saw the enemy flying, and, forgetting the earnest injunction of Achilles, he bade Automedon lay on
the lash, and followed in hot pursuit. Even to the very
walls he drove; but then he found awaiting him one
mightier than Hector, even Apollo himself, who shook
the ægis in his face, and warned him back. Patroclus
retired a little, and while he hesitated Apollo went to

the gates of the city, where Hector was lingering, in doubt whether to continue the battle, or to withdraw behind the walls.

"What doest thou here, son of Priam?" said the god; "come with me, and I will show thee where the path of glory lies." When he heard Apollo's voice, Hector's courage returned, and he commanded Cebriones, his charioteer, to drive back to the battlefield. Avoiding the other Greeks, Hector made straight for the place where Patroclus had been left standing by Apollo. Patroclus came to meet him, holding his spear in his left hand, while in his right he grasped a jagged stone. And as the car approached, he flung the stone with all his force, and struck Cebriones on the forehead, shattering the bones. The reins dropped from his hands, and without a single cry he fell from the car, striking the ground with his head. "How bravely the man tumbles!" cried Patroclus. "He would make a rare diver, and earn a good wage by bringing up oysters from the sea. I perceive that the Trojans can dance, as well as the Cretans."

Thereupon he leapt upon the prostrate charioteer, and Hector sprang forward to defend his comrade's body. So there they met, like two hungry lions fighting for the carcass of a stag; and the Greeks and Trojans thronged on either side to their support, like two winds from opposite quarters, which shatter the boughs of beech and ash in a mountain forest. All the ground about the corpse was set thick with javelins and arrows, and heaped with the stones which crashed upon corslet and shield. And there lay the giant Trojan, while the battle raged above him, mighty and mightily fallen, and all his horsemanship forgot.

Never had the arm of Patroclus dealt such havoc among the foemen's ranks as then; for his doom was near, and Zeus gave him honour in this, his latest hour. Thrice he made an onset, fierce as the god of war himself, and thrice he slew nine men. But when for the fourth time he sprang to the encounter, Phœbus made after him, and smote him on the back with his open hand. Patroclus reeled and grew dizzy, like one who has received a sunstroke. Then Apollo struck the helmet from his head, and it rolled clattering among the horses' feet, that mighty brazen helm, whose plumes, now soiled with dust and gore, had once waved above the princely brow of Achilles. The spear was shivered to pieces in his hand, and his shield slipped from his shoulder to the ground. And as he stood thus, defenceless and amazed, a Trojan, whose name was Euphorbus, wounded him between the shoulders with his spear. The blow was not mortal, and Patroclus drew back, to mingle with the press; but Hector followed after him, and drove his spear deep into his side. And as a lion overpowers a wild boar, fighting with him in the lone mountains for the possession of a little spring, and slays him by his might, so slew Hector the valiant son of Menœtius, and stayed the ravage of the Trojan ranks.

"Ah! Patroclus," said he, gazing in triumph on the dying hero, "thou thoughtest this day to have taken our city by storm, and led captive the women of Troy. But they have in me a defender who is too strong for thee. Vain man! Achilles, I doubt not, bade thee bring back to him the bloody spoils of Hector, and now thou liest slain by Hector's hand."

"Boast not," answered Patroclus faintly. "It is small glory for thee to have slain the slain. I received my death blow from Apollo and Euphorbus, not from thee. And thine own fate shall overtake thee soon, when thou shalt die by the hands of Æacides."

Even as he spake the shadow of death fell upon him, and his soul took wing for the realm of Hades, bewailing her lot, leaving all that beauty and manly bloom.

16

THE FIGHT FOR THE BODY OF PATROCLUS

I

MENELAUS WAS THE first to mark the fall of Patroclus, and he came with a rush and stood over his body to defend it, like a young mother of the herd when she stands lowing plaintively over her calf, the first that she has borne. Shield on shoulder and spear in hand he stood, glaring defiance at the foe; and Euphorbus, the Trojan who had dealt the first blow at Patroclus, took up the challenge, addressing Menelaus with these haughty words: "Make way, son of Atreus, and leave me to take my lawful spoil. 'Twas I that wounded Patroclus first, and his armour belongs by right to me. Back, or thou shalt die the death."

"If big words could kill," answered Menelaus, with scorn, "then wert thou and thy brethren the most dreaded warriors of all thy nation; for there are no such windy braggarts in Priam's army. Away with thee, if thou wouldst have breath left in thee to boast again."

But Euphorbus, though a boaster, and a mere novice in war, was no coward. He thrust manfully at Menelaus, who parried the blow with his shield, and then, striking in his turn, and throwing all his weight into the stroke, drove his spear into Euphorbus' throat, so that the point came out at the back of his neck. Down he went, and his armour clattered upon him, and his love locks, curiously adorned with gold and silver, were dabbled with blood. As when a man tends carefully a green olive-shoot, in some sheltered spot, near a gushing fountain-head; and now it is a comely tree, just bursting into blossom, and lightly rocked by all the airs of heaven: then comes a sudden tempest, and uproots it from the soil, and all its promise is marred: so stricken and cut off in the dawn of his manhood lay that gallant lad. And as a lion comes down from the mountains, trusting in his might, and strikes down a young heifer feeding in a meadow, the fairest of the herd, breaking her neck with his mighty teeth, and then glutting himself with her blood and her flesh; and the herdsmen with their hounds stand apart, making great uproar, but not one dares to interrupt him in his meal: so dared not one of the Trojans to stand against Menelaus face to face.

Hector, who after slaying Patroclus had gone off in pursuit of the car of Achilles, was recalled from that fruitless chase by the tidings of Euphorbus' death.

With a loud cry of rage he turned back, and hastened to the place where the young Trojan lay, side by side with Patroclus. Menelaus stayed not to abide his coming, but fell back upon the ranks of his comrades, and there halted, and scanned the fighting line, looking for the great Telamonian Ajax. Observing him at last on the extreme left of the battle, he ran up to him, crying eagerly: "Make haste, Ajax, and aid me to recover the body of Patroclus, that we may carry it back, naked as it is, to Achilles; for the armour Hector has taken already."

So together they went, and stood side by side over the body of Patroclus; and Hector in his turn shrank back, when he was confronted by the towering form of Ajax, with his massive, sevenfold shield. But he took with him the armour, and gave it to two of his men to carry to the city.

Glaucus was full of anger when he saw Hector quail before Ajax, and he reproached him bitterly, calling him faint-hearted, and false to his great office. "It is a thankless task," he said, "to fight under such a leader. Henceforth let the Trojans make shift to defend their city without our aid, for we of Lycia at least will fight their battles no more. Basely hast thou dealt with us, after all our good service, leaving our great captain Sarpedon in the hands of the Greeks. If ye of Troy had the spirit of men, ye would aid us to capture the body of Patroclus, that we might keep it to exchange for Sarpedon's corpse. But thou art a prudent warrior, and fearest the face of Ajax, knowing him to be a far better man than thou art."

"O folly of the wise!" answered Hector scornfully. "'Tis Glaucus can talk thus, who hath the rarest wit, as we are told, among all the men of Lycia. Come and stand by me, and thou shall see if I fear the face of Ajax, or any other Greek. But first I will put on the armour of Achilles, which was given, men say, by the gods, as a wedding gift to his father Peleus." And with that he ran and overtook the men who were carrying the spoils of Patroclus towards the city, and taking off his own armour began to put on that of Achilles.

When Zeus beheld him thus gaily equipping himself in the spoils of the mighty, he shook his head, and spake thus to his own heart: "Ah! wretch, thy triumph will be short lived, and the hand of doom is stretched out already to take thee. But thou shall have thine hour, and Andromache shall hear of thy deeds, though never more shall she welcome thee returning from battle."

He said it, and confirmed it with a nod, and forthwith the very demon of war entered into the heart of Hector, and with a fierce cry he ran back to the field, glittering in the armour of Pelides, which seemed to have been wrought for himself, so well it fitted his limbs.

Even the great Ajax felt a cold touch of fear as Hector bore down upon him, with the most famous warriors of Troy and Lycia at his back. "We are lost," he said to Menelaus, "unless we can get some other succour to beat back this tempest of war." Then, raising his voice, he shouted: "To the rescue, ye captains and princes of the Greeks! Let not Patroclus become a prey to dogs in the streets of Troy." His cry was heard, and soon he was joined by Idomeneus, and Meriones, and the lesser Ajax.

Like the roar of the advancing tide, when it meets the torrent waters at the mouth of the mighty river, such was the shout of the Trojans as they rushed to the onset. And the Greeks stood firm to meet them, making a fence with their shields over the body of Patroclus. At the first shock of that tremendous charge they were forced to give ground a little, and one of the Trojans fastened a thong to the ankle of the corpse, and began to drag it away. But he had not gone far when Ajax sprang upon him, and with one blow of his sword shivered his helmet, and clave him to the chin. This gave time for the Greeks to rally, and the battle was renewed in that narrow space round the body of Patroclus, where many a valiant deed was wrought, and many a hero bit the dust, fighting for the possession of a helpless corpse. Over this struggling mass of warriors in the centre of the field was spread a thick curtain of darkness, for Zeus had ordered it so, while the rest of the Greeks and Trojans were fighting in the broad sunlight. Far away on the border of the fight were Antilochus, the son of Nestor, and his brother, who had not yet heard that Patroclus had been slain.

But in that dark kernel of the battle the ruthless tug of war went on. There was no stay, no pause, while they hewed, and thrust, and strove, till the blinding sweat poured down into their eyes, and their knees shook with weariness. As when a master currier gives to his journeymen a great bull's hide, well drenched with fat, to be stretched, and they stand in a circle, and tug with all their might, straining it equally on all sides, until all moisture departs from it, and the fat penetrates to every pore; so they tugged the body between them, this way and that, the Trojans haling it towards the city, and the Greeks towards their camp. "Die, ye Greeks!" cried Ajax, who was fighting like twenty men; "die, rather than give up the body to the Trojans."

II

After the fall of Patroclus, Automedon had driven his car out of the press of battle, flying from the fury of Hector. When Hector was recalled from the pursuit, Automedon strove in vain to stir his horses from the spot where he had halted. In vain he plied the lash, in vain he coaxed and threatened; still as a monumental pillar on a tomb they stood, with their heads drooping to the earth, and their glossy manes streaming over their eyes, while the hot tears dropped fast in the dust, as they wept for the gentle prince, whom they had borne so often to battle.

Zeus pitied them in their sorrow, and spake thus

within himself: "Ah! hapless pair, why did we give you to a mortal master, while ye know neither age nor death? What part or lot have ye with human misery, or with man, the most wretched thing that breathes and moves on earth? But Hector shall never mount the car behind you, or put the bit in your mouths—I will not suffer that. Be strong, and bear your driver safe, until the battle be done."

Therewith, he breathed new vigour into the steeds, and they shook the dust from their manes, and galloped lightly with the car back to the fighting lines. Singlehanded, Automedon could take no part in the hand-to-hand battle with the Trojans, and for some time he contented himself with making rapid charges with his chariot, swooping down here and there, like an eagle pouncing on a flock of geese, and easily avoiding every attack. At last he found a helper in a comrade named Alcimedon, and handing the reins to him he dismounted himself to fight on foot.

When Hector saw the car of Achilles in charge of a strange driver he called to Æneas, and said: "See, there are the steeds of Æacides, ill-guided, and ill-defended; let us not miss the occasion to win so glorious a prize." So together they went, Æneas and Hector, and two other Trojans, in high hope to slay Automedon, and take the car. But Automedon, uttering a prayer to Zeus, flung his spear, and slew Aretus, one of his assailants; and before Hector, who missed his cast at Automedon, could come to close quarters with his sword,

Ajax interposed, and drove him back.

The arrival of Automedon had interrupted the struggle for the possession of the body of Patroclus; but it was resumed with new fury on both sides, and the Greeks now received a new ally in the person of Athene, who obtained permission from Zeus to bring aid to her old allies. Disguised in the form of the aged Phœnix, she went and stood by the side of Menelaus, and said to him: "Courage, son of Atreus! We shall win the battle yet, and save the noble comrade of Achilles from the foeman's hands."

"Ah! Phœnix," answered Menelaus, "I would that Athene would put strength into my arm; then might I, as far as it is now possible, retrieve the bitter loss which we have suffered this day."

Athene was glad that he had named her before any other god, and she filled him with an indomitable spirit, and gave him the stubborn courage of a fly, which returns again and again to the attack, in its fierce desire for blood. And, seeing a good mark for his spear in the back of a flying Trojan, Menelaus flung, and pierced him in the waist. The man whom he slew was Podes, a son of Eëtion, and a friend and boon companion of Hector. Provoked beyond measure by the death of his comrade, Hector led such a determined charge against the Greek centre that even the bravest began to flinch; and to affright them the more there came a deafening peal of thunder from the heights of Ida, now wrapped in a pitchy cloud.

The first to fly was Peneleos, the bravest of the Bœotians, whose shoulder had been cut to the bone by the spear of Polydamas. Then Idomeneus, coming to succour a wounded Greek, broke his spear on Hector's breastplate, and it would have gone hard with him had not Cœranus, a Cretan, driven up to the rescue in the car of Meriones; for Idomeneus had come to the field on foot, leaving his own car in the camp. The brave Cœranus paid for this good service with his life, sustaining a fearful thrust from Hector's spear, which struck him just at the angle of the jaw, and severed his tongue at the root. He fell from the car, and dropped the reins on the ground; but Meriones picked them up, and gave them to Idomeneus, who drove off at full speed towards the ships.

Thus deprived of his bravest supporters, Ajax cast a glance of dismay at Menelaus, who was still fighting at his side, and said: "Alas! even a blind man might see that Zeus himself is aiding the Trojans. Every weapon of theirs finds its mark, let it be hurled by ever so weak a hand; but our spears fall idle to the ground, one and all. Yet, abandoned though we are, let us take thought how we may save the body of Patroclus, and ourselves return alive to gladden the eyes of our faithful comrades, who methinks are in sore distress, thinking that the might and the murderous hands of Hector shall no more be stayed until they have hurled destruction on our fleet. Also I would fain despatch a messenger to bear the bitter tidings to Pelides, who dreams not that his beloved Patroclus has perished. But I cannot see anyone to whom I might deliver this charge, for men and steeds alike are covered by thick darkness. Dread sire of heaven, at least from darkness deliver the sons of Greece! Bring back the day, and give us the sight of our eyes. Slay us, if die we must—but slay us in the light!"

Zeus had compassion on that brave man in his agony, and forthwith the thick cloud of darkness was removed, and the sun shone out, and all the field of battle was disclosed to view. "Now haste, Menelaus," said Ajax. "Go thou, and find Antilochus, who is very dear to Achilles, and bid him carry this message, which none other may dare to bring."

Menelaus was very reluctant to leave his place among the defenders of Patroclus. Slowly, and with many a backward glance, he turned to go, like a lion who is driven off at dawn by a shower of javelins and burning brands, after he has prowled all night round the stalls where fat oxen are housed. "Ah! remember," he said earnestly, pausing once more, "remember how dear, how gentle he was to us all, this poor Patroclus, who now lies cold in death. Forsake him not, but stand by him till I come back."

After this fervent appeal he made all haste, and ran along the fighting line, looking about him with a piercing glance, like an eagle soaring high in the heaven, who spies out a hare as she crouches in the shadow of a thicket. So did the keen eye of Menelaus soon discern where Antilochus was fighting, on the extreme left of the field. "Dire is the news I bring," said Menelaus, halting by his side: "Patroclus is slain, Hector has his armour, and thou art chosen to tell Achilles of his loss, that if it be possible he may yet save the body."

With parted lips, and eyes staring with horror, Antilochus stood gazing at the bringer of the message of woe. Then dashing the tears from his eyes, and drawing a deep sobbing breath, he flung down his shield and sped away on his mournful errand.

"I have sent him," said Menelaus, when he had returned with all speed to the defenders of the fallen Patroclus. "I know not what Achilles will do—he cannot fight without armour. But to our task." "The Trojans have drawn off a little," answered Ajax. "Now is the time: do thou and Meriones take the corpse on your shoulders, while I and my brother-in-arms hold the foe in play."

Without a moment's delay Menelaus and Meriones hoisted the body on their shoulders and began to carry it towards the camp: which when the Trojans saw, they raised a great shout, and rushed after, like hounds attacking a wounded wild boar; but as the hounds are scattered when the great brute wheels to the charge, so fled the Trojans before the determined stand of Ajax and his comrade.

But only for a moment: on they came again, fierce as a mighty conflagration, which sweeps through the streets of a town, driven before the gale, while the houses melt away like wax in the flames: with like furious uproar came horse and foot hard at their heels, as they bore the body from the field. But stoutly and stubbornly they plodded on with their burden, panting and sweating like a pair of mules which drag a heavy beam down a rugged mountain path: and behind them those two doughty champions opposed an impassable barrier to the Trojans, like a long wooded mountain spur, which hurls back the fierce assault of a swollen stream, and cannot be broken.

Yet even now the issue seemed doubtful; for just as the bearers reached the barriers of the camp Hector and Æneas led a vigorous charge, scattering the Greeks as a hawk scatters a noisy mob of starlings or daws.

17

THE NEWS IS BROUGHT TO ACHILLES

I

"Why tarries Patroclus so long?" asked Achilles of himself, as he sat waiting by his tent. "Alas! I fear that he hath disobeyed me, and lost his life by his rashness. Did not my mother tell me that the noblest of the Greeks should fall in battle with the Trojans while I lived?" His alarm increased when he saw straggling parties of the Greeks entering the camp, with every sign of panic and defeat. Presently the roar of the struggle drew nearer and nearer, and he had just determined to rush to the ramparts, and learn the worst, when Antilochus came running up, and in broken accents panted out his dreadful message.

As when a thunderbolt descends, laying low some giant of the forest, so fell the mighty Pelides, laid prostrate beneath that stunning blow. Then that proud head, which had never bowed to mortal man, was defiled with dust, and those heroic limbs, the very mould of manly strength and beauty, grovelled and writhed on the ground. He tore his hair, cast ashes on his head, and moaned like a wounded beast in his agony. And all the handmaids whom he had taken in war gathered round him, wailing and beating their breasts; for sorrow was their portion, and their tears were ever ready to flow. By his side knelt Antilochus, holding his hands, in fear lest he should do violence to his life.

Then Achilles shook off the grasp of Antilochus, and started to his feet with a fearful cry, glaring wildly, like one about to do some desperate act. But just at this moment a sound of female voices came floating over the placid sea, and Thetis glided into his presence, with all her band of Ocean nymphs attending. Achilles flung himself down again when he saw her, with a fresh burst of grief; and kneeling by him she embraced him tenderly, and weeping cried: "O child of my sorrow, what new cause of mourning hath reached thee now? Hath not Zeus fulfilled his promise, and avenged thine honour?"

"What avails his promise, or the fulfilment thereof?" answered Achilles, groaning bitterly. "What care I for honour, if I must pay for it with the life of my best beloved? He lies in his blood, and Hector, his slayer, has taken the glorious armour which the gods gave to Peleus when they made thee his unwilling bride. 'Twas a woeful match, for thee and for me, and soon thou shall reap the bitter fruit, for Hector must die by my hand, to appease the ghost of Patroclus, and thou hast told me that, when Hector falls, my own end is not far off." A mournful silence followed, broken only by the sobs of Thetis, who knew her son had pronounced his own doom. Then Achilles burst out again, in louder and angrier tones: "But let me die, when that task is done! What has life been to me?—a burden to myself, and a curse to others! Here have I lain, like a useless trunk, encumbering the sod, and left my comrades to perish, and given him, the very light of mine eyes, to be a prey to the spoiler. Accursed, and thrice accursed, be the spirit of strife, which trickles, sweeter than honey, into the hearts of men, and rises up again, in words more bitter than gall!—even as Agamemnon provoked me to fierce anger, which now comes back upon me, with thrice envenomed sting. But past is past—we will speak no more of that. My fate calls me to vengeance— and after that the grave. Then away, soft visitings of love and gentle sorrow! And thou, fond heart, become a stone! I will strew with havoc the path which leads me to mine enemy, and the streets of Troy shall be filled with lamentation, and women wailing for their dead."

"I know that I cannot shake thy purpose," answered Thetis sadly, "and it shall be as thou hast said. But unarmed thou canst not go into battle. Remain here therefore until my return, and by to-morrow's dawn I will bring thee such armour as never mortal wore."

II

While these events were passing, the struggle over the slain Patroclus raged fiercer than ever. Slowly the Greeks were driven back to the very gates of their camp, and at the eleventh hour that pitiful prize which had cost so much blood would have fallen into the hands of the Trojans, had not Hera intervened and sent Iris to summon Achilles to the rescue.

"Rouse thee, son of Peleus!" said Iris, appearing at his side. "Hector hath sworn to set the head of Patroclus on the battlements of Troy, and he will accomplish his threat if thou sittest idle here."

"How can I go unarmed to the field?" answered Achilles. "I know of none whose armour I might wear, save only Ajax, and he is fighting at the front."

"No more words," replied Iris. "Do as thou art bidden, and heaven will find a way." Then Achilles arose, and went to the ramparts; and Athene drew near him, and threw her tasselled ægis over his shoulders, and on his head she caused a golden cloud to descend, which shot forth rays of angry light. As in a beleaguered city, where a thousand watch-fires are lighted, and all day long the pillars of smoke ascend, but in the darkness the red blaze is seen afar, a signal of distress to distant allies—so shone that unearthly fire on the head of Achilles, as he stood on the brink of the moat. Then he lifted up his voice, and shouted; and the sound was as the sound of a trumpet summoning to arms.

When they saw the dreadful light, and heard the brazen voice of Pelides, the Trojans were astonished, and halted in the midst of their wild assault; and while they wavered the Greeks fell upon them, and drove them back in disorder. The tide had turned at last, and the long day of battle, so full of strange revolutions of fortune, came to an end.

Slowly and reverently the body of Patroclus was laid upon a bier, and carried to the tent of Achilles. But a few short hours before he had gone forth, with horses and with chariots, to battle, in the pride of youth and strength; and now he lay cold in death, gored with hideous wounds by Trojan spears. And all night long Achilles and his comrades mourned for their slaughtered hero, the gentlest and the best of all their band. Like a lion who leaves his whelps in their dark forest lair, and returns to find his bed empty, and his young ones gone; roaring with rage and grief he tracks the footsteps of the robber along many a mountain path, and all the forest is filled with the sound of his wrath: such was Pelides in his sorrow, and such the voice of his mourning. "Vain, alas! was the promise which I made to thy father Menœtius, that I would bring thee back safe to thy home in Locris, loaded with the spoils of Troy. Thy blood is red on the Trojan sod, where mine too shall flow before many days are passed. Now hear my vow, Patroclus, and take comfort, even in death I will not pay the last rites to thy corpse until I have brought Hector's body hither, with the armour which he has taken, and slain twelve Trojan captives as a sacrifice to thy shade. Till then thou shalt lie as thou art, and the women of Troy, whom we won with the might of our hands, shall mourn thee night and day."

Then they washed the body, and anointed it with fragrant oil, and laid it, wrapped in fine linen, on a bed to wait for burial.

III

The Trojans still kept the field, though with far other feelings than when they lit their camp-fires, only the night before. Before ever they thought of supper the chiefs met in council, and stood about in anxious groups, waiting until some recognised leader should advise them in their present strait. Then Polydamas, who was esteemed the wisest head among them, came forward and commanded silence; and all listened attentive to hear what he should say. "Friends," he began, "ye had best take heed what ye do; as for me, I have but one thing to advise—back to the city, and let not to-morrow's dawn find us here! We have all had our hopes, and I among the rest; but all those hopes are fled now that Achilles has arisen again; and if we abide his coming we shall learn too late what it means to face him in the open field. Here, where we stand, dogs and vultures will hold their foul revel, and batten on our flesh, at the going-down of the sun. Therefore, I say again, back to the city, and put a stout bulwark of stone and oak between yourselves and this terrible man. To-morrow we will man the walls, and laugh at his fury if he seeks to assail us there. Yea, his steeds shall weary with drawing his car, and he himself shall sicken of the vain attempt, for he knows well that Troy is not destined to fall by his hands."

So ran the counsels of prudence; but another spirit was there also—the spirit of rash confidence and unauthorised ambition—and it found passionate utterance in the voice of Hector, who was the next to speak. "I like not thy words, Polydamas," said he, with an angry look; "I like not the cowardly counsel which bids us skulk behind our walls. Who is not sick of our long confinement in that pinfold there? We have drained our treasury, and scattered abroad the wealth for which Troy was once famed throughout the world, wherever human speech is heard. But now that we have been vouchsafed the glorious promise of carrying the war into the enemy's camp, and driving these hounds of war out of our land—now, I say, unlock no more the thoughts of thy base soul, to damp our courage, and quench the bright flame of hope which has been kindled in our breasts. Now hear what I advise: to-night we will hold our camp here, and keep watch in turn; and to-morrow at first peep of day we will put on our armour and march against the Grecian stronghold. Achilles is arisen, sayest thou? The worse for him: I will not fly before him, but will meet him face to face, and slay him, or be slain."

The fiery eloquence of Hector carried his hearers with him, and they resolved with one accord to remain where they were, and abide the issue.

18

THE SHIELD OF ACHILLES

MINDFUL OF her promise, Thetis, when she left Achilles, went straightway to Olympus and entered the dwelling of Hephæstus. It was a wondrous structure, all of brass, which the lame god had planned and fashioned by his own skill and labour. She found him in his forge, blowing up the fire with his bellows; for he was hard at work, setting the finish to twenty brazen vessels, for use in his house. Each vessel ran on golden wheels, and moved to and fro of its own accord, coming and going at the master's bidding. With him sat Charis, his wife, watching her husband at his toil; and when she saw Thetis enter she came forward to greet her, and placed a chair, inlaid with silver, for her to sit on. Then she called to Hephæstus, who was stooping over his forge, and said: "Leave thy work, and come and welcome this honoured guest."

"Welcome indeed she is, and honoured too," said the hospitable god, limping across the stithy with outstretched hands. "Did she not save me from my shrewish mother, who was ashamed of her crippled son, and sought to put me out of the way, when I was but a child? Then it would have gone hard with me if Thetis had not received me into her home, the deep cavern, round which Oceanus wraps his watery coils, foaming and thundering everlastingly. There I dwelt in peace for nine long years, and many a pretty jewel I wrought for my preservers—brooches, and bracelets and necklaces. And none of the gods knew where I was, save only kind Thetis and Eurynome, daughter of Oceanus. Therefore thrice welcome, sweet lady of the sea! I owe thee my life, and shall be rejoiced if I can pay part of the debt. Take her, dear Charis, to the guest-chamber, while I put away the implements of my trade."

Thetis left the forge with her hostess, and when they were gone Hephæstus gathered up his tools, and turned the bellows away from the fire. The tools he placed in a vast silver chest, and then taking a sponge he cleansed his face and hands, his brawny neck, and hairy chest. Then he put on a clean tunic, and went to join Charis and her guest. His huge heavy frame was ill supported on a pair of thin, crooked legs; but his own inventive genius had enabled him to supply this defect, for on either side of him walked a wonderful creature, wrought by himself in gold, with the form and face of a maiden, a human voice, and human wit. Leaning on these strange supporters, he entered the guest-chamber, and sat down by the side of Thetis. "What need," he asked, "has brought thee to my poor house—an angel's visit, indeed, to me, both rare and dear?"

Encouraged by the cordial tone of the good-na-tured god, Thetis poured out afresh all the tale of her woes, beginning from the time when, sorely against her will, she became the bride of Peleus. He was now an old man, broken and infirm, and she a goddess, radiant in her immortal bloom, was still chained to the human wreck, and Achilles, her son, still in the prime of his splendid manhood, was a perpetual source of trouble and grief. "Few indeed," she went on, "and evil, are the days of his life. First foully insulted by his sover-eign, and now broken-hearted at the loss of his dearest friend! Help me to do what I can to comfort him in this bitter hour; lend me thy skill, and make him a suit of armour such as never mortal man hath worn before."

"If that be all," answered Hephæstus cheerfully, "thy prayer is granted as soon as uttered. Arms he shall have, which shall make him the wonder of the world when he goes forth to battle."

Then leaving Thetis in charge of his wife he went back to his forge, and having stripped to the waist ad-dressed himself to his work. Round the furnace in the centre of the stithy were twenty pairs of bellows, each serving a separate smelting oven. These he now turned to the fire, and commanded them to blow, for they were endowed with a consciousness of their own, and obeyed the master's will, now sending forth a tremen-dous blast, which made the fire roar with fury, and the flames leap upward to the roof, now breathing low, like some huge monster in his softer mood. Into the smelting ovens he cast bronze and tin, silver and gold; and when his metal was ready he placed a ponderous anvil on the anvil block, and took in one hand a mighty hammer, while in the other he grasped the tongs.

And first a shield he fashioned, vast and strong, with threefold rim, and baldric of silver. The shield was of five folds; and on it he wrought many a pictured scene with wondrous skill.

There were imaged earth and sea, the unwearied sun, and the moon in her waxing and her waning, and the heavens with all their starry crown—Pleiades, and Hyades, and Orion's might, and the Bear, whom men likewise call the Wain, who turns on the same spot, and watches Orion, and alone has no share in the baths of Ocean.

And there was fashioned many a scene from human life, peace and war, pastime and industry. The first was a city, and along the streets a bridal procession was passing, with blazing torches, and the loud hymeneal song, and the whirl of dancers, and the music of flute and harp; and the women stood at their thresholds, admiring that gay company. But in the market-place was heard the voice of loud dispute; for the elders were met in their session, to decide a quarrel concerning the blood-price of a murdered man. The slayer brought witnesses to prove that he had paid the whole amount; but the plaintiff denied that he had received a doit. Outside the circle stood the clamorous mob, eager partisans of either side, and held in check by the heralds with their rods of office, and in the midst sat the elders in solemn conclave on their seats of polished stone, rising up in turn to give sentence. And he whose judgment was held wisest was to receive a reward of two talents of gold.

A second city there was, hard beset by stress of war. For about it lay two armies encamped, whose counsels were divided: in one the leaders were for taking the city by storm, while in the other they would have made a treaty, by which the citizens were to buy off the attack with half their goods. But while the besiegers were disputing, the citizens left their walls to be defended by the old men and the weaker sort, and sallied out in full force to lay an ambush for a convoy which was on its way to the enemy's camp. So forth they marched, with Ares and Athene at their head, distinguished by their towering stature and golden armour. And when they came to the chosen place of ambush, by the riverside, where was a watering-place for flocks and herds, they crouched down among the bushes, leaving two scouts to warn them of the convoy's approach. Soon they heard the lowing of cattle, and the bleating of sheep, and the sound of the herdsmen's pipes, as they came on, dreaming of no harm; then forth rushed the armed troop, and cut down the herdsmen, and began to drive off the beasts.

The cries of the herdsmen, and the bellowing of the affrighted beasts, reached the ears of the besiegers, as they sat in council, and seizing their arms they mounted their horses, and hurried to the rescue. Then began a furious struggle, in which all the demons of war—Strife, and Confusion, and deadly Fate—held high carnival, and drank deep of human blood.[16]

Then followed diverse scenes of happy toil. The first was a fair fallow land of rich tilth, where ploughmen were driving their teams to and fro, drawing long furrows, straight and deep, and pausing now and then to refresh themselves with a cup of wine, which was handed to them by a man who stood ready at the end of the field. Dark rose the curling furrow, as the ploughshare passed, and the sods seemed of rich black soil, though wrought in gold; for therein was displayed the artist's skill.

The next was a harvest of yellow corn, and a row of busy reapers with sharp sickles in their hands. Others stood ready to bind the sheaves, and these again were supplied by a willing troop of boys, who gathered up the swathe as fast as it fell, and handed the ripe bundles to the binders. Near at hand stood the master, rejoicing in his wealth; and under a tree at the border of the field the henchmen were slaughtering an ox, to make savoury meat for him and his guests, while women were preparing a mess of pottage for the reapers.

Likewise he fashioned a vineyard, heavy with great clusters of grapes, and along the rows moved a merry

16. It should be observed that the poet gives the whole succession of incidents which are merely hinted at by the artist, who is confined to one moment in the story.

troop of boys and girls, with baskets in their hands, gathering the luscious fruit; and when their baskets were full they brought their burdens home with dancing steps, led by a boy who played the harp and sang the sweet dirge of summer in his shrill, childish voice.

Then came a herd of oxen going to pasture, and lowing as they went along the waving rushes, along the murmuring stream. Four herdsmen followed, and with them were nine dogs. But lo! a noble bull, the leader of the herd, falls suddenly in his tracks, struck down by the claws of two ravening lions. They begin to drag him off, and the herdsmen follow at a distance, cheering on their dogs, which leap and bay wildly, but will not close with those terrible robbers.

The last scene of all was a dance of youths and maidens, the youths clad in close-fitting doublets, and wearing hangers at their sides, and the maidens wearing light garments of linen, and circlets of gold on their heads. Holding one another by the wrist, they first moved in a giddy circle, swift and true as the wheel flies in the potter's hands, and then they parted in two rows, and met again, weaving and unweaving all the mazy figures of a Cretan dance, while two tumblers whirled among them, and a singer gave the time with his voice.

Framing this rich succession of pictures ran the broad stream of Oceanus, rolling his waters round the outer rim of the shield.

Corslet, and greaves, and helmet with crest of gold, were fashioned next, and when the great work was done, Hephæstus brought it and laid it at the feet of Thetis. After due thanks, she took leave of her generous friends, and then sped on her way to the Grecian camp, bearing the costly gift of Hephæstus to her son.

19

THE
RECONCILIATION

I

Dawn was beginning to redden the waters of the Hellespont when Thetis reached the tent of Achilles. She found him sitting, lost in a gloomy reverie, by the side of the bed on which the body of Patroclus lay. "Come," said Thetis, touching him lightly on the shoulder, "let the dead bury their dead, and behold the glorious armour which Hephæstus has wrought for thee."

With that she set down the dazzling panoply, fresh from the forge of the god; the ethereal metal rang with a dreadful sound, and from the burnished surface darted angry beams of light, blinding the eyes of the Myrmidons who had drawn near to gaze, so that they fled in terror from the sight. But the eyes of Achilles flashed with an answering fire, and his heart burned with fierce joy, as he handled the work of the immortal armourer. "Mother," he said, when he had scrutinised every piece, "the work is worthy of the artist—I can say no more.

And now to battle! Yet one thing I fear—lest the body of my friend be marred by decay before my vow is accomplished and I am free to bury him."

"Let not that care disquiet thee," answered Thetis, "I will find a means to keep off the destroying hordes of the air, that breathe corruption in the limbs of fallen warriors. Though he lie unburied for the space of a whole year, his flesh shall remain pure and clean, as the flesh of a little child. Now go thou and summon the Greeks to the place of assembly, that when thou hast renounced thy feud with Agamemnon, thou mayest gird thee with might and go forth to battle." Then she brought nectar and ambrosia, and embalmed therewith the body of Patroclus, that his flesh might remain sound and whole.

But Achilles strode rapidly along the strand, shouting as he went to call the people to the assembly. And forthwith from every tent the multitude came flocking, and not one remained behind, no, not even those who pursued peaceful crafts, and were not wont to take part in the councils of the armed host. For not one was willing to be absent from that memorable meeting.

As he passed on, he overtook Odysseus and Diomede, who were limping painfully along, leaning on their spears; for they were still sore with their wounds. After a few words of greeting, he left them to follow, and went forward to the place where the chiefs were sitting round the throne of Agamemnon, which was still vacant. It was a level spot, in the centre of a natural hollow, whose sides rose gently, until they were closed by a background of waving woods. And now all the slopes were black with a swarming multitude, armed and unarmed, stout spearmen, and noisy rabble. At last Agamemnon was seen approaching, moving slowly and with pain. He took his seat on the royal throne, and then a dead hush fell on all that vast company, as Achilles rose in his place, and began to speak.

"Great King," he said, "we are met to end the lamentable feud which arose out of our quarrel for the sake of the maid Briseis. Would that she had never been born, or had been stricken with sudden death by the gentle shafts of Artemis, before ever she had put enmity between me and thee! So would many a brave man have been alive and well who now lies sleeping an iron sleep. Yes, for many a year to come the Greeks will speak of the wrath of Achilles, and of him who was the cause. But here it ends: my wrath is now aimed at another mark, and once more I am thy faithful friend and ally. War, war without quarter or mercy—that is all I ask for now. Let us see if the Trojans will hold their camp at our gates when they stand beneath the shadow of my destroying spear."

Right glad were the Greeks to learn that the tremendous passions of Achilles were now enlisted on their side. But their joyful cries were changed to murmurs of resentment when Agamemnon rose to answer; for they saw in him the author of all their disasters. Signs of remorse and confusion appeared in his face; and the first words of his speech were heard with difficulty amidst the tumult. "Friends and comrades in arms," he began, "I beseech you to hear me with patience, while I make confession of my fault. I have sinned, I cannot deny it, through the dread power of Ate,[17] who blinded my heart, and maimed my wits, on the day when I took from Achilles his prize. Ah! she is a fearful goddess, this Ate, a fiend to vex mankind. Soft is her tread, and her path lies on the heads of men: unseen, unheard, she approaches, and enters into the soul of him whom she has marked for ruin. Once she dwelt among the gods in Olympus, but she dared to lay her foul spells on Zeus himself, so that he fell into grievous error; and when he learnt how he had been deceived, he swore a mighty oath that never again should that abhorred witch set foot in the celestial abode. So he caught her by the hair, and flung her down to earth, to plague the tribes of men. And she it was who made me her victim, whereby all this mischief befell. But now I am ready to make all good, and heal the wrong which I have wrought. And all the gifts which I promised yesterday by the mouth of Odysseus are thine, Achilles, without abatement of one jot. Wait awhile, before thou goest into battle, and my squires shall bring them to thy tent."

"As for the gifts," replied Achilles, "they are thine to give or to withhold as thou choosest. But of that hereafter; for the present, I have work to do which admits of no delay. No more of talk, but let us away to the field

---

17. A personification of moral blindness.

at once."

But here the voice of prudence intervened, checking the fiery impetuosity of Achilles. "Hear me a moment, valiant prince," said Odysseus. "We must not lead the people fasting to battle, for an empty man hath little heart for the fight, which methinks will be neither short nor easy to-day. Let the people first eat their fill, for a man cannot face the foe from dawn till eve without tasting meat. However willing his spirit, his flesh is weak; his limbs are soon overtaken with weariness, his mouth is parched with thirst, and his knees totter as he goes. Therefore, I say, let us eat, and after that to battle. And thou, Achilles, shalt receive the gifts of Agamemnon, and partake of a banquet of honour with the other chieftains in his tent. The King knows what is fitting, and he cannot do less."

Agamemnon willingly assented, and was proceeding to give the order to bring the gifts when Achilles started up again, in eager protest against this delay.

"Illustrious King," he said, "surely there will be time enough to speak of these lesser matters when we have humbled the pride of the Trojans, who are waiting for us on the plain. My friend lies slaughtered, pierced by Hector's spear, and ye talk to me of meat and drink! By my will the whole army should keep a solemn fast, until we have washed out the stain on our honour in a sea of blood, and then, after the great act of vengeance is complete, we will feast and make merry. I at least will suffer no morsel or drop to pass my lips as long as my comrade lies in my tent with his feet to the door, and the women mourning round. No; far other thoughts fill my heart—blood and slaughter, and the groans of dying men."

But these desperate counsels found no favour with the veteran heads of the army, and a deep hum of approval greeted the more sober eloquence of Odysseus, who now rose again to reply. "Mighty son of Peleus," he said, "thou art stronger far than I, and thy spear writes deadlier record on the foemen's ranks; but I have lived longer than thou, and seen more: bear with me, then, while I speak what reason and experience hath taught me. Soon weary grows the hand which toils in war's barren harvest, where the swathe is so thick, and the yield so scanty when the day is done. We cannot keep a fast for every Greek that falls—where would be the end? The warrior's dirge is short, and he is honoured enough if he is mourned for a day. And those who are left must eat, that they may have strength to fight on the morrow. To your tents, then, every one! And when ye have eaten, come quickly, armed for the fight, and await no second summons."

For all his fierce impatience, Achilles was compelled to yield. With great effort he controlled himself while the gifts were brought, and the ceremonies performed, with no circumstance of solemnity omitted, to ratify the covenant of forgiveness and reconciliation between him and Agamemnon. And so the first act in the great drama of his wrath is concluded.

II

Seven youths of princely rank, attended by a long train of bearers, were despatched to the tent of Achilles, loaded with the costly gifts of atonement from the King. With them went Briseis, thus returned to her former lord. When she saw Patroclus on the bed where he lay, she beat her breast, and, embracing the cold body, burst into a passion of weeping. "Friend of my sorrow!" she cried, "I left thee living, and I find thee dead. Woe, and more woe, is all my portion. When I came hither, an orphaned captive, bereaved of all, thou didst comfort me in my great affliction, promising, when the war was over, to make me Achilles' lawful wife. Thy gentleness and thy knightly courtesy shed balm upon my wounded spirit, and now thou art gone, and my last comfort is gone with thee."

So mourned Briseis, and all the captive ladies wept afresh when they heard her, having cause enough for tears, every one. The sound of their lamentation reached the ears of Achilles where he sat, but he remained unmoved by the tragedy of these lesser spirits, being absorbed in the sense of his own great loss. The tide of his passion had ebbed again, leaving his heart cold and desolate. His men brought him food and drink, but he repulsed them sternly, and would touch nothing. He thought of the happy past—when he and Patroclus had partaken together of many a cheerful meal—and then of the bitter present, when the sight of bread and meat filled him with loathing. He thought of his father Peleus, growing old in his solitary home, waiting in sad expectation to hear of his son's death, and of the young Neoptolemus, his own child, growing up among strangers in the island of Scyros. "Lost, lost, all lost!" he murmured; "I shall never see them again."

But the gods had not forgotten their favourite. Zeus beheld him as he sat thus stricken and forlorn, and sent Athene to inspire him with new comfort and strength. Unseen, she alighted at his side, and fed him, though he knew it not, with heavenly food, filling his heart with more than mortal vigour and courage. Meanwhile the clash of arms rang through the camp as the Greeks marched out, column after column, to battle, thick as autumnal leaves, or hovering snowflakes in winter. The air seemed on fire with the flash of myriads of spears, and the earth shook beneath the thunder of their tread.

Roused by the sound, Achilles sprang to his feet, and buckled on his corslet, and clasped the greaves to his ankles. Then he flung the sword over his shoulder, and thrust his arm through the strap of his shield, which shone like the full-orbed moon, or a beaconlight blazing afar over a stormy sea. Last of all, he lifted his mighty helmet, with its nodding, golden plume, and set it on his head. And now, being arrayed in his harness from head to foot, he raised himself to his towering height, and stretched his fleet limbs, to prove the armour; and it became unto him as wings, making him lighter and nimbler than ever before.

Grasping in his right hand his spear—the mighty Pelian ash, pointed with death—he went forth before the tent, where Automedon stood waiting with his car. "Now hear me, ye children of the wind!" he cried, addressing his steeds, "see that ye play me not false to-day, as when ye left Patroclus dead on the field, and came back with an empty car."

Then there befell a wondrous thing; for the good steed Xanthus, drooping low his head, answered with a human voice, and spake thus unto his master: "Yea, we will carry thee safe back, most dread Achilles, when the fight is o'er. It was by no sloth or tardiness of ours that thy brave comrade met his death; that deed was wrought by the hand of Apollo, using Hector as his instrument—even as thou too shalt be cut off by a human weapon, but by no human power."

So spake the immortal courser, for the first and the last time; for fate suffered it not again. And Achilles answered him, and said: "Waste not thy prophecies on me, good steed! I know my fate—death on the battle-field, far from my home: but ere that hour comes I will send many a Trojan to herald my coming among the dead."

Then, shouting his dread battle-cry, he sprang into his car, and drove headlong to the front.

20

ACHILLES IN
THE BATTLEFIELD

I

BY HIGH PERMISSION of all-ruling Jove the gods were
now free to take part in the war, and they all with one
accord came down from Olympus to mingle with the
fray. Only Zeus remained behind, as supreme arbiter of
the final issue. All the rest took sides with the Greeks
or Trojans, and five rival pairs confronted each other in
the field—Poseidon found a match in Apollo, the great
ally of the Trojans—Hera, who loved the Greeks like
a mother, was confronted by the archer-goddess Artemis—against Athene stood Ares, whose fickle mind
now inclined to the Trojans—Hermes, who favoured
the Greeks, was met on the other side by Leto, the
mother of Artemis and Apollo—and lastly Hephæstus
and Scamander, the opposing powers of fire and water,
took the field, the former for the Greeks, the latter for
the Trojans.

All nature was in uproar as these tremendous allies entered the scene of conflict. Earth shook, and the mountains reeled to their foundations, and the towers of Troy and the Grecian ships reeled as in an earthquake. Then trembling came upon Hades, the monarch of the dead, and leaping from his throne he cried aloud in fear, lest the earth, rent by Poseidon's trident, should disclose to mortal and immortal eyes the dank and dreary mansions of the dead, which even the gods abhor.

Far in front of the Grecian line was seen the glittering form of Achilles, who scanned the Trojan ranks like a lion who seeks his prey, having but one thought, but one aim—to meet Hector, and slay him. But Hector's hour was not yet come, for Apollo stood near to shield him from his great enemy, and delay the fatal stroke which sooner or later must lay him low. And first the god put it into the heart of Æneas to defy Achilles to battle, and gave him unwonted courage and strength, that he might not flinch in that fearful encounter. Then Æneas heard a voice which whispered within him, and seemed to say: "Art thou not the son of Aphrodite, who is the daughter of supreme Jove? Why fearest thou then this upstart child of Thetis, of far meaner lineage than thine? Go face him, and let him learn that neither are the Trojans forsaken of heaven."

So between the advancing lines they met, both sons of gods, but far different in their fate. At first Achilles had not observed his approach, but stalked, heedless of all lesser foes, before the embattled host of Troy, like a lion bent on ravage, against whom a whole township is gathered, with purpose to slay him and at first he goes on his way, disdaining the menaces of that rabble rout—but then, being pricked by the point of a random spear, he gathers himself, foaming and gnashing his teeth, for the spring, and his mighty spirit groans within him, and he lashes his flanks on both sides with his tail, goading himself to battle—then glaring and roaring he launches his vast weight at the foe, resolved to kill or be killed—so sprang Achilles against Æneas, in wrath at his presumption.

"What wouldst thou of me, Æneas?" he cried, in disdainful mood. "Have the Trojans promised thee a fair estate, if thou take my life? Or hopest thou, perchance, to sit in the seat of Priam, if thou accomplish this great deed? I thought thou hadst had enough of me and my spear. Hast thou forgotten when I chased thee through the glades of Ida, having caught thee alone among the grazing herds? Then didst thou never turn thy head to look back, until thou hadst reached the shelter of a fenced city. And I sacked the city, and led captive the women; but thou didst escape me again, through the special mercy of Zeus. Go back, vain man, and join the press of thy comrades or thou shalt not escape me now.

"Who art thou?" answered Æneas, undaunted, "that thinkest to affright me with boastful words, as if I were a witless boy? Know, proud man, that I am of higher descent than thine, for in my veins flows the royal blood of Dardanus, mingled with the blood of gods. Go to, let us wrangle no more like women in the market-place, but decide the quarrel with our spears."

As he spoke, he cast his spear, which struck with strong impact against the shield of Achilles; and he, when he felt the shock, held the shield away from his body, fearing that the point would pass through and reach his flesh. But immortal armour is not easy to be pierced by mortal weapons, and the spear dropped harmless to the earth. Then Achilles flung in his turn, and the spear tore its way through the upper rim of Æneas' shield: and he, stooping low, heard the rush of the mighty lance, as it flew over his head, and buried itself in the ground behind him. Having thus both missed their cast, they prepared to renew the struggle hand to hand. Achilles drew his sword, and rushed to the encounter with a fierce cry: while Æneas lifted a heavy stone, and stood ready to hurl it as his antagonist drew near.

But that combat, which must have ended fatally for the Trojan, was not destined to be fought out to its end. "Behold," said Poseidon, who was watching the unequal duel, to Hera, who sat near him, "my spirit is troubled because of Æneas, whom his own rashness, and the evil counsels of Apollo, are leading to his doom. But this must not be: he is reserved for a better fate, which shall be accomplished after the towers of Troy have been levelled with the dust. In him shall the line of Dardanus be preserved, and from him shall be born a mighty race, to found a new empire on the ruins of the old."[18]

"Do as thou wilt," answered Hera. "As for me, I have sworn a great oath that I will never save a Trojan from perishing, no, not in the last fatal hour when Troy shall be consumed with fire."

When Poseidon heard that, he went and stood between the fighting champions; and on the eyes of Achilles he shed a thick darkness, that he might not see what was done. Then he drew the spear from the shield of Æneas, and threw it at Achilles' feet; and catching up the Trojan prince in his hand he bore him aloft over the heads of the Greeks and Trojans, until he reached the utmost verge of the battlefield. There he set him down, and, becoming visible in all his divine majesty, addressed him in these solemn words of warning: "Æneas, what put this mad thought into thy heart, to fight against Achilles, who is both stronger than thou and dearer to the gods? Tempt not thy fate again, but when thou meetest him avoid his spear; and after he is slain, then mayest thou boldly encounter the bravest of the Greeks, for no other hath power to do thee hurt."

II

When the darkness fell from the eyes of Achilles he looked round about him, and saw his spear lying at his feet, but sought in vain for Æneas. "What wonder is

---

18. These lines contain the germ of the *Æneid*.

this?" he said to himself; "the spear is returned to me, but mine enemy is vanished. Surely the gods love him also, though I deemed that he boasted idly. Let him go! It will be long before he desires to face me again."

Then, shouting to the Greeks to support him, he fell upon the main body of the Trojans, seeking everywhere for Hector; and finding him not (for Apollo as yet withheld the Trojan patriot from his eyes) he began to deal out indiscriminate slaughter wherever he went. A brave Lycian, the son of a mountain nymph, who rushed to attack him, was his first victim; with one blow of that tremendous spear his head was shattered as with a battering-ram, and he fell beneath the feet of the horses, and the wheels of the car passed over his body.

Among the many who went to swell the list of the slain that day was Polydorus, a favourite son of Priam, who loved him as his youngest born, and who had forbidden him to go into battle. But he, trusting in the speed of his feet, had come to the field the day before, and now appeared in the van of the Trojans, a graceful and agile youth, lovely and pleasant to behold. But as he pursued his gay career a javelin from the hand of Achilles pierced his armour at the waist, and he fell, torn in the midst by a hideous wound.

Hector saw his brother fall, and full of rage and grief sprang forward to avenge his death. When Achilles saw his great enemy at last within his reach he leapt towards him with a loud and exultant cry: "Draw near, and pay the price of my comrade, whom thou hast slain!" "Proud man, I fear thee not," answered Hector, undismayed: "I know that thou art far mightier than I, but nevertheless I defy thee, and trust that heaven will lend keenness to my spear."

But the end was not yet. Apollo intervened to save the gallant Trojan, and bore him away wrapped in a cloud of darkness. Three times Achilles struck, and three times his spear smote idly on the empty air. "Thou dog!" he cried at last, finding his efforts unavailing, "Thou hast avoided me now, but I will destroy thee yet, for I have friends among the gods as well as thou. Till then, let my vengeance fall upon thy countrymen."

And as a fire rages in a forest on a mountainside, licking up the underwood, and thrusting out its red fangs to devour the tall trees, so raged Pelides in the fury of slaughter, and the earth ran red with blood. And as two broad-browed steers move to and fro on a threshing-floor, treading out the corn, so trampled the steeds of Achilles on corpses and shields and broken armour, as he passed on, raining wounds and death on every side.

III

The Trojan army was now split into two divisions, one of which was flying across the plain towards the city, while Achilles drove the other before him towards the banks of Scamander. Into the stream they flocked, without pausing in their flight, like a cloud of locusts driven by a fire to seek refuge in the nearest water; and Scamander's bed was choked by a huddled multitude of horses and men.

Leaning his spear against a plane-tree, Achilles leapt into the river, sword in hand, and struck right and left, until the waters were crimsoned with blood. And as a shoal of fish flies before the onset of a dolphin, seeking the shallow waters near the shore, so shrank the Trojans from the sword of Achilles, and hid themselves under the arching banks. Then he remembered his promise to Patroclus, and, choosing twelve comely youths from that panic-stricken throng, he drove them before him, and gave them, bound, to his men to be brought alive to the ships. This done, he went back to continue the work of slaughter; and as he reached the river's brink he saw a Trojan, who had just left the water, and was preparing to fly towards the city. "Aha! are we met again?" cried Achilles, recognising in the fugitive a certain Lycaon, one of the numerous family of Priam, whom once before he had taken prisoner, having caught him during a night foray, when the luckless youth was busy cutting the young shoots of the olive, to make a rim for a chariot. On that occasion he had spared his life, and sold him into captivity to the King of Lemnos, from whom he had been ransomed by a friend of Priam, and so found his way back to Troy. For eleven days since his return from Lemnos he had taken his pleasure among his friends, and on the twelfth his fate threw him into the hands of Achilles for the second and last time.

Lycaon had flung away shield and helmet and spear, that he might be lightened in the race for his life. But Achilles was upon him before he was aware, threatening him with uplifted spear. "So thou hast returned from Lemnos?" he said mockingly. "We will now send thee on a longer journey, and we will see if thou come back again this time." The wretched youth flung himself down, and avoiding the spear-point crawled on his knees to Achilles, and clinging to him said: "Have pity on me, great warrior, and have respect for the sacred tie between host and guest; for I was thy guest, illustrious chieftain, and have broken bread under thy roof, on the day when thou madest me captive. Thou hast no cause to hate me, for I was not born of the same mother as Hector, who slew thy friend."

But there was no sign of relenting in the stern face which was bent over him, and he received a foretaste of the pangs of death as he heard the answer of Achilles. "Talk not to me," said he, "of ransom or redemption. As long as Patroclus was alive I was well pleased to make prisoners and release them for a price, but now not one shall escape of all those who fall into my hands, and least of all the sons of Priam. Thou must die, my friend! Why seems it to thee so hard? Patroclus met his fate with the rest, and he was a far better man than thou art. Look upon me; am I not a tall and proper man? Yet the shadow of death is creeping nearer and ever nearer to me, and soon the hour of my doom shall strike, whether at morn, or at noon, or at eventide."

At these words Lycaon's heart froze within him, and leaving hold of the spear he sank down on his knees, stretching out both his hands in mute entreaty. Then Achilles lifted up his sword, and clove him to the waist, and seizing his body by the foot flung it into the river. "Lie there among the fishes!" cried that ruthless man: "They will tend thy wounds, until Scamander bears thee to the deep, where thou shalt find fit burial in some sea monster's maw. Death, death to all your accursed race! Naught shall avail you your silver-eddying stream, to whose deity ye offer sacrifice of bulls and horses, but ye shall pay threefold and fourfold the debt of blood which ye owe me for the lives of the Greeks whom ye have slain."

The river-god heard him, and, waxing exceeding wroth, began to consider how he should stop the murderous career of Achilles. And while he was still debating within himself Achilles was confronted by Asteropæus, a brave Thracian chieftain, and the son of the presiding deity of Axius, a broad and noble stream. This man now barred the way of Achilles, brandishing a spear in each hand. "Whence and what art thou?" cried Achilles, amazed that anyone should dare to oppose him; for he knew not that Scamander had steeled the heart of Asteropæus to do this deed. "Art thou weary of thy life?" he asked again, as the Thracian still came on. "I will tell thee what I am," answered Asteropæus boldly: "I am the son of a deity, even as thou art, and my father was Axius, the fairest river on earth. Now let us fight, great son of Thetis."

With that he flung both spears at once, for he was equally skilled with both hands; and one of the spears struck against the shield of Achilles, but could not penetrate it, while the other grazed his right arm, and drew blood. Then Achilles hurled his spear, which missed Asteropæus, and buried itself to half its length in the river bank. Asteropæus grasped the shaft, and strove with all his might to tear the weapon from the ground. Failing in this, he next tried to break it in the middle, to use as a club; but by this time Achilles was upon him, and with one stroke of his sword clove him almost in twain. "Thou hast found thy match, thou river's brood!" he cried, stripping off the bloodstained armour. "Fool, that comparest thyself with me, whose fathers sprang in a direct line from Jove! He, methinks, is mightier than any river, yea, mightier than Oceanus, the great father of floods, who trembles before the red lightning, and the voice of the thunder, when it crashes through the skies."

So saying he lightly plucked out the embedded spear, and went in pursuit of the men of Asteropæus, who were crouching in terror along the river's banks. Seven of them he slew, and was about to continue the work of carnage when he received a check. From the depths of the stream a mysterious voice arose, in tones of protest and complaint: "Achilles, thine arm is exceeding mighty, and thy prowess more than mortal; for the gods are ever near to aid thee. If Zeus hath given thee leave to slaughter all the Trojans, at least drive them away from my bed and butcher them on the plain. My waters are choked with corpses, and I cannot roll my current any longer towards the holy sea, because my channel is straitened by the multitude of thy miserable victims. Give place, great chieftain, and cumber me no more."

"It shall be as thou sayest, thou god revered," answered Achilles. "But suffer me yet a little while until my task is done." And without further parley he sprang down again into the river bed. Then the god was wroth, and prepared to expel that daring intruder from his domain. He gathered all his waters, which rose up in surging billows, and washed the corpses ashore; and to the living he gave shelter, hiding them away in great hollow eddies. Then, collecting himself in one towering wave, he rushed upon Achilles, buffeting his shield, and eating away the ground under his feet. Achilles grasped an elm, a tall and stately tree, and clung to it for support; but the torrent had undermined its roots, and the next moment it fell, tearing a huge gap in the bank, and damming back the waters with its leafy boughs. Then he leaped from the yellow, swirling torrent, and darted across the plain in head-long flight; for he was sore afraid. But Scamander followed hard at his heels, roaring and arching his crest. In vain Achilles ran and doubled, and doubled and ran; the river pursued him everywhere, until his strength began to fail him; and if he stood still for a moment the waves rose instantly as high as his shoulders, threatening to swallow him up. Then he gave himself up for lost, and with a groan he gazed upward to the broad heaven, and uttered this despairing cry for help: "O all ye gods, is this then to be my end? Am I to perish thus, drowned like some nameless churl, who is swept away while crossing a ford in winter?"

Some friendly power heard his wild appeal, and lent him new strength and courage to continue the struggle. So on he panted across the plain, which by this time was covered with floating corpses, helmets, and shields. But Scamander raged the more furiously when he saw his prey still eluding his clutch, and he called aloud to Simocis, his brother stream, to join in the pursuit. And Simocis answered to his call, and mustered all his waters from every fountainhead and every tributary stream. Then the twin rivers roared together in unison, and came down upon him, battering him with uprooted trees and rolling rocks, which they swept along in their course, "We will quell thee," they shouted, "thou godless man, for all thy beauty and thy strength, and thou and thy gleaming panoply shall be wrapped in a thick shroud of mud, at the bottom of our blackest and deepest pool. Thy dirge shall be sung by our rolling waters, and thy monument none shall behold."

Achilles was now in extremity, and would surely have ended as ignobly as the river-god had said, if another power had not come to his aid. "Where art thou, my son, Hephæstus?" cried Hera, seeing that Achilles could hold out no longer. "Thou art he who should save our champion in this strait, for thou and Scamander are natural enemies. Haste thee to the rescue, armed with thy proper element; and I will summon the blasts of the West and the South to fan thy flames. Let fire fight with water, and spare not, nor cease thy fury until I give thee the signal to desist."

Hephæstus made haste to obey his mother, and forthwith he caused a sheet of fire to sweep across the plain, burning the corpses, and drying up the flood. Then he turned his flames upon the river himself, and all the trees which fringed his banks—elms, and willows, and plane-trees—were soon ablaze. Speedily the fire spread to the rushes and water plants, and at last the very waters began to grow hot, so that the fishes leapt into the air in their agony, and Scamander himself was in dire distress.

"It is enough," he cried, yielding to a superior power. "Torment me no more, Hephæstus! Let Achilles destroy the whole nation of Trojans, if he will—I will not seek to prevent him."

By this time the waters were beginning to boil and bubble, and clouds of steam rose into the air. Seeing that the river was thoroughly quelled, Hera gave the signal, and Hephæstus drew off his forces, and left Scamander in peace.

IV

After his escape from the river, Achilles went in pursuit of the other Trojans, who had fallen back towards the town. Then began a second rout, and a second slaughter, and Priam, who was watching the field from his citadel, soon beheld the whole remnant of the Trojan army flying before Achilles towards the city. With a cry of alarm he hastened down to the gates, and gave directions to the warders to draw bolt and bar, and admit the flying multitude. "But stand ready," he said, "to make all fast, as soon as the people are safe within, for fear lest this terrible man should enter the town."

The warders did as they were bidden, and held the gates ready; and before long the first of the fugitives came panting in, their lips parched with thirst, and their armour powdered with dust.

Still unsated with slaughter, Achilles came on in hot pursuit, and Priam's fears might have been realised if Agenor, a young Trojan noble, had not been inspired by Apollo with sudden courage, which prompted him to cross the destroyer's path. "I will face this man," he said, halting from his flight. "He too is of mortal flesh, and has but one life to lose. I will face him, though Zeus fight on his side."

As a leopard comes forth from his thick covert to meet the hunter, when he hears the baying of the hounds, and, even though sorely wounded, fights on till he is slain, so stood Agenor to meet Achilles, with shield on breast, and spear poised for the throw. "Thou thoughtest to have taken Troy this day," he cried. "Thou fool! This deed is not for thee; thou shall not read to the end the story of her woes, but here, on this spot, I will end thy life of blood."

With that he cast his spear, which struck him on the greave above the knee, but rebounded from the tempered metal; but before Achilles could return the attack Apollo removed Agenor from his reach, and putting on the likeness of Agenor fled away towards the river, luring Achilles after him. The Trojans were thus given time to make good their escape, and the city was soon filled with a frightened and disordered host, thankful to have escaped with bare life. All along the battlements were seen groups of exhausted men, who wiped the sweat from their brows, and drank deep draughts of wine to quench their burning thirst. Only one was left outside: This was Hector, who remained of his own free will, resolved to decide the issue in single combat with Achilles.

21

THE DEATH OF HECTOR

I

HAVING ACHIEVED his purpose, Apollo now resumed his own shape, and halting before Achilles thus addressed him: "Knowest thou not me, Achilles? See, the Trojans are safe from thy fury, gathered within their gates. What wouldst thou have? Is it my life thou seekest? Cease, presumptuous mortal, and remember what thou art!"

"Thou hast foiled me, archer-god," answered Achilles, perceiving that he had been tricked. "Thou hast robbed me of my prey, or many another Trojan would have bitten the dust. I would make thee rue this wrong to mine honour had I but the power." Then, like a fiery courser starting in the race, he sped away towards the city, bent on high designs. Like the red rays of that sultry star whose rising heralds in the fierce heat of summer, the season of drought and fever, such was the bright but fearful gleam which flashed from his armour as he ran.

Priam was the first who saw that ill-omened ray, from the place where he stood, on the wall above the gate. And when he marked the destroyer's approach he groaned aloud, and beat his head, and then, stretching out his hands over the battlements, thus spake unto Hector, beseeching him earnestly, and with tears: "O Hector, my son, my son, remain not there, thus deserted and alone, to abide the coming of that fearful man, seeing that he is mightier far than thou. He hath robbed me of many a noble son, whom he hath killed or sold into captivity in distant isles. Spare me this last and bitterest blow! Fling not thy life away, to bring glory on Pelides, and on us sorrow and loss unspeakable. Alas! will it never cease, the storm of misery which rains without pause on this white, distracted head! No, I see them flocking, the spectres of worse evils yet to come, sorrow on sorrow, and woe on woe—murdered sons and daughters dragged into bondage, a violated home, and little children dashed to the ground in the fury of battle. Last scene of all—an old man slaughtered on his own hearthstone, and the dogs who fed at his table and guarded his door now maddened by sights and sounds of horror, and lapping his blood!"

The old man broke off, overpowered by the dark vision which his fancy had conjured up; and the appeal was taken up by Hecuba, the venerable Queen of Troy. "By this breast which nourished thee," she cried, "by the sacred name of mother, I implore thee to abandon thy rash purpose. Fly from this man, or he will slay thee, and dogs will devour thy flesh in the Grecian camp."

But all the anguished entreaties of his father and mother had no power to shake the resolution of Hector. He could not go back now; he had rejected with scorn the prudent advice which Polydamas had given the night before, and had thereby caused the death of a legion of Trojans. How could he face the taunts of the women whom his rashness had made widows, and the mute reproaches of the children now orphaned by his act? He had openly defied Achilles, and it was too late to recall the challenge. A wild plan crossed his mind, only to be instantly rejected: should he lay aside shield, and helmet, and spear, and go unarmed to Achilles, offering to make an end of this lamentable war at the cost of half the city's goods, and the free restitution of Helen with all her wealth? "No," he said, convinced at once of the desperate folly of such an enterprise: "I should then be guilty of self-murder: he would butcher me without mercy, before I had time to utter a word. This is no time for gentle parley, as between maid and youth sitting in soft dalliance under rock or tree: I must meet him with sword and spear, for victory or death."

Achilles was now close at hand, with the mighty Pelian ash swaying on his right shoulder, and his armour blazing like the light of the rising sun. When Hector saw him advancing, like an incarnate spirit of vengeance, all his heroic resolves forsook him, and seized with sudden terror he turned and fled. And as a falcon swoops down on a hare, and pounces, and pounces again, as his victim leaps and doubles, to escape from the fatal clutch, so Achilles darted after Hector, following all the turns and windings of his flight. Past a low hill they went, whence the Trojan scout had espied the advance of the Greeks not many days before, and past the wild fig-tree, following a beaten road, which led to two fair springs, the double source of eddying Scamander. One of the springs is of hot water, and a cloud of steam hangs over it, like the smoke of a burning fire; but the other is cold as ice. Here were broad washing-pits, lined with stone, in which the wives and daughters were wont to tread the clothes, in the old peaceful days, before ever the Greeks had landed on the shores of Troy. Leaving these behind them, they sped on, and still on, pursuer and pursued. Noble was the quarry, but the hunter was nobler far, and never before had he run in so keen a chase. Like mettled steeds, which strive for the mastery, where the prize is a vessel of gold or of silver, they flew; but here they were running for a far higher stake, even the very life of Troy's bravest son.

Three times they compassed the whole circuit of the walls, and again and again Hector tried to draw his pursuer within range of the spears of the Trojans who lined the battlements; but each time his effort was defeated by Achilles, who barred his way to the city, and drove him back into the open plain.

As one who pursues his enemy in a dream, and cannot catch him, though he seems ever within reach, so was Achilles ever baffled, when he strove to overtake Hector, and Hector, when he strove to escape. All the Greeks stood near in their ranks, watching the chase— and many a time a spear was levelled at Hector, to strike him down; but Achilles beckoned with his hand, and forbade his comrades to come between him and his victim.

For the fourth time they came to the place of the washing-pits, and here by mutual consent they paused to draw breath; for both were sore spent with running, and could not go a step farther. As Achilles stood panting, and leaning on his spear, Athene drew near to him, unseen of all the rest, and said: "He cannot escape us now, though Apollo should grovel in the dust at the feet of Zeus, begging for his life. Remain awhile and recover thy strength, and I will go and persuade him to fight thee face to face."

About an arrow's flight distant, Hector had come to a standstill, and drooped heavily, resting his hands on his knees, half strangled by his efforts to breathe. Suddenly, to his amazement, he saw Deiphobus, his brother, standing by his side, and heard the familiar tones of his voice. "Dear brother," said Deiphobus, "thou art hard beset, and driven to bay by this fierce son of Peleus. But lo! I am here to aid thee, and I will not fail thee in this strait."

"Deiphobus," answered Hector, "thou wert ever dearest to me of all the sons whom Hecuba bore to

Priam: but now thou art dear and honoured too, since alone of all my nation thou hast dared to leave the shelter of the walls."

"Ay," answered the pretended Deiphobus, "my mother and my father, and all my friends, strove to hold me back; but my heart yearned towards thee in thy mortal need. But come with me, and together we will try the fortune of war. Go thou first, and I will follow."

Hector accordingly advanced to meet Achilles, who was already moving towards him. "I will fly thee no more," he said, when they were within a spear's cast of each other, "I will either slay thee, or be slain. But let us first make a covenant, and call the gods to witness it: swear thou that, if I fall, thou wilt restore my body and my armour to the Trojans—and I will swear to do the like by thee."

"Talk not to me of covenants, thou villain!" answered Achilles fiercely. "As there is no treaty possible between lions and men, no concord between wolves and lambs, but only fear and hatred, so is there hate unending between me and thee, which naught but death may cancel or abate. Summon up all thy manhood, and prepare to pay the price of my comrades whom thou hast slain."

This said he poised and flung his spear; but Hector stooped low, and the spear flew over his head, and sank deep into the earth. Unobserved by Hector, Athene drew it out, and gave it back to Achilles. "Take now my spear!" shouted the Trojan, "take it to thy heart, thou braggart, that thinkest to dismay me with boastful words!" The weapon flew straight to its mark, and, striking the centre of Achilles' shield, rebounded to a distance, and fell rattling on the ground. Then Hector called anxiously to Deiphobus, bidding him bring another lance. But no answer came, for the real Deiphobus was safe behind the walls, and he who had appeared to Hector was a false Deiphobus, concealing the person of Athene.

"Alas! I have been deceived," said Hector. "My last bolt is shot, and my fate summons me to death. Let me not die inglorious and without a struggle, but in such wise that I shall be named with honour by generations yet unborn."

Then, drawing his sword, he rushed upon Achilles, who came on slowly, towering above the rampart of his shield, nodding his golden plumes and brandishing high his spear, whose point twinkled and flashed like the light of the evening star. Scanning every joint in Hector's armour, at last Achilles spied a point, between the shoulder-blade and the neck, which was undefended; and at this mark he hurled his spear with all his force and pierced him through the neck. But the passage of his voice was left untouched, so that he was still able to speak.

"Thou hast paid thy debt to Patroclus," said Achilles, standing over his fallen enemy, "and now thou shalt pay the usury. Dogs and vultures shall give thee burial, but he shall lie in an honoured tomb."

"By thy life," answered Hector faintly, "by thy father's name, I implore thee, give not my body to be devoured by dogs, but restore it to my friends, who will pay thee a heavy ransom, that I may receive my due in death."

"Thou dog!" replied Achilles, with a furious look, "talk not of thy dues, nor name my father to me! Would that I could find it in my heart to carve and devour thy flesh, as surely as thou shalt not escape the hounds and vultures, no, not if Priam were to offer thy weight in gold, after what thou hast done unto me and mine."

"I knew that I should not persuade thee," said Hector, with his dying breath. "Thou hast a heart of iron. But vengeance shall reach thee in the day when Apollo and Paris shall subdue thee at the gates of Troy."

As he uttered this prophecy a shudder ran through his limbs, and the gallant spirit fled to the land of shadows.

"Die!" said Achilles, as Hector uttered his last sigh. "As for me, I am prepared to meet my fate whensoever heaven wills its accomplishment."

Then he drew out his spear, and laying it aside, began to strip off the armour which Hector had taken from Patroclus. And the Greeks came crowding round, to gaze on the beauty and stature of Hector, and stab the helpless body with their spears. Far other had he seemed to them when he came with fire and sword to burn their ships, and fill their camp with slaughter!

When Achilles had finished stripping the corpse, he stood up and spoke thus to the assembled host: "Princes and counsellors of the Greeks, now that the gods have granted us to slay this mighty champion, who hath done us more harm than all the rest together, shall we not advance in full force against the city, and end the war at one bold stroke? But alas! what am I saying? We have another and a sadder duty to perform. Patroclus lies among the ships, unburied, unwept, and shall I forget him in this hour of triumph? No; not in the hour of death, not in the grave itself, which brings, they say, oblivion to all, shall my love for him grow cold. Therefore follow me, sirs, to the ships, and raise the song of victory. We have gained great glory, we have slain Troy's chief defender, to whom all the Trojans prayed as to a god."

Then, in fulfilment of his horrible menaces, he prepared to take hideous vengeance on his slaughtered enemy. Stooping down he pierced the dead man's feet from heel to ankle, and passed a leathern thong through the holes; then he made fast the thong behind the chariot, and, taking up the armour, he sprang into the driver's place, and lashed his horses to a gallop. So amid a swirling cloud of dust the fallen hero was dragged along, with his dark locks streaming, and that comely head marred and defiled; and Zeus delivered him to injury and outrage at the hands of his enemies in his own native land.

II

But what were the feelings of the Trojans watching on the walls when they saw their great champion fall, and with what eyes did the aged king and the fond mother behold their Hector, their joy and pride, and chief defence, butchered, mutilated, and dragged through the dust! Through all the city arose a great cry of lamentation, and such horror was written on every face as if the Greeks had carried Troy by storm, and were filling her streets with fire and slaughter. Priam was hardly restrained from going forth at once, with the purpose of entering the Grecian camp, and throwing himself at the feet of Achilles.

But there was another, bound by an even nearer and dearer tie to the slain, who was the last to learn the fearful news. This was Andromache, Hector's wife, who was sitting at her loom in the retirement of her chamber, weaving a piece of flowered tapestry. Presently she left her task, and calling her handmaids bade them prepare the bath for their master against his return from battle. Her face was cheerful and serene, and she smiled as she thought of the happy meeting which seemed so near. But in the midst of these pleasant household cares a dreadful sound reached her ears—a shrill note, as of women shrieking, mingled with the deeper groans of men. "Hark!" she said, turning deadly pale, and dropping the shuttle, which she had been holding in her hand: "What mean these cries?" Then, as she paused again to listen, she heard the voice of Hecuba, raised in loud anguish above the rest. With a woman's quick instinct she divined that the worst had befallen her, and shrieking: "Hector, my Hector, is slain!" she hastened, with ashy cheeks, and tottering knees, to the walls. The crowd fell back at her approach, and every voice was hushed when they saw her bending over the battlements, and gazing with wild eyes across the plain. Then she saw Achilles in full career towards the ships, dragging her husband's body behind his car. At that sight she gave one gasping cry, and reeling back fell swooning into the arms of her kinswomen who were standing ready to aid. Thus for awhile she lay, motionless and lifeless, with her long hair, escaped from its bands, streaming about her. At last she drew a deep, sobbing breath, and opening her eyes looked into the anxious faces bent over her. Then the full consciousness of her loss rushed back upon her in a bitter flood, and breaking from the gentle hands which held her she made as if she would fling herself down from the battlements. She was prevented by kindly force, and led away, moaning and weeping, to her widowed home.

22

THE FUNERAL GAMES OF PATROCLUS

I

WHEN ACHILLES reached the camp, he commanded his men to remain under arms, and led the whole company, with horses and with chariots, in solemn procession, three times round the couch on which the dead Patroclus lay. When the strange rite was ended, the couch, which had been brought out for this purpose, was carried back with its burden to the tent, and they unyoked their horses, and prepared to take their supper. Hector's body was flung into a corner, where it lay exposed to the burning sun, and the cold dews of night. Achilles feasted his men bountifully, and then went, attended by a special guard of honour, to partake of a banquet in the royal tent. Being invited to refresh himself with a bath, he stubbornly refused, and swore a great oath that he would never wash the stains of battle from his person until Patroclus had been buried with all the pomp of woe. At the banquet he seemed ill at ease, and as soon as it was ended he prayed his kingly host to have him excused, and went back to the quarters of the Myrmidons.

Night came down, and silence fell on the sleeping camp. Achilles had not sought his bed, but had laid himself down on the sand, in a clear space, where the billows broke at his feet. There sleep soon overtook him, stilling the dull ache of sorrow; for his limbs were very weary, after that tremendous fight, and still more tremendous race. And as he slept the ghost of Patroclus came and stood by his side, like to the living man in stature and in face and in voice, and in the very garments he had on; and thus spake the spectre, in hollow and mournful tones: "Ah! fickle heart, oblivious of the dead, canst thou sleep, Achilles? Has death broken the bond which united us in life? Bury me with all speed, and let me wander no more, a homeless ghost, at the gates of Hades, disowned and rejected by the other spirits who have crossed the dark river. Give me thy hand, sweet friend, I entreat thee! For never again shall I return to earth, when ye have given my body to the flames—never more shall we sit retired from our comrades, as once in life, and take sweet counsel together. My fate hath seized me, and cast me down into the pit which was prepared for me when I was born; and for thee too the bolt is prepared, which shall lay thee low beneath the walls of Troy. And one more charge have I to lay upon thee: let not our bones lie apart, Achilles, but let us be joined in death, even as we were united in life. One home, one love, we shared, and thy father was to me as mine own, from the day when I slew my playmate in a childish brawl, and was brought by Menœtius to the house of Peleus. Therefore, when thy fate hath reached thee, let our ashes be mingled in one urn."

"Wherefore, beloved," answered Achilles in his sleep, "hast thou come hither to remind me of my duty, and seemest to doubt my love? Come nearer, that I may embrace thee! Yet a little while let my heart beat against thine, and ease its heavy burden of sorrow."

With these words he stretched out his eager arms to clasp Patroclus to his breast; but the ghost eluded his grasp, and with one piercing wail melted away like smoke into the darkness. "Alas!" cried Achilles, springing up in amaze, and summoning his comrades, "I perceive that, even in the house of Hades, there is a spirit and a phantom of the dead—but understanding none at all—for all night long the ghost of the hapless Patroclus stood by my side moaning and lamenting, and straitly charging me concerning all that I must do. And the phantom was in aspect as the living man himself."

II

At earliest dawn a long train of mules was seen ascending the lower slopes of Ida, attended by a numerous company of men, all carrying axes and ropes of withes.

The whole troop was under the command of Meriones, the squire of Idomeneus, on whom the task had been laid of providing fuel for the funeral pyre of Patroclus. A large grove of pines was felled, the trunks were divided into logs, and these were bound into bundles and laid on the backs of the mules. Then down the slope they were driven at a quick trot, the men running beside them; and when they reached the camp the mules were unloaded and the logs piled up in an open space pointed out by Achilles. A thousand willing hands aided in the work, and soon a huge stack of pinewood towered in the midst of the ships and tents.

When the pyre was raised, Achilles gave the order to the Myrmidons to gird on their armour and harness the steeds to their cars. The whole army stood waiting, drawn up in silence on either side of the way by which the funeral train was to pass; and presently the procession was seen approaching. First came the chariots, each carrying two men—the driver, and the man-at-arms; behind these followed a numerous troop of infantry, marching slowly in dense array; and in the space between the corpse was borne, covered with locks of hair which the Myrmidons had cut off as a last tribute to the dead.

Achilles walked behind the bier, supporting the head of Patroclus in his hands, and moving heavily, as one that mourns for a brother; and so they passed on, through the long lane of mailed warriors, until they came to the place where the pyre was built.

Then Achilles took a sharp knife, and cut off from his forehead a long lock of hair, and, placing the lock in the dead man's hand, turned round and gazed wistfully across the dark gulf of waters which divided him from his home. "Alas for the hopes of men!" he said, in a voice of distress. "My father Peleus designed this lock for another purpose, as an offering to thee, Spercheus, my native stream, if ever I returned safe from the war. But now thine altar, which stands in thy grove near thy sacred source, shall never smoke for me again. A foreign grave awaits me, far from my home and kindred, and Peleus is absolved from his vow. Therefore to thee, Patroclus, I dedicate this lock."

The Greeks now dispersed to their quarters leaving those who were nearest to the dead, by birth or by station, to perform the last rites. The chief mourners approached the bier, and lifting it with the corpse placed it on the top of the pyre. Many sheep and oxen were slaughtered and flayed, and the body of Patroclus was wrapped from head to foot in the fat taken from the carcasses. Then the carcasses of the victims were heaped up round the bier, with jars of honey and olive-oil. Four horses were next slaughtered, and two favourite hounds of Patroclus, and their bodies added to the rest. Last of all the twelve Trojan captives whom he had taken in battle the day before were led in chains to the spot, butchered by Achilles with his own hands, and flung upon the pyre.

"It is done!" cried Achilles, when this last savage

tribute was paid to his friend, "I have accomplished my vow, and the fire may now do its work—but for thee, Hector, no fire shall be lighted, but dogs shall devour thee."

That cruel threat at least was not to be fulfilled. Unseen hands were busy about the fallen Trojan hero, guarding him day and night from the prowling dogs of the camp. Aphrodite embalmed his body with a heavenly essence, which closed all his wounds, and kept his flesh pure and unharmed; and Apollo covered all the place where he lay with a dark cloud, to shield him from the scorching rays of the sun.

Meanwhile torches had been brought to kindle the pyre. But the huge mass smouldered sullenly, and the victims remained unconsumed. Then Achilles took a golden bowl, and pouring a libation to Boreas and Zephyrus, the twin gods of the winds, prayed them to lend their blasts and blow the fire to a blaze. Iris heard his prayer, and went swiftly to call the winds to his aid. She found them seated at table with all their brethren in the house of Zephyrus; and thus spake Iris to that boisterous company: "Why sit ye here feasting and making merry, when there is work for you to do? Hear ye not the prayers of Achilles, who needs your help, that the pyre of Patroclus may burn freely, and consume him to ashes, with all that lies about him."

Prompt at the summons, the winds arose, with clamour and uproarious din, and rushed down the mountainside, chasing the clouds before them. Over

the complaining sea they swept, and flew whistling onward till they reached the shores of Troy. There they fell
upon the smouldering pyre, and the flames leaped and
bellowed in response to the roaring blast. So all night
long they lashed the fire to fury, and all night long
Achilles paced to and fro before the pyre, pouring li-
bations from a golden bowl on the ground, and calling
aloud to the ghost of his ill-starred friend. As mourns
a father when he burns the bones of his son, a young
bridegroom cut off by death on his wedding-day, so
mourned Achilles as the fire devoured his comrade's
body—so pitiful were his cries, so faltering his gait.

Towards dawn the fire began to die out, and nothing was left but a vast heap of glowing ashes. Then the
winds went back to their home, and earth and ocean
sank to rest, beneath the gentle light of the morning star. Soothed by the calm influence of the hour,
Achilles fell into a fitful slumber, but was soon aroused
by the sound of footsteps and the murmur of voices.
Starting up, he saw a goodly company of nobles approaching, with Agamemnon at their head; and with
their assistance the ritual ceremonies due to the dead
were completed. First, they poured wine on the glowing mass of embers, till the last spark was extinguished;
then they collected the ashes of Patroclus, which lay
by themselves, surrounded by the charred remains of
beasts and men. A costly urn of gold received the few
handfuls of dust which were all that remained of him
whom they had so cherished and honoured; and the

urn was buried in a low mound of earth, which was one day to be raised to a commanding height, as a monument to the great Achilles.

III

When the last tribute of sorrow had been paid, the rest of the day was devoted to sport and festivity. In heroic times funeral games were an important part of the honours assigned to a fallen warrior; and those of Patroclus were celebrated on a scale of unrivalled magnificence.

The great event of the day was to be the chariot race, and splendid prizes were offered by Achilles, who was the sole patron and prize giver, for the winners. When the gifts were set in order, Achilles rose and invited all who prided themselves in their horsemanship to take part in the friendly contest. "If," he said, "we were keeping this festival in honour of any other Greek, I myself must needs carry off the first prize; for no steeds in all the army can vie with mine, the immortal coursers which were a gift from Poseidon to my father. But this is a day of mourning both to me and to them; for they have lost their gentle charioteer, and now stand, sorrow-stricken, with manes drooping to the ground, in their stalls, deprived of his loving care. Therefore take your places, all ye who would prove the mettle of your horses, and your own mastery of this gallant game."

Four chieftains brought their cars to try their fortune in the race: Eumelus, a prince of Thessaly, a land renowned for its breed of horses; Diomede, who drove the horses which he had taken from Æneas; Menelaus, with a mare of Agamemnon's, named Arthe, and his own horse Podargus; and Antilochus, whose car was drawn by a pair from his father's stables. Nestor, who knew their quality, which was indeed but poor, accompanied his son to the starting-point, and as they were the first to arrive he improved the occasion by proffering a world of good advice, reinforced by many a pithy saw, showing Antilochus how the want of speed may be remedied by cunning and skill. "Art," he said, "is far greater than force. Art drives the axe, though aimed by a weaker arm, deep into the heart of the oak; art controls the motions of tall ships, by means of a very small helm; and art may save thee from reaching the goal last in this race."

In the ancient chariot races the starting-point and the winning-post were always the same, as it was the custom to run a certain distance, and then wheel round a certain point, and return on the homeward track, which was parallel to the other. The turning-point was marked by a pillar, or some other conspicuous object, and here a desperate struggle often took place between the rival cars for the inside place, taxing the skill and courage of the drivers to the utmost. Nestor had been over the course, and gave his son minute directions as to the appearance and position of the turning-post, which was far off on the plain, and invisible from the starting-point. "You will see," he said, "a withered stump of oak or fir, rising to about a fathom above the earth, with a white stone leaning against it on either side. There you must turn; and see that you lose no ground in wheeling round to the homeward track. Give your right horse the reins, and urge him to full speed with voice and lash, but rein in the other, and hold him back; and let the nave of your left wheel just seem to graze the stump. If you can pass another car in turning, there is no fear that he will catch you again. Thou hast my counsel: go, and prosper—be wary, and be wise."

At the last moment a fifth chariot appeared on the scene, driven by Meriones. Lots were cast for the stations, and Antilochus was so fortunate as to obtain the inside place. The cars drew up in a line, Achilles gave the word, and away they went in a cloud of dust, the horses' manes streaming, the drivers shouting, and the cars gliding smoothly, or leaping and plunging at the uneven places.

Soon the cars began to separate by wider and wider intervals, and a keen struggle ensued between the Thracian horses, driven by Eumelus, and the Trojans, driven by Diomede. Eumelus took the lead, but Diomede followed him so close that he felt the hot breath of the pursuing horses on his back. So they ran for about a bowshot; then Diomede dropped his whip, and his horses, wanting the lash, began to fall back. This accident befell him by the malice of Apollo, who owed him a grudge for the havoc which he had wrought among the Trojans. But Athene had not forgotten her favourite, and she contrived that he should recover his whip, and put fresh mettle into his steeds. Nor did she stop there, but, overtaking the car of Eumelus, she broke the yoke which coupled his horses, so that they reared violently in opposite directions, and the pole of the car was dashed to the ground. Thus suddenly arrested at the height of his speed, Eumelus rolled headlong from the car, and sustained woeful damage. The skin was torn from his elbows and nose and mouth, his forehead was severely bruised, and he lay for a while senseless where he fell. This mishap secured an easy victory for Diomede. Avoiding the wreck, he pressed onwards, leaving the whole field far behind, turned the goal successfully, and drove at an easy gallop along the homeward track.

He was followed at a long distance by Menelaus, now second in the race; and the third place was held by Antilochus, whose ambition had been fired by the unlooked-for good fortune of Diomede, so that he hoped by some similar accident to obtain at least the second prize. Cheering on his horses, he went hard in pursuit of Menelaus, who was just then approaching a difficult piece of ground, where the course had been hollowed out by the winter rains. The place was too narrow to allow two cars to pass, and Antilochus determined to secure the lead before Menelaus had time to reach the broad course on the other side of the ravine. Accordingly he plied the lash unsparingly, and overtook Menelaus at the moment when he was about to enter the neck of the dry watercourse. "Keep back!" shouted Menelaus in alarm. "Do not try to pass me here, or you will wreck both our cars."

Antilochus pretended not to hear, and drove on harder than ever, so that Menelaus, who was a timid driver, was compelled to rein in his horses and let him go by.

While the race was being thus run, with varying turns of fortune, the chieftains assembled round Achilles were sitting in their places, waiting for the return of the cars, and discussing the chances of the drivers. Presently Idomeneus, who sat somewhat apart from the rest, in a position which gave him a long view over the course, cried out excitedly: "Diomede is leading! I can see the white mark on the face of one of the horses, which shows that he is one of the Trojan stallions—the red chestnut, with a mark like a half-moon on his forehead. Look out, some of you who have younger eyes than mine, and see if I am right."

"Hold thy peace, old prater!" said Ajax, son of Oileus, roughly. "We can see nothing yet—neither canst thou. Eumelus was leading when we saw him last, and doubtless he is leading still."

"Thou mannerless fellow!" answered Idomeneus hotly. "Foremost in a brawl, and in all else the least of the Greeks! Come, let us lay a wager, and Agamemnon shall hold the stakes; or art thou afraid to back thy saucy tongue?"

Ajax started up in a rage, hurling abuse at the Cretan veteran, and words would have soon led to blows, had not Achilles interposed his authority to put an end to the quarrel. "For shame!" he said, rising from his seat, "I wonder to hear you, two men of name and high station, wrangling like boors. What avails this idle contention? Wait but a moment, and the winner will be here to answer for himself."

Even as he spoke, a loud huzza was heard, and a moment after, the Trojan car, driven by Diomede, turned the last corner, and came racing lightly down the last straight stretch of the course, until it was pulled up before the chair of Achilles. Sthenelus was standing ready to welcome his comrade, and the first prize—a female slave, and a huge cauldron for heating water for the bath—was forthwith delivered to the victor.

After a long interval Antilochus came in, driving at a heavy gallop, and hotly pursued by Menelaus, who was gaining at every stride, and had by this time reduced the wide gap which had separated them to a mere hand's-breadth. His horses were displaying splendid mettle, especially the mare Arthe, who had been given to Agamemnon by a wealthy noble of Sicyon, as the price of his exemption from serving in the war; and if the course had been a bowshot longer he would have passed Antilochus, and taken the second prize. As it was, he came in third, but those who stood near as he was dismounting could see that he was red with indignation, and big with some grievance, real or supposed.

The fourth was Meriones, who was a poor driver, and whose steeds were the weakest; and last of all came Eumelus, with face sorely disfigured, dragging his wrecked car behind him, and driving before him his horses. "The last man is the best!" cried Achilles, moved to pity by his ill-fortune. "How say you, sirs? Shall we not give him the second prize?" The proposal found general approval, excepting, of course, with Antilochus, who loudly protested against such an award. "Thou art no friend of mine, Achilles," he said angrily, "if thou deprive me of the gift which I have fairly earned. Prizes are given to reward the winners, not to console the unlucky. If you wish to be generous, you can make Eumelus happy by bestowing on him some other gift, of equal or greater value, out of the rich store which is laid up in your tent. But this prize is mine, and I will not give her up no, not if I have to fight for her."

So saying, he seized the halter of the mare, who was tethered near, with her foal, to be given to him who won the second place.

The great Achilles smiled indulgently at the defiant attitude of Antilochus, who was very dear to him. "It shall be as you say," he replied. "The prize is yours, and to Eumelus I will give the corslet of Asteropæus, which I won in the battle yesterday." Automedon brought the corslet—a curious piece of work, finely fashioned in brass, with a casting of white metal—and Eumelus' eyes glistened with pleasure as he received it.

But the storm which had been lowering in the face of Menelaus ever since Antilochus had passed him now burst. Having caused the herald to proclaim silence he took the staff from his hands, as a sign that he had an important statement to make, and standing up before the whole assembly proclaimed his wrongs to the ears of all. "I am astonished," he said, "at the conduct of Antilochus. He has beaten me in the race by a trick, though his horses are far inferior to mine in any fair trial of speed. I appeal to all those present to say whether it is not so. If he denies it, let him take his whip in his hand, and holding his horses by the rein swear a solemn oath, in the name of Poseidon, the god of horsemanship, that he did not hinder me by fraud in the race."

Menelaus was clearly in the wrong, indeed, his whole plea was absurd; for nothing but his own faint-heartedness had lost him the second prize. But out of respect to his high rank and amiable character Antilochus was willing to appease him. Accordingly he brought the mare with her foal to Menelaus, and placing the bridle in his hand said respectfully: "Spare me thy reproaches, gentle prince! I yield to thee the prize, and would sacrifice much more than this, rather than lose thy favour and incur the anger of heaven."

As falls the refreshing dew on the bristling ears of barley, when the crops are ripening, so fell the soft answer of Antilochus on the Spartan prince's heart, and the sharp stings of resentment pricked him no more.

"Thou shalt have the prize," he said mildly, "though it is mine by right. Thou art not wont to be so heedless of what is due to others: but this time thy young blood didst get the mastery of thy better sense. Take heed that thou art not so reckless again. I have yielded to thee in this for thy father's sake, and for thine also; for ye have both suffered many things in my cause." And so the dispute, which threatened to disturb the harmony of the meeting, was happily ended.

Five prizes had been offered for the race, and as Eumelus had received a special gift, the fifth prize, a drinking goblet, still remained unclaimed. Observing this, Achilles seized the occasion of showing his esteem for the venerable King of Pylos. So he took the cup, and going to the place where Nestor was sitting put it in his hands. "Take this, father," he said, "as a memorial of our lost Patroclus, in whose honour we are met to-day. Thou art full of years and honours, and deservest the highest prize of all, though thou canst not strive with young men in boxing, or in wrestling, or in speed of foot."

"Thou sayest truly, my son," answered the old man, "my feet are heavy with age, and my arms dart not nimbly from the shoulder, as they did of yore. Yet the day has been when none could vie with me in feats of strength and skill. Well do I remember the funeral games of a noble prince of Elis, where I won the prize in every contest, except only in the chariot race, and then I was overmatched by numbers, for the winning car had two drivers, one plying the lash, and the other managing the reins. Alas for my youth! Alas for my vanished strength! Now I must be content to see others excel, though once I was mighty among the mightiest. Let then the games proceed, and receive an old man's blessing for thy kindly gift."

IV

"Now let the boxers try their skill and hardihood," said Achilles, when he had returned to his seat. "Here is a stout mule of six years old for the winner, and for the loser there is a silver cup."

In answer to the challenge a huge champion named Epeus strode into the ring, and, laying his hand on the mule, cried boastfully: "Come on, whoever wishes to win the cup! The mule is surely mine, for there is no boxer here who can match me. If there be anyone who would dispute the prize with me, let him stand up, when he has made all ready for his funeral—for I will pound his flesh, and batter his bones, until he is fit only for burial."

Epeus, with his massive frame and brawny arms, seemed quite capable of performing his threats, and it was some time before anyone was found willing to face him. At last Euryalus, an Argive, whose father had been a famous boxer, was encouraged by his friend Diomede to try his chances in this painful and dangerous sport; and having stripped to the waist, and bound their hands with tough leathern thongs, the two combatants confronted each other in the centre of the ring. The struggle was very short, for after they had fenced a little with their fists Euryalus received a crushing blow on the side of his jaw, and dropped in a heap where he stood, like a great fish flung by the waves on the beach. Spitting out blood, and rolling his head from side to side, he was led away by his friends, and Epeus carried off the mule in triumph.

Then followed a hard-contested match between Odysseus and Telamonian Ajax, for the championship in wrestling. Stripped, like the boxers, to the waist, they clutched each other in a fierce embrace, and remained thus locked together, their strong arms crossed like the rafters in a roof, and their sides growing black under the iron pressure. They seemed rooted to the ground, and neither could stir the other an inch. Then Ajax, suddenly exerting his enormous strength, lifted Odysseus bodily into the air; but Odysseus struck him with his heel behind the knee, and they fell together, Odysseus above, and Ajax below. Rising again to their feet they wrestled a second bout, and this time Odysseus, though foiled in his attempt to lift the huge bulk of his antagonist, succeeded in tripping him by a crook of the knee, and they came down again, and lay side by side. Once more they would have renewed the struggle, but Achilles put an end to the contest, and awarded them an equal prize.

A beautiful silver bowl, the work of Sidonian art-
ists, which Achilles had once received as the ransom of
the unhappy Lycaon, was now offered as the first prize
for the foot race. The second prize was a fat ox, and the
third one half of a talent of gold. There were three com-
petitors: the lesser Ajax, who was famed for his speed
of foot, Odysseus, and Antilochus. The distance was
about a furlong, and Ajax took the lead from the start,
though Odysseus pressed him so hard that he seemed
glued to him; and so they ran, without changing their
positions, over half the course, the Greeks shouting to
encourage Odysseus, who was a popular favourite. Still
Ajax held the lead, and seemed about to win, when he
slipped in a miry place, where the ground was wet with
the blood of the oxen slaughtered by Achilles at the
funeral of Patroclus, and pitched head foremost in the
horrid mire, which filled his mouth and nostrils. But
he was on his feet again in a moment, and though he
could not overtake Odysseus he succeeded in obtaining
the second prize. "It is an old story," he said, holding
the ox by the horn, and spitting out the slime which
filled his mouth; "Odysseus was helped by Athene,
who watches over him as a mother over her child."

The Greeks laughed at his discomfiture, and found
fresh matter for mirth in the humorous excuses of Antilochus, who had been left far behind in the race. "You
know," he said, "that the gods are always on the side of
the elder men; Ajax is a little older than I, and Odysseus belongs to another generation. But he is in a green

old age, and none can vie with him in speed, except only Achilles."

"Thy praise shall not be spoken for nothing," said Achilles, smiling, and he gave him one half of a talent of gold as a reward for his good words.

Contests in archery and throwing the weight succeeded, and an encounter with sword and spear took place between Ajax and Diomede. Then Achilles offered two prizes for throwing the javelin, and Agamemnon, in recognition of his high rank and known skill in this exercise, was allowed to take the first prize without a trial. With this incident the games came to an end.

23

PRIAM RANSOMS THE BODY OF HECTOR

I

THE BUSY DAY was over, and night sank down on the Grecian camp, bringing to all, save one tormented spirit, the blessed gift of sleep. With silence and solitude the pangs of sorrow awakened with new keenness in the heart of Achilles, and he lay tossing and turning on his uneasy pillow, seeking rest, and finding none. A thousand memories of his friendship with Patroclus—gallant adventures, hairbreadth escapes, moving accidents by flood and field—coursed through his mind, bringing home to him the immensity of his loss. After some hours of sleepless misery he sprang to his feet, and throwing on his clothes went down to the sea, and roamed distracted along the sand. With the first glimmer of daylight he yoked his horses to the car, and drove round and round the tomb of Patroclus, dragging after him the body of Hector. Having made the circuit of the tomb three times, he unyoked his horses, and retired once more to his tent, leaving his lifeless victim face downwards in the dust.

Twelve days passed; and every day the same outrage was repeated. All the gods, except Poseidon, Hera, and Athene, whose hatred of all things Trojan was inveterate, were indignant at his senseless barbarity, and they began to urge Hermes to steal Hector's body, and restore it to his friends. But nothing was done until, on the twelfth day, Apollo rose up and reproached the gods, who were met in full assembly, for their cruel indifference. "Is there no pity," he said, "is there no justice, left in heaven, that ye suffer this inhuman son of Peleus to wreak his brutal fury on the body of a man of stainless life, constant all his days in sacrifice and prayer? All your favour is lavished on Achilles, who has the heart of a ravening lion, nourished in havoc and carnage. Death lies about the paths of mortals, taking their nearest and their dearest; yet sorrow must sleep at last, for patience is the best gift which the gods have given to men. But this man is more cruel in his love than in his hate, and because he has lost a friend his rancour burns on like an unquenchable fire."

"Thou forgettest," answered Hera, "that Achilles is the son of a goddess, and shares the privileges of divine descent. His father also was a favourite of heaven, and thou thyself, Phœbus, didst lend the music of thy harp to grace his nuptials; but now, it seemeth, thou takest delight in baser company."

"Fair consort," said Zeus, "be not thus implacable. Granted that Achilles stands higher in honour, yet Hector hath also his claim on our regard, for none was ever more pious than he. Therefore, that we may end this miserable coil at once, let Iris go and summon hither his mother Thetis, that we may contrive some way of restoring Hector to his people."

Iris hastened to obey the command, and, stooping from Olympus to the surface of the sea, dropped like a leaden plummet into the purple depths, until she reached the grotto where Thetis dwelt. She found her sitting among the Nereids, mourning the lot of her matchless son, whose death was near at hand. "What wants the monarch of heaven from me?" she asked, when she heard the summons from Zeus. "I am ill prepared to attend the happy session of the gods, for grief has clouded my mind and marred my face." Nevertheless she rose to go, and putting on a veil of funereal blackness followed Iris, who brought her speedily to the assembly of the gods.

"We thank thee, Thetis," said Zeus, beckoning her to a seat next to his throne, "that thou hast answered so promptly to our call. We know thy sorrows, and have respect for thee and thy son; and for this cause have we sent for thee. For nine days there has been strife among us, concerning the body of Hector, which Achilles still keeps in his possession. Some there were who would have had Hermes steal it away, but this I would not suffer, out of regard to thy son's honour. But go thou to the camp, and tell him that we are sore displeased with him, because in his madness he keeps the corpse of his enemy and will not ransom it. And I will send Iris with a charge to Priam, that he may go with acceptable gifts to the tent of Achilles, and redeem the body for burial."

II

Still nursing his wound, still torn by the demons of rage and grief, Achilles sat moodily in his tent, while his comrades were busy about him, preparing the morning meal. Suddenly he felt a gentle touch on his shoulder, and looking up he saw his mother's face bent over him, with looks of sympathy and love. "My son," she said, in a low sweet voice, "how long wilt thou devour thy heart in bootless anguish, refusing meat and drink, and spurning the tender offices of human affection? O darken not the little remnant that remains to thee of life, but take what good thou canst, and at least live as a man. I have come with a message to thee from Zeus, who bids thee to give up Hector's body, and receive the ransom which his friends will offer thee."

"Be it so," answered Achilles. "Let them bring the price, and I will give back the body." Overjoyed by his ready consent, Thetis bade him farewell, and returned to her ocean home.

Meanwhile the ever-active Iris was gone on another errand, carrying the commands of Zeus to Priam.

Swiftly she passed through the streets of Troy, and entered the house of woe, where the voice of sorrow had never ceased since the day when Hector had fallen by the hands of Achilles. Priam himself was lying prostrate on the ground in the courtyard, with his white locks defied with dust and ashes. Round him were gathered his sons, trying in vain to rouse him from his stupor; and at the windows were seen from time to time the white faces of women, when any of his daughters paused in their household tasks to glance at the sorrow-stricken group outside.

Lying thus, mute and motionless, Priam was startled to hear a still, small voice, which seemed to be speaking at a great distance, addressing him in these words: "Take comfort, son of Dardanus, and be not dismayed! I who speak have not come to foretell thee harm, but only good. Thy cries and thy groanings have gone up to the ear of Zeus, and he hath sent me to comfort and advise thee. Hearken now, and do as I shall tell thee: let them prepare thee a wain, loaded with precious gifts, and go thou in thy car to the tent of Achilles, and let only a herald go with thee, a man stricken in years like thyself, to guide the mules. Fear nothing, for heaven is near thee, and the gods have put it into the heart of Achilles to hear thy prayer."

To the amazement of those who stood near, and who knew nothing of the cause, new life and energy were seen to enter the palsied limbs of Priam, and starting to his feet he ordered his sons to prepare the mule car, and make fast to it the great wicker basket which was used for the carriage of goods. Then, without staying for question or reply, he hastened into the house, and calling to Hecuba made known to her his purpose. When she heard what he intended, Hecuba lifted up her hands, and answered in tones of astonishment and terror. "Is it Priam who speaks—the monarch revered for his wisdom even in distant lands—or is it some madman who has taken upon him Priam's likeness? What, wilt thou go into the presence of that butcher, whose savage hands have made thee all but childless? Faithless and ruthless as he is, thinkest thou that he will reverence thy grey hairs? No, he will slaughter thee without pity, and give us new cause for tears. Hector hath received the portion appointed to him at his birth, and dogs shall eat his flesh where he lies in the tent of that man of blood. May the curse of heaven light on his slayer! Would that I could tear his heart with my teeth, and devour it! Then would my noble son be avenged, who died bravely before the face of all his people, with no thought of flight or escape."

But Priam was not to be shaken in his resolve. "Seek not to hinder me," he answered, "and vex me not with thy evil forebodings. I go not at the bidding of any earthly prophet, but with direct assurance of the aid and countenance of heaven. If I have been deceived, I am prepared to die, so that the stroke but find me holding my son in my arms, and clinging to him in a last embrace."

With that he went to his treasure-chamber, and opening the chests of cedarwood took from them rich robes, choice tapestries, and costly raiment. To these he added ten talents of gold and a bowl of silver, which he had received as a gift of honour when he went on an embassy to Thrace. And having set the gifts in order he went forth again into the courtyard, to hasten the preparations for his journey. Finding there a crowd of Trojans, whom some rumour had drawn to the palace, he drove them all out, beating them with his staff, and crying: "What make ye here, idle caitiffs? Have ye not sorrow enough at home that ye come hither to chatter and pry into my grief? Ye will soon learn what ye have lost in my Hector, when ye fly like sheep without a shepherd before the wolves of Greece." The Trojans fled before the old man's anger, and he looked about him, seeking his sons. "Where are ye," he cried, "children of my shame? Would that ye had all perished, and Hector alone were left! Alas! the best are ever taken first, and in those that remain there is neither comfort nor strength, but only dishonour and reproach. Liars, dancers, devourers of the people—these are my children now."

Roused by the loud rebukes of their father, the young princes made haste to bring forth the mule car and harness the mules. Then they loaded the car with the gifts to Achilles, and yoked to the chariot the horses which Priam himself was to drive.

When all was ready, Hecuba came and stood by the chariot, bearing a golden cup filled with wine. "Take this," she said to Priam, "and pour a drink-offering to Zeus, if so be that he will vouchsafe thee a sign, and show thee whether it be by his will or not that thou goest on this journey."

"Thou sayest well," answered Priam. "It is a good thing to hold up our hands to heaven in prayer." Thereupon he washed his hands in water, which was brought by a handmaid, took the cup from his wife, and standing by the altar in the middle of the courtyard lifted up his voice and prayed: "Lord of Ida, most glorious, most great, grant that the heart of Achilles may incline in pity towards me, and send thy messenger, the swift eagle whom thou lovest best of all fowls, that having seen him we may go with good heart and courage to the Grecian camp."

Even as he spoke, a mighty eagle was seen soaring over the city on the right hand, with his vast wings outspread, like the folding doors of a rich man's house. Rejoicing in the omen, Priam mounted his chariot, and drove through the echoing porch, preceded by the herald Idæus, who drove the mule car. Along the streets they passed, making what speed they could, through the multitudes who had flocked out to see them depart, and who mourned them as already dead.

Night had fallen, and all the sky was thick set with stars, as they left the city gates, and turned their faces towards the sea. When they reached the ford of the river they paused to let the animals drink: and while they halted Idæus suddenly cried out in tones of terror: "My lord, we are undone! I see a man approaching, and I fear he means us no good." Priam peered out into the darkness, following with his eyes the pointing finger of Idæus, and saw a tall figure moving with rapid steps towards them.

"What doest thou here?" said the stranger, who was a graceful and comely youth, and whose voice sounded like the chiming of a silver bell. "Why art thou here unguarded, at the very gates of the foe? But be of good cheer—I will not harm thee, nor suffer others to do so. I see in thee a likeness to my dear father."

"Fair youth," answered Priam, whose alarm had vanished before the gentle mien and kind words of the young Greek, "surely some god has sent thee in my way, in pity for my helpless state. Tell me, who art thou, and who is the father who is blest with such a son?"

"I am a follower of Achilles," was the startling reply, "and came hither in the same ship. My father is Polyctor, a wealthy man, and of like age with thee. I am the youngest of seven sons, and the lot fell upon me to follow the host to Troy. And this night I came out to spy upon the movements of the Trojans."

"If thou art a comrade of Achilles," said Priam, "thou canst tell me concerning my son Hector. Lies his body still by the ships, or has Achilles given it already to his dogs to devour?"

"Neither dog," answered the other, "nor unclean fowl hath approached him, nor hath the worm had power over his flesh. Unmarred by violence, untouched by decay, he lieth, without soil or stain, and all his wounds are closed. This miracle the gods have wrought, in the great love which they bear him."

"Glad news thou tellest me," said Priam, "and now I know that piety hath its reward, even in death." Then he took out a silver cup from the mule car, and offering it to the stranger said: "Take this for thyself, and conduct me safe to the ships of Achilles, that I may see the face of my son."

"Tempt me not, old man," replied the Greek. "This cup belongs to Achilles, and if I should steal it from him what thinkest thou that he would do unto me? But come, give me the reins, and I will guide thee to thy goal—yea, though it were in distant Argos, thou shouldst reach it safe and sound, and none should molest thee."

So saying, he sprang to the side of Priam, and took the reins. Under his guidance the horses seemed to be endued with wings, and in a very short time they reached the main entrance of the camp. The gates flew open, as if by magic, and all the sentries were sleeping at their posts. On to the extreme verge of the camp they went, still unchallenged, and drew up at length before a high stockade, within which were the quarters of Achilles. Once more the gates opened at a touch, and they entered. Here the mysterious stranger dismounted from the car, and turning on Priam a countenance which shone with a celestial radiance he said: "I have brought thee to the place where thou wouldst go, and now I will leave thee, for the task is finished which Zeus my father gave me to do. For know that I am Hermes, the herald of the gods, and the strong helper of those that are in need."

III

The dwelling of Achilles, which, for want of a better word, we have called a tent, was in reality a roomy building, constructed of solid pine trunks, and thatched with moss and rushes. On this memorable evening Achilles was sitting in the main apartment of the dwelling, and two of his squires were removing the vessels used at the evening meal. The light of the fire gleamed fitfully on his face, and he seemed in a gentler and more placid mood than had been usual with him for many days. He had partaken freely of food and wine, and conversed cheerfully with his attendants. He was now silent, and sat musing quietly by himself, when suddenly, to his amazement, an old man of tall stature and regal port entered the room, and throwing himself on the ground before him clasped his knees and kissed his hands—those terrible murderous hands!—bathing them with his tears. Like a man who has slain a fellow-countryman, and enters the house of some wealthy noble, where a great company is gathered, to implore shelter and protection—for the avenger of blood is at his heels—so seemed that aged man to Achilles and those that were with him, so trembling, helpless, and forlorn.

And as they gazed in deep wonder, murmuring to each other the name of Priam, he began, in a voice broken with weeping, to urge his petition: "Pity me, Achilles, for thy father's sake, an old man like me, standing on the brink of the grave. Maybe he is in sole straits, oppressed by those that dwell about him, for want of thy succouring arm. Yet still he has hope, as long as thou livest, and looks forward to the joyful day of thy return. But what hope have I, what solace, what refuge from the blows which fate aims without ceasing at mine afflicted head? Fifty sons I had, when the sons of Greece first came to these shores, and of these the greater part have paid their last tribute to the stern god of war. And he, the bravest and the best, the bulwark of my city, fell by thy hand not many days since. Him have I come to ransom at a great price. In the name of thy father, in the name of the gods whom we both adore, have mercy on me, Achilles—on me, who have found it in my heart to do what mortal never did before, to lift to my lips the hand that slew my son!"

Then at last that iron-hearted man was melted into compassion when he saw the renowned King of Asia prostrate at his feet, humbled to the dust for the sake of one poor boon—permission to give his son's body to the grave. And the sight of all that misery awakened anew the thought of his own sad lot, his recent loss, his brief and troubled life, soon to be ended by a coward's hand, the desolation of his home, and his father pining in solitary old age. Surely he also had cause enough for tears!

So the two great enemies were united for the time by the common bond of human sorrow. Then Achilles rose, and, taking the old man by the hand, led him to a seat, and placing himself by his side said to him: "O marked by sorrow's seal before all the children of men, what a heart must thou have, to meet me face to face, who have given to death so many of thy valiant sons! But thou knowest that it is the common lot: only the gods know neither care nor grief, but mortal life is encompassed with ills. Two caskets there are which stand by the throne of Zeus, one filled with good gifts, and the other with evil gifts. And for the more part Zeus mingles the gifts, and tempers much evil with a little good; but now and then some wretch receives naught but evil, and wanders from land to land as misery's thrall, branded by the malice of fate. To Peleus, my father, good things were given at first—wealth, power, and prosperity, and a goddess for his bride. But now he is receiving his portion of ill. And thou too, Priam, wast in old times renowned for the number of thy blessings, and men called thee great king, happy father, and envied thine abundance. But in thy latter years thou hast seen naught but wars and fightings, losses and deaths. So shifts the tide, so turns the scale, now up, now down, and naught that we can do will avail to raise or diminish by one tittle the sum of our fate."

Up to this point Priam had prospered in his mission beyond his hopes. But now he obtained a glimpse of the fearful passions which were smouldering in the breast of Achilles, and ready at any moment to leap up in devouring flames. Being invited by Achilles to stay and rest awhile before resuming his journey, he would have refused, alleging that he could not rest until he had the body of Hector safe in his keeping. But that fierce and imperious nature brooked not the slightest hint of opposition. "Provoke me no further, old man," said the terrible chieftain, with a dark glance at his guest. "Hector's body thou shalt have—but there must be no unseemly haste. My heart is exceeding sore; touch not thou the galled spot, lest I should do thee mischief, and break the ordinances of heaven."

Then, leaving Priam where he sat, Achilles went out with Automedon and another of his squires, and, bidding Idæus attend his master, they unyoked the mules, and brought in the ransom. "Now, haste thee, Automedon," said Achilles, in a low tone, "go with the handmaids to the place where Hector's body lies, and when they have washed and anointed it return with it hither. Be silent, and be wary; for if Priam sees what ye are doing—if he catches sight of Hector's body, where now it lies—I fear that he will break out into anger against me, and becoming outrageous provoke me to slay him."

Having carried out their orders with all due caution, they brought the body, wrapped in fine linen, and Achilles with his own hands placed it in the mule car. But he groaned in spirit when he thought of his promise to Patroclus, and cried aloud, invoking his ghost: "Take it not amiss, my Patroclus, when the news reaches thee in the house of the dead, that I have restored the body of thy slayer. His father hath paid me no mean ransom, whereof thou shalt have thy share."

The laws of hospitality required that Priam should not leave Achilles' roof without breaking bread. Accordingly, on his return to the house, Achilles urged his guest to take some food. "Remember," he said, "that Niobe herself, so constant in her sorrow that even now, though turned to a stone, she weeps and weeps for ever—even she tasted food when the first anguish of her grief was passed. Thou knowest her sad story—how she boasted that she had borne twelve fair children, six stalwart sons and six lovely daughters—and taunted Leto that she had only borne two. But those two were Apollo and Artemis, a god and a goddess, and they slew all the children of Niobe, to avenge the insult to their mother. Apollo slew the sons with his silver bow, and Artemis, the archer-goddess, slew the daughters. For nine days they lay in their blood, with none to give them burial; but on the tenth day the gods buried them with their own hands. And if she, that stricken mother, could sit down to meat, so do thou also, Priam; after that, thou shall take some sleep, and at dawn I will send thee back in safety to Troy."

The meal was prepared, and they sat down face to face at the same table, joined as host and guest, after all that had passed between them. But Priam's eyes were exceeding heavy, for he had hardly closed them in slumber since the awful day when he saw Hector stricken to death before his sight; and after tasting a morsel he begged Achilles to show him the place where he was to rest.

IV

Priam's bed was laid under the portico which ran round the outside of the dwelling, for fear lest any chance visitor to Achilles should see him if he lay within. Overcome by weariness, he soon fell into a deep sleep. But in the dead of night he was roused by the voice of Hermes, whose watchful eye had never left him, and who now came to warn him of the perils by which he was surrounded. What if Agamemnon should hear that the King of Troy was lying asleep in the midst of the Grecian camp! All the wealth of Troy would hardly suffice to ransom such a prisoner.

Priam rose in haste, now fully alive to his danger, and found the horses ready harnessed, and Idæus waiting with the mule car. The same powerful hand which had brought them to the dwelling of Achilles now smoothed the way for their return, and day was just breaking as they crossed the ford of the river.

The first to observe their coming was Cassandra, a daughter of Priam, who was watching from the highest tower of the citadel; and the report soon spread throughout the city that Priam was returning, bringing with him the body of Hector. Then not a man nor a woman was left in the city, but all with one accord streamed out through the gates to meet the strange procession. There was seen Hecuba, the mother of the slain, leaning on the shoulder of Andromache, his faithful wife; and following them at a distance, with downcast eyes, avoiding the looks of hate which were cast at her, went the fatal Helen. During all the years that she had lived as an unwelcome guest in the house of Priam, Hector had never reminded her by a look or a word of the miseries which she had brought on his country. He was all gentleness, all goodness, even to her, who had sinned so grievously against him and his people; and when hard words were aimed at her by any of his kinsfolk his patience and charity had ever been her shield.

By the authority of Achilles a truce of eleven days was granted to the Trojans to celebrate the obsequies of Hector. For nine days he lay in the chamber prepared for him in the palace, and all the city was given up to mourning. On the tenth day they buried him, and on the eleventh they raised his monument.

And so, after long delay, that knightly spirit passed into its rest.

PRONOUNCING LIST OF NAMES

Abydos (abī'dos)
Abas (ă'-bas)
Achilles (akil'les)
Æneas (eenee'as)
Æacides (eeă'cidees)
Ægæ (ee'gee)
Æthe (ee'thee)
Agamemnon (agamem'non
Agenor (agee'nor)
Ajax (a'jax)
Alœus (alō'yūs)
Alcathous (alcă'thŏ-ŭs)
Alcimedon (alkī'mĭdon)
Anchises (ankī'sees)
Antenor (antee'nor)
Antiphus (an'tĭfŭs)
Antea (antee'ă)
Andromache (andrŏ'măkee)
Antilochus (antil'ŏkŭs)
Antimachus (anti'măkŭs)
Aphrodite (ăfrŏdī'tee)
Ares (ā'rees)
Artemis (ar'tĕmĭs)
Asclepius (asklee'pĭŭs)
Astyanax (asti'ănax)
Asius (ā'sius)
Ascalaphus (ascăl'ăfŭs)

Asteropæus (asterŏpee'ŭs)
Athene (athee'nee)
Atreus (ā'trūs)
Ate (ā'tee)
Aulis (au'lis)
Automedon (autŏ'mĕdon)
Axius (ax'ĭŭs)

Balius (băl'ĭŭs)
Bathycles (băthĭ-clees)
Bœotia (beeō'tĭă)
Bellerophon (bellĕ'rŏfŏn)
Boreas (bŏr'ĕās)

Calchas (cal'kas)
Castor (cas'tōr)
Cebriones (kĕb'rĭŏnees)
Charops (kā'rops)
Chiron (kī'ron)
Chrysa (krī'să)
Chryseis (krī'see'is)
Chryses (krī'sees)
Chimæra (kĭmee'ră)
Clytæmnestra (clīteemnes'tră)
Cœranus (kee'rănŭs)
Cronos (crŏn'ŏs)

Dares (dărees)
Deiphobus (deeĭf'ŏbŭs)
Democoon (deemŏk'ōōn)
Diomede (dī'ŏmeed)
Dione (dio'nee)
Dolon (dŏl'ōn)
Dodona (dōdō'nă)

Eëtion (ee-ĕt'ĭōn)
Epeus (ĕpee'ŭs)
Eris (ĕ'ris)
Euchenor (ūkee'nōr)
Eumelus (ūmee'lŭs)
Euphorbus (ūfor'bus)
Euryalus (urī'ălŭs)
Eurybates (ūrĭ'bătees)
Eurydamas (ūrĭ'dămas)
Eurypylus (ūrĭ'pĭlŭs)
Eurynome (ūrĭ'nŏmee)

Ganymede (gănĭmeed)
Gargarus (gar'gă'rŭs)
Glaucus (glau'cus)

Hades (Hā'dees)
Harpalion (harpăl'ĭōn)
Hecuba (hĕc'ŭbă)
Hebe (heebee)

Helenus (hĒl'Ēnŭs)
Hephæstus (heefees'tŭs)
Hera (hee'rā)
Hermes (her'mees)
Heracles (her'āclees)
Hippolochus (hippōl'ō-kus)

Idæus (īdee'ŭs)
Idomeneus (īdŏm'enyŭs)
Ilios (ī'lĭŏs)
Iphidamas (īfī'dămās)
Iris (ī'ris)
Ithaca (ĭ'thăcă)

Laertes (lāĕr'tees)
Laodice (laŏ'dĭkee)
Laodocus (lāŏ'dŏkŭs)
Laogonus (lāŏ'gŏntĭs)
Lemnos (lem'nos)
Leucus (loo'kŭs)
Locris (lŏ'cris)
Lycaon (līcā'ōn)

Machaon (măkā'ōn)
Menœtius (měnee'tĭŭs)
Menelaus (měnělā'ŭs)
Menestheus (měněs'thyŭs)
Meriones (mee'rĭŭnees)

Mycenæ (mīsee'nee)
Myrine (mĭrī'nee)
Neoptolemus (nĕ-ŏptŏl'ĕmŭs)
Nereus (nee'rūs)
Nestor (nes'tōr)
Nireus (nī'rūs)

Oceanus (ōsee'ănŭs)
Odysseus (odis'syŭs)
Œneus (ee'nyŭs)
Oileus (ŏī'lyŭs)
Othryoneus (ŏth'rĭŏnyŭs)

Pæan (pee'an)
Pandarus (pan'dărŭs)
Paphlagonia (păflăgŏnĭa)
Patroclus (pătrŏ'clŭs)
Pedasus (pee'dăsŭs)
Pelops (pĕl'ops)
Peneleos (peenĕl'ĕōs)
Phænops (fee'nops)
Phegeus (fee'gyūs)
Phereclus (fĕrĕ'clŭs)
Philoctetes (fĭloctee'tees)
Phocis (fō'kis)
Phthia (fthī'ă)
Podalirius (pŏdălī'rĭŭs)
Podargus (pŏdar'gŭs)
Podes (pŏ'dees)

Polydeuces (pŏlĭdyū'kees)
Polydamas (pŏlĭ'dămas)
Polyctor (pŏlic'tor)
Polydorus (pŏlĭdōr'ŭs)
Polyidus (pŏlīī'dŭs)
Poseidon (pŭsī'dōn)
Priam (prī'am)
Protesilaus (prōtĕsĭlā'ŭs)
Prœtus (pree'tŭs)
Pylos (pī'los)
Pyræchmes (pīreek'mees)

Samothrace (sămŏthrā'kee)
Sarpedon (sarpee'dōn)
Scamander (scăman'dĕr)
Scamandrius (scăman'drĭus)
Scyros (skī'ros)
Sicyon (sĭk'ĭŏn)
Simoeis (sĭm'ŏeis)
Simœisius (sĭmŏei'sĭŭs)
Sisyphus (sī'sĭfŭs)
Solymi (sŏl'ĭmĭ)
Socus (sō'cŭs)
Spercheus (sperkee'ŭs)
Stentor (sten'tōr)
Sthenelus (sthĕn'ĕlŭs)

Talthybius (talthĭb'ĭŭs)
Telamon (tĕl'ămōn)

Telemachus (tĒlĕ'măkŭs)
Tethys (tee'thĭs)
Teucer (tyū'ser)
Thetis (thĒ'tĭs)
Thersites (thersī'tees)
Tiryns (tī'rins)
Tydeus (tī'dyūs)

Zephyrus (zĕf'ĭrŭs)
Zeus (zyŭs)